monsoonbooks

OPERATION TIPPING POINT

Lt. Col. JP Cross is a retired British officer who served with Gurkha units for nearly forty years. He has been an Indian frontier soldier, jungle fighter, policeman, military attaché, Gurkha recruitment officer and a linguist researcher, and he is the author of twenty-four books. He has fought in Burma, Indo-China, Malaya and Borneo and served in India, Pakistan, Hong Kong, Laos and Nepal where he now lives. Nearing his century, he still walks several hours daily.

Operation Tipping Point is the eighth in a series of historical military novels set in Southeast Asia including *Operation Black Rose*, *Operation Janus*, *Operation Red Tidings*, *Operation Blind Spot*, *Operation Stealth*, *Operation Four Rings* and *Operation Blowpipe*. The series features Gurkha military units, and the author draws on real events he witnessed and real people he fought alongside in various theatres of war in SE Asia and India.

'Nobody in the world is better qualified to tell the story of the Gurkhas' deadly jungle battles against Communist insurgency in Malaya in the 1950s. Cross spins his tale with the eye of incomparable experience.'

John le Carré

'... a gripping adventure story ...
learn the ins and outs of jungle warfare from a true expert'

The Oldie (on *Operation Janus*)

Also by JP Cross

OPERATION TIPPING POINT

JP CROSS

monsoon

monsoonbooks

First published in 2023
by Monsoon Books Ltd
www.monsoonbooks.co.uk

No.1 The Lodge, Burrough Court,
Burrough on the Hill, Melton Mowbray LE14 2QS, UK

ISBN (paperback): 9781915310149
ISBN (ebook): 9781915310156

Cover design by Cover Kitchen.

A Cataloguing-in-Publication data record is available from the British
Library.

Printed and bound in Great Britain by Clays Ltd, Elcograf S.p.A.
25 24 23   1 2 3

List of Characters

Historical characters:

Briggs, Sir Harold, Lieutenant General, author of the 'Briggs Plan'

Brooke, Charles Vyner, last British ruler of Sarawak

Brooke, Duncan Stewart, successor-designate of the above

Capone, Al, famous mafia executive during prohibition in USA

Chien Tiang, chief confidant of Chin Peng (q.v.) and propaganda expert

Chin Peng, alias of Ong Boon Hua, Secretary General of the Malayan Communist Party

Churchill, Winston, English politician

Empikau, Iban 'Pengara' in the Ulu Ai area of Sarawak

Besarionis dze Jughashvilia, a.k.a. Joseph Stalin ('Steel'), Georgian revolutionary and General Secretary of Soviet Communist Party

Kirill Novikok, Soviet Ambassador to India

Lai Tek, triple agent

Lee An Tung, Head of the Central Propaganda Department, Malayan Communist Party

Lee Kheng Kwoh, Chinese monk based in Darjeeling

Lu Dingyi, Chinese Communist Party spokesman

Mao Tse-tung, Chairman, Chinese Communist Party

Nagano, Major General, General Office Commanding 16th Japanese Imperial Army

Ng Chen, second-in-command of the killer squad of the Malayan Races Liberation Army

Ong Boon Hua, real name of Chin Peng (q.v.)

Padamsing (Padam) Rai, member of All-India Gorkha League and Sergeant, 1/12 Gurkha Rifles [Note: this is not the real name of the historical person your author knew]

Pahalman Rai, Rifleman, 1/10 Gurkha Rifles

Sharkey, Lawrence ('Lance'), Secretary General of the Australian Communist Party

Svetlana Allilueva, Stalin's daughter

Taylor, Grant, Federal Bureau of Investigation officer during prohibition in USA

Templer, Sir Gerald, General, High Commissioner and Direcor of Operations, Malaya

Too Chee Chew ('C C Too') brilliant propagandist, Special Branch, Malayan Police

Ulyanov, Vladamir Ilych, a.k.a. Lenin, Soviet revolutionary saint

Westerong, Raymond, Dutch officer with Dutch 'Shock Troops'

Wilhelmina ,Queen of the Netherlands

Yap Piow, Commander 7 Company, Malayan Races Liberation Army

Yerzin, Pavel Dmitrevch, Soviet handler for Sharkey (q.v.)

Zdhanov, Andrei A, Colonel General, Russian theoretician

Names either born in the author's imagination or changed to avoid family embarrassment:

Ah Fat, police 'mole' and non-voting Central Committee member, Malayan Communist Party

Ah Ho, pseudonym of Xi Zhan Yang, secret Communist courier (q.v.)

Akbar Salleh, Indonesian delegate at Calcutta conference

Atmaji Anugerah, Indonesian delegate at Calcutta conference

Basnet, Mansing, Nepalese Vice Consul in Rangoon

'Bear', Hung Lo, nickname of Wang Ming, (q.v.)

Bugga, Vikas, Indian Communist agent

Chan Man Yee, Malayan Communist Party 'mole' in Police HQ, Kuala Lumpur

Cheng Fan Tek, grocer in Taiping

Chen Geng, Communist in Singapore

Dutt, Anil, Indian Communist

Hemlal Rai, Gurkha Captain, Chief Clerk, 1/12 Gurkha Rifles

Heron, James, Lieutenant Colonel, Defence Attaché, Rangoon

Hinlea, Alan, Captain, turncoat officer in 1/12 Gurkha Rifles

Hutchinson, Mr, Warrant Officer, Class 1, Movement Control.

Hutton, Reggie, Special Branch officer, Singapore

Jaslal Rai, Sergeant, 1/10 Gurkha Rifles

Jones, Peter, manager of Everton Estate

Kamal Rai, worker on Bhutan Estate

Kulbahadur Limbu, Rifleman, 1/12 Gurkha Rifles

Lam Wai Lim, Captain of SS *Eastern Queen*

Lau Beng, Negri Sembilan Regional Commissar

Law Chu Hoi, Purser of SS *Eastern Queen*

Lee Kheng Kwoh, member of the Chinese Security Service, Kwok Ka On Chuin Bo

May, Dougie, Major, Officer Commanding Gurkha Transit Camp, Barrackpore

McGurk, James, Major, Reserve Officer attached to 1/12 Gurkha Rifles

Mole, Rodney, Officer in charge Police District

Oli, Dhruba Kumar, Nepalese consul in Rangoon

O'Neal, Peter, Major, Second-in-Command, 1/12 Gurkha Rifles

Pahalsing Gurung, Gurkha Lieutenant, 1 Platoon Commander, A Company, 1/12 Gurkha Rifles

P'ing Yee, Flat Ears, nickname of Ah Fat (q.v.)

Rance, Jason Percival Vere, Captain, 1/12 Gurkha Rifles,

Shandung P'aau, Shandong Cannon, nickname of Jason Rance (q.v.)

Sim Ting Ong, Secretary General of the Sarawak United People's Party

Sobolev, Leonid Pavlovich, Soviet 'Rezident', Calcutta

Tsarkov, Dmitry, a member of the Soviet consulate, Calcutta

Abbreviations

2 ic	Second-in-Command
ADC	aide de camp, personal staff officer to a senior officer
ADO	Assistant District Officer
CO	Commanding Officer, commander of major unit
CPO	Chief Police Officer
CMP	Corps of Military Police
CQMS	Company Quartermaster Sergeant
CRW	Communist Revolutionary Warfare
CSM	Company Sergeant Major
CT	Communist Terrorist/s, official name for guerrilla/s
DA	Defence Attaché
DSO	Distinguished Service Order, the second highest bravery award
FARELF	Far East Land Forces
GHQ	General Headquarters
GM	Gurkha Major
GR	Gurkha Rifles
HQ	headquarters
ID	identity
Int	intelligence
KL	Kuala Lumpur
MA	Military Adviser
MCP	Malayan Communist Party

MGB	Soviet Ministry of State Security, Ministerstvo Gosudarstvennoi Besopasnosti (1946-54)
MRLA	Malayan Races Liberation Army
MT	mechanical transport
NCO	non-commissioned officer
OC	Officer Commanding, commander of sub-unit
OCPD	Officer in Charge Police District
'O' Group	'Orders Group', sub-commanders for whom any orders are relevant
Red Cap	nickname for British Army police from the colour of their hats
RSM	Regimental Sergeant Major
sitrep	situation report

Signals jargon

roger	understood
sunray	commander of unit or sub-unit concerned
sunray minor	deputy commander of unit or sub-unit concerned

Glossary

Chinese
I sincerely thank Mr Bernard C C Chan, MBE, AMN, for his unstinting help in matters Chinese.

char sui	crispy roast pork belly
fei toh	bandit
Goo K'a bing	Gurkha soldiers
gwai lo	foreigner, literally 'devil chap', 'old devil'
HakWa	Hakka language
ham saap kwai	'salty wet', randy devil
juin jit dim	turning point
kung toh	Communist bandits
Kwok Ka On Chuin Bo	Security Service
Loi Pai Yi	Nepali
mi	vermicelli
Min Yuen	Masses Movement
Sinsaang	Mr, 'sir' (in Hak Wa the pronunciation is Sin Saang)
tung chi	'equal thinkers'

Hindi
hazur	term of respect, inert conversational response (literally 'presence')
machan	elevated platform for hunting or watching game

Iban
Pengara	senior headman of a district

Indonesian

bakwan	vegetable fritters
dalang	proverbial puppet master
krupak udang	prawn crackers
Permuda	Fatherland Defence Force fighters
tempeh	deep-fried, fermented soya beans

Japanese

genchi shobun	on-the-spot punishment
genju shobun	punishment by law
romusha	forced labour

Malay

atap	palm thatch, *Nipa fruticus*
jalan	road, street
kampong	village
-lah	tag for emphasis
makan	food
Mat Salleh	name Malays give to Europeans
orang	man
parang	chopper, knife
seladang	wild bison, Bos gauruss
Selamat petang	Good evening
songkok	hat
Terima kasih	thank you
tuan	official, 'sir'

Nepali (Gurkhali)

chamché	one like a spoon, can turn either way
daku	'dacoit', guerrilla
keta	lad
gaur	wild bison, *Bos gaurus*
gora	fair-skinned, word for British troops
hajur	term of respect, inert conversational response (literally 'presence')

hunchha	is, okay
-ji/-jyu	polite suffixes, used after a person's name
Major-ba	one way of addressing a Gurkha Company Sergeant Major
mijhar	formal name for a monk
namasté	Nepali greeting, made with joined hands in front of the lower face
S/sarkar	government, officialdom word used to address or to refer to royalty
shikar	game
shikari	hunter
tagra rahau	may you remain strong
ustad	'teacher', non-commissioned officer

Note: the '-bahadur' at the end of names is often shorted to '-é' when talking, so, instead of Kulbahadur, it is Kulé etc

Russian

I thank Prof. em Dr. George van Driem for his unstinted help in the vocabulary used in the narrative.

aktivnyye meropriyatiya	active measures
gazvedka	intelligence-gathering
maskirovka	deception
Rodina	motherland, Mother Russia
vlasti	the elite
vnezapnost	surprise

General
cane bamboo	*Aurindibaria falcata*

Malayan Peninsula

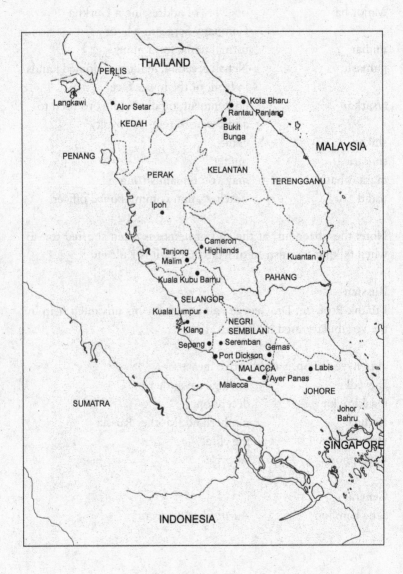

Malayan Railway

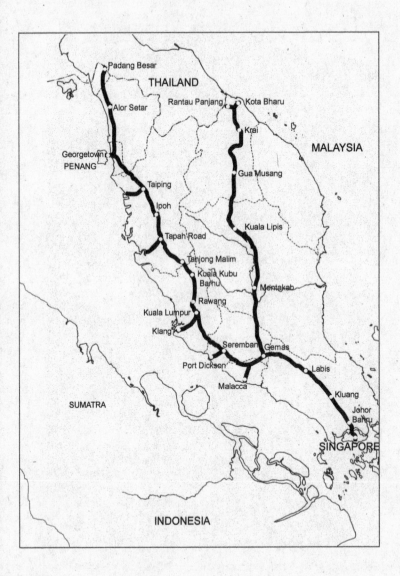

Preface

It has happened times without number, most likely unknown at the time by those involved the most. Some put it that 'history turns on a very small point'; others, less careful in expressing themselves, ask whether it was God's law or sod's law? However described, 'it happens'. In the story I have written for you, disguised as it is to save reputations and to keep law suits off me, I tell how one night in August 1951 during the 10-year-long Malayan Emergency, a senior, highly experienced British major commanding a rifle company of Gurkhas, went to bed with 'too much on board'. This was not the first or last time that such was the case. However, on the night in question he was woken up in the small hours by an excited Special Branch officer's phone call – the line was not a clear one – to be told that a large party of guerrillas was at such-and-such a place. 'I recommend you move *now*,' the excited man said after passing the six-figure grid reference.

In his haze the Major wrote the last two figures in the wrong order so went where he had not been directed. Dame Fortune, that ever fickle lady, also decreed that the Special Branch officer's information was out-of-date when he phoned and that by then the guerrillas had moved quite some way away. Against millions of odds, the two parties met up and the guerrillas suffered their greatest loss ever during the Emergency.

As the Major was a friend of the author's he shall remain nameless.[1]

If, Gentle Reader, that intrigues you, please read on to learn what actually happened and how that one isolated incident became the 'tipping point' of the Malayan Emergency in favour of the Security Forces. Fully to appreciate the significance and the irony of that one incident, background events in Moscow, Darjeeling, Delhi and Calcutta must first be brought to your notice.

Your humble author.

---

1 The official version of the incident is on pages 31 to 41 in the *History of the 2nd King Edward VII's Own Gookhas* (*The Sirmoor Rifles*) Volume IV, 1948-1994.

1

Tuesday 4 October 1946, The Old Arsenal Building, The Kremlin, Moscow: 'You have done well, Comrade Colonel General. I want our revolutionary struggle in Asia to prevail before that Mao Tse-tung wins the civil war in China, which I believe he surely will. Your suggestion has many merits. Once we have Politburo approval you will put your plan into action.'

The man known to the world as Stalin, 'Steel', the Secretary General and Chairman of the Council of Ministers of the United Soviet Socialist Republics, the homicidal and illegitimate son of a Georgian shoemaker, was probably unaware that Mao's spokesman, Lu Dingyi, had, nine months earlier, already produced his own theory and plan for similar action. Had Stalin – arch-realist, brutal and unpredictable despot, psychologically warped and capable of much evil – known that, his praise might not have been so warm as he looked up, eyes hooded, at the man standing in front of him whose son, Juri, would marry his daughter Svetlana Allilueva as her second husband. He was clearly pleased with his protégé, who should never be, nor was, allowed to become too strong.

'Thank you, Comrade Secretary General. Your words mean a great deal to me and, indeed, I feel that my offering can only do the Party much good,' answered Colonel General Andrei A Zhdanov,[2] the younger by twenty years, trying, not very successfully, to hide his obvious pleasure. It was never wise to show anything that might be taken as exuberance in front of the Secretary General, especially when his dark, cruel eyes – eyes that hooded as he spoke and seemed to know too much and to see farther than the line of vision permitted. 'My life's work is for Cause and Country,' he said, adding, for good measure, 'under the creative genius of your leadership.'

That merely drew a shrug: it was to be expected. His peers recognised that the Secretary General was a man out of proportion, his cunning, his conceit, his strength and his dreams – all were larger than life, exacerbated by megalomania. He was a man who thought and acted in absolute terms; patience and guile hiding his vainglory so successfully that many took him for normal.

Zhdanov, now the Party's ideologue and theorist, had become a candidate member of the Central Committee in 1930 at the unusually young age of thirty-four and a full member of the Politburo in 1939. To be a political Colonel General was a rarity and reflected his great potential. Of medium height, his hairline had receded. His round face, with its small nose and wide-set

---

2 The announcement of Zhdanov's new policy was only made public in September 1947, in Poland, at Szklarska Poreba, formerly a German resort town, previously known as Schreiberhau. It signalled the end to wartime cooperation between the Soviet Union and the 'Western' allies. Susanne S Lotarski, *The Communist Takeover in Poland*, in Thomas T Hammond (ed.), *The Anatomy of Communist Takeovers* (Yale University Press, New Haven, 1973), quoted in *The Rise and Fall of Communism*, Archie Brown, London, 2009, pages 157 and 158, and note 24 on page 642.

eyes, belied his inner toughness. His tight lips under his clipped moustache and a protruding chin showed a firmness of character and his still lithe body reflected a strapping youth. In fact, he was as tough as any, more dedicated than most and as hard an exponent of the Stalinist line in all matters as there could be.

The members of the Politburo, sitting either side of a long, heavy, oak table, looked on with tolerance at the praise, so seldom given, now being bestowed on this potentially all-powerful individual who wore his authority with a bland good will that masked a subtle intelligence and dominating resolve. Older Politburo members, whose ideology had been the tiniest bit suspect or who had opinions of their own, had long vanished, shot in the head in the Lefortovo jail, bodies disposed of, leaving bereft families suffering hardships by being 'tainted', so under lifetime suspicion.

That left clever, fawning toadies to rise to senior level. Zhdanov's potential was, however, a cause for Stalin's jealousy – no one at that meeting would have guessed that he would die under mysterious and unexplained circumstances the following year.

'Comrade Zhdanov, before the other Comrades open the folder in front of them and a full discussion starts on what you have prepared, I want you to tell us, in outline, what your new policy recommendation is and why you have made it.'

With a dismissive nod of his head, Stalin indicated the empty chair at the end of the table. Zhdanov took his seat and addressed the meeting, first taking some notes out of his briefcase.

With his face lit by a fleeting smile, the Colonel General

said, 'Comrades, the world is divided into two camps: the anti-democratic, imperialist camp on the one hand and the anti-imperialist, democratic camp on the other. My proposed doctrine is purely anti-imperialistic in concept. It adds a dimension to our struggle as world liberators of the oppressed. The Great Patriotic War, which we won virtually single-handed at such a cost in blood and treasure, left the imperialist nations in ruins after their initial defeat in the case of France and Holland (Belgium doesn't count), or seriously weakened and floundering in debt, in the case of Great Britain. Look how our clever propaganda managed to persuade British voters to discard that drunken and arrogant Churchill in his fumbling twilight, even though he had been Prime Minister for most of the war, and elect a socialist government with many members sympathetic to our Cause and our beloved motherland, our *Rodina*.'

His listeners, seated in thick leather-covered chairs, nodded their approval. Indeed, the tempestuous traumas and sulks of their Chairman that made life so difficult and dangerous for them were unknown about in Britain where a popular 'Uncle Joe' was how the public saw him. It had made his long-term planning immeasurably easier.

Overseeing them at the far end of the room was a full-length portrait of Vladimir Ilych Ulyanov, 'Lenin', the revolutionary saint of Soviet Communism, his domed forehead thrown back as though in a fresh breeze, his piercing eyes looking towards the glorious future which his stern face confidently proclaimed and which Marxism-Leninism called an historic inevitability.

'Our fundamental aim,' the Colonel General continued, 'is

to ensure that all colonies, starting in Asia rather than in Africa, have anti-imperialist comrades running them after ejecting the current imperialist, colonial governments, by stealth or force. Our chief targets are Indo-China, the Dutch East Indies, Malaya and Singapore, and finally Hong Kong. The "tipping point" for the first two will be sooner than for the others. After that the remainder should fall into our hands like ripe plums.'

'How long do you reckon before all this happens?' someone asked.

'Comrade, that is difficult to say. My guess is four to five years without our assistance. Shorter with it.' That vague answer seemed to satisfy.

The Minister in charge of munitions, cracking the joints of his fingers, tritely observed 'Surely you don't envisage any overt aid, do you? I have some stock not used during the war but I feel it will be safer to have it nearer to hand.'

He glanced at Stalin who did not even bother to look at him or to take his pipe out of the sunken crack of a mouth that his walrus moustache half-concealed.

'No certainly not. I believe that no overt help and no surplus wartime stocks are necessary, certainly not to start with anyway. There are more than enough weapons already in the hands of those natives who fought against the feudalist Japanese.'

The knuckle-cracker looked relieved. Zhdanov continued, 'before I show you on the map where the places I am talking about are, I want to emphasise why I have also said "no physical presence". Over the years our Party has managed to get a firm footing among the imperialists' colonies. As an example from

India I mention one Mr Vikas Bugga who is a linchpin for our work there. This quaintly named Indian, a Captain in the Disinformation Department of the First Chief Directorate of the International Department of the Central Committee, is fully trained in *aktivnyye meropriyatiya*, active measures, run, of course, by the Ministry of State Security, the MGB.'

Stalin butted in. 'Comrade Zhdanov will not mind if I say that speed is of the essence. I want this done before those yellow monsters, the slit-eyed Chinese, try to get comrades with their way of thinking into power.'

Zhdanov, sensing impatience, blenched visibly and quickly covered some more details before saying, slightly more robustly than before, 'You will notice that I have not mentioned the two white countries, Australia and New Zealand.' He went and pointed out on the map the counties so far mentioned before returning to his seat. He looked firmly at each member in turn and continued: 'Let me explain. Recently I have had the General Secretary of the Australian Communist Party, Comrade Lawrence Sharkey, "Lance" to his friends, with me. He has gone back to Australia, where he needs no help from us at the moment, with our Chairman's orders to brief all potential leaders in the colonial countries concerned that I have mentioned through their trusted intermediaries. The last I heard from him was that he had indeed managed to contact all relevant comrades who need to be involved. Now, with the help of his Indian comrades, Sharkey has arranged to attend an innocent-sounding gathering, a Southeast Asia Youth Conference, to take place in early 1948, probably in February, followed by a full Indian Communist Party Plenum, both in Calcutta. The delegates will be fully briefed on how they should put their anti-imperialist plans into action, each according to circumstances in their own particular country and reinforced by our concept. Comrade Lance Sharkey will be our link and his intimate knowledge of the Orient will be the main means of that concept being successfully promulgated in full and final detail. We can do no better than that. The Calcutta conference will be our "tipping point" to eventual victory.'

He looked around the table, expecting acknowledgement, nor was he disappointed. There was nothing in his project to upset any hardliners. He had everyone's attention.

'It is my opinion,' Zhdanov continued, 'as soon as the Indians have punched the British out of the ring, the time will be ripe for a knock-out blow in the rest of their Asian colonies to push them through the ropes. The virulent anti-British propaganda employed by the Indian Congress Party has been immeasurably helped, in fact, from this very room, as indeed has the basis of all anti-colonial rhetoric.' And he allowed himself the ghost of a smile of satisfaction. 'So you can see that Comrade Lance Sharkey's efforts will merely be pushing at an open door. Not only that, I have persuaded him,' he added proudly, 'on his way back to Australia to have a full meeting with Singapore's and Malaya's comrades about starting the armed struggle soon so that matters can come to an early and successful conclusion before any more British troops can get there after leaving India, probably in early 1948.'

'Excuse me, Comrade,' broke in the Foreign Minister, an elderly man whose face was all angles and planes. 'Surely British troops will have gone back to the United Kingdom when India has self-rule and not to Malaya where, my understanding is, there are only two British Army infantry battalions and one gunner regiment at most.' He paused, shrugged and made a grimace of superiority. 'Nothing local guerrillas can't cope with, and the colonial Malay Regiment is no threat either.' He brushed a lank forelock from his forehead with a smile as warm as a skull.

The Director of the Joint Planning Staff, who worked at 19 Frunze Street, broke in. 'We have nothing on our books or in our files as a counter to any threat posed in that context.'

'Comrade,' continued Zdhanov, with a nod at the Director, 'I agree with you but I have had it from my chief source in India, Mr Bugga, that great efforts are being made to get some of those excellent fighters, the Gurkhas, from the Indian Army transferred into the British Army. Most are due to go to Malaya, some to Hong Kong. Comrade Sharkey's visit will not be before the British Army Gurkhas are deployed there but my sources have other plans to delay Gurkha deployment.'

'So, it will be so much easier if Gurkhas don't go to Malaya' another member commented.

'So much the easier, I agree, but go they will. I am planning that one of my Indian agents will try and postpone their leaving India by one year so that our Malayan comrades can get a firm, unshakeable foothold that a late Gurkha arrival won't be able to dislodge. In any event I have already made another plan to scupper any permanent lodgement there. I plan to use an asset, cultivated by our man Vikas Bugga in Darjeeling,' he rose again and pointed it out on the map. 'He is our link both with comrades there and the delicious tea that the British started setting up commercially in 1852.' He felt he had to show the others the extent of his research. 'Our man there has his own network of young anti-British, Darjeeling-based Gurkhas he can use.'

'I thought the Gurkhas came from Nepal, not India,' someone objected.

'Correct, Comrade, they do but there are some Indian-domiciled men from Nepal who have been working in the Indian tea gardens for fifty or sixty years. I understand that they have lost their innate Himalayan robustness by living in British India but they are the better educated for living there. I really do have the right person to ensure that our project goes as we wish it to. Also, I have recently found out that, when was it now?' a pause while he thought, 'yes, in 1904, some Gurkhas from those tea gardens went to Malaya to work on the rubber plantations there. I have heard there are three such British-run places with Gurkha labour. Comrade Sharkey has enough knowledge to ensure they must be used as an essential link in our task of influencing the British Army Gurkhas favourably to our cause after their arrival.'

'Just one more point,' said someone else. 'Surely, with our potential in India, we could arrange for a cessation of any British Gurkhas by "leaning on" the Indian prime minister who will, in turn, "lean on" the government in Nepal. It will not have escaped anyone's attention that India has its fingers on Nepal's jugular, Nepal being land-locked.'

He laughed and the assembled company clapped in appreciation, both of the concept and the amount of planning detail that had so obviously been achieved to put it into action. The participants had to pretend that their approval was needed although everyone knew such was only a formality. Indeed, Zhdanov would never have started on the project in the first place had it not initially received the Secretary General's 'blessing'.

The Head of the MGB, which had its main office at 2 Bolshaya Lubuanka Street, said, 'What is needed is a secret office for intelligence-gathering, *gazvedka*, which was, as we all know, a critical part of operational doctrine during the Great Patriotic War.' Well into his stride he continued '*Vnezapnost*' – surprise – 'and *maskirovka*' – deception, concealment – 'must be our permanent watchwords. It was those two aspects that immeasurably helped our victory against the Germans.'

He looked around: there was no dissent. 'I can't say where but somewhere in Asia where it can act as a point both for the collection of and dissemination of information essential to helping our cause and so hindering the colonialists. Is Darjeeling suitable for this?'

At that Zhdanov felt he had lost some ground in his presentation so, to make up, said, 'I have ordered some Darjeeling tea to be made ready if you would like to use that as a token toast to our potential victory.'

Stalin raised his hand in pleasure. 'I agree. Tell the Duty Officer to have it brought in. We will drink it as it has been drunk in our *Rodina* for as long as we can remember.'

Two white-coated orderlies brought it in on silver trays. 'With no Germans in the queue there'll be plenty more of it later even if we run out of it soon.' Seldom had the Secretary General been seen in such a good mood.

Tea was poured out into cups with a small amount of white-cherry preserves. They drank it in the traditional way, first putting some of the sweetened cherries into their mouth, then letting the tea wash around them. It made conversation awkward, but it was Russian in style and taste. As they sipped, Zhdanov started to give more details but was interrupted by Stalin, 'Let me sum up for Comrade Zhdanov. Before now the sun never set on the British Empire with their colonies coloured red on maps. The colour will still be the same but the red will be the red of our flag and of the sun that will never set on any of our devoted comrades, only on our bourgeois and beatable enemies.' Zhdanov was the hero of the hour.

It was after dark when the meeting broke up. The inside perimeter of the Kremlin walls was lit with harsh, blue-white light floods. MGB troops and soldiers of the Taman Guards Division, ceremonial troops with minimal weapon training stationed at Alabino outside Moscow, appeared and disappeared in splashes of floodlights as they patrolled the area. As the black Chaika limousines, with their distinctive Central Committee number plates beginning with the letters MOC, carrying their senior Comrades, rolled out of the front entrance, they were smartly saluted. They sped down the centre lane reserved for the *vlasti*, the elite, the fat cats in what had become of Marx's dreamed of classless society; a society rigidly structured with layer upon layer of ossified, hypocritical inefficiency and class-ridden as only a vast bureaucratic hierarchy can be. But as long as the way these people ran affairs, *Rodina* would be safe for ever, surely? – but, like so many other plans made by the Soviet Union, there was less in this one than met the eye, with appearances having more weight than reality and perceptions seen as more important than facts.

Friday August 1947, Darjeeling, Bengal, India: The British and Indian communities celebrated Indian Independence Day in their own fashion and inclinations, the British ineffably sadly and the Indians gloatingly gladly. The only Englishman to be glad was a Captain Alan Hinlea, a Gunner officer on leave there. He and his father in England were both devout card-carrying Communists and son Hinlea was so thunderstruck by Britain's leaving so many in India dirt-poor that he just knew that India would redress affairs now it was independent. He had happened to hear someone, a young Nepali, addressing a crowd saying that it was wrong to have Gurkha soldiers in the British Army in Hong Kong and Malaya. It should be stopped if it had started and prevented if it had yet to start. It so cleared Hinlea's mind that he followed the Nepali when he left, to try and find out more of his ideas.

He saw him stopped by a hirsute Indian outside a teashop and addressed as Padamsing Rai and the Gurkha answering, calling the other man Mr Bugga. They went into a tea shop and Hinlea followed. Upstairs he sat at a table in hearing distance of the other two men who ordered a pot of tea and some honey sandwiches. When he overheard the conversation turn to Padamsing Rai being ordered by the Party to join the British Gurkhas in Malaya in his role of influencing them against the British Army to such an extent that they'd be disbanded, Hinlea could hold his patience no longer and joined them, showing them his Communist membership card that he always carried.

He learnt that before joining up Padamsing was due to attend a South East Asian Youth Conference in Calcutta. 'I have an idea, please listen,' He broke in excitedly, 'Let's work together. I hear 12 Gurkha Rifles is to be made into Gunners. I am a Gunner. I'll volunteer so you also try to join that regiment. Together we'll manage to disrupt matters so efficiently, we'll both be Politburo heroes.'

And in the fullness of time that is what did happen.[3]

Friday 28 November 1947. Red Fort, Delhi: The senior British Army officer left in India was a Brigadier, known as Commander, British Gurkhas India. A tall, handsome man, honoured with several bravery awards, a natural leader, tense, responsive and one hundred per cent dedicated, he had served with the Gurkhas his whole career. Now his task was to liaise with the Indian authorities, pricklier by far than any hedgehog ever knew how to be, to arrange for the five remaining Gurkha battalions and four regimental centres, with some still in West Pakistan, to leave India for pastures new. Three battalions detailed for Crown service were already in Rangoon. The difficulties were almost insurmountable, with problems unending. Scheme QUIM, Quit India Immediately, had 31 December 1947 as a deadline for all British military personnel to have left, a seemingly impossible date to meet. Relevant queries, all of the highest priority, were ridiculously slow in being answered, if answered at all. Payment, correct and timely, for everything was now the norm: for clothes worn, stores to be taken, food eaten, fuel for vehicles, fodder for

---

3 See *Operation Janus*.

mules, handing over barracks lived in, in one case for more than a hundred years, and paying for any damages – cracked windows seemed unnecessarily expensive! – transport to railway stations, then for trains, then finally for shipping all had to be paid in full before any movement was authorised. The Brigadier had a minuscule staff of Indians, not Gurkhas, and was completely overburdened.

His small office was on the third floor of one of the buildings near the entrance of the Red Fort complex.

Came a knock on the door.

'Come in,' he called out, wearily and warily.

His Indian clerk entered. 'Sahib, a visitor has come to see you. Here he is.'

In walked a middle-aged, suave Indian whom the Brigadier had met before but knew only slightly. 'I am sorry to disturb you, Brigadier sahib. I know how frantically busy you are.' The man's English was perfect. 'My name is Dutt, Anil Dutt.'

'Not at all, not at all.' The Brigadier had stood up, glad to stretch his legs. 'Please sit down, Mr Dutt,' the Brigadier said, pointing to a chair to one side of his desk. 'I can certainly spare you some of my time.'

The Indian visitor had a beak-like nose and strange, jutting mouth with a thin upper and a thick lower lip which protruded beyond a sullen, bony jaw, a rugged, ugly face. The Brigadier felt that there was something about him that did not ring true, hard to pin down quite what. For his part, the Indian, now seated, saw one whose eyes demanded attention, cool wells of reserve, flanked not by laughter lines but creases of careworn deliberation, belonging to one who was having a running battle without knowing who or what awaited him.

He's on the defensive and a hard one. Will I be successful? Mr Dutt thought, refusing an offered cigarette, came straight to the point. 'Brigadier. I am an advisor to a cabinet sub-committee. I have come to see you in your role of Commander, British Gurkhas India. We, too, are overburdened with new problems, to say nothing of a completely unwanted struggle over Kashmir. We can fully appreciate how hard you are finding moving your Gurkhas overseas.'

The Brigadier, a man of few words, nodded.

'We have heard, true or false but probably true,' the Indian continued coyly, 'that standard accommodation both in Malaya and Hong Kong will not be ready for most units for at least another year.'

'Yes, Mr Dutt. Indeed that is a problem but I don't think it is as severe as you are making out.' *What business is it of his? What's behind this? Why now when everything has been settled?*

'The purpose of my visit is, so far unofficially, to get your reaction to my government offering your government accommodation and all facilities, on payment of course, for a year while your accommodation is being built.'

The Brigadier, ever courteous as only an English gentleman can properly be, stood up. 'I thank you, Mr Dutt, for your kind offer which I can tell you here and now I totally reject. It will not be worth my reporting it to the War Office in London,'[4] and,

_____

4 The Brigadier related this to your author when he visited him a day later to hand in recommendations for the Viceroy's Commissioned Officers

making for the door, opened it.

The Indian left without a word and neither man offered his hand. *I knew it would be hard to sell. I'll have to alert Sharkey and let Pavel Dmitrievich Yerzin know.* This last was Dutt's MGB handler who had recently arrived in a 'trade' guise.

Friday 19-Tuesday 30 March 1948, Calcutta, India: The Conference of Youth and Students of Southeast Asia Fighting for Freedom and Independence, familiarly known as the Southeast Asia Youth Conference – a youth being anyone up to thirty-five years old – lasting from the 19th to the 23rd of March, took place in Wellesley Street under the ægis of the Indian Communist Party but orchestrated by the Soviet MGB. Its organisers had thought that the shortened and unassuming title was a way of avoiding suspicion and undue scrutiny. Its genesis lay as far back as 1946 when Soviet anti-imperialist policy was formulated with the aim of indoctrinating those whose job would be to spread Communism all over colonial southeast Asia by teaching the participants how best to prepare for and then launch the Communist-inspired risings against the imperialist colonialists.

Apart from such representatives, the rough-tongued Secretary General of the Australian Communist Party, 'Lance' Sharkey, had accepted an invitation to attend and, as he was rated as a 'star', to address the meeting. He was a tactless, forceful bully, hostile to his own government and had never allowed anyone or thing to stand in his way. His face chimed in with his character, frowning,

---

(VCOs) of his battalion, 1/1 GR, to be fully commissioned.

bellicose and alert for insults.

He had flown from Australia to Singapore and now, aboard the SS *Rajula* alongside Keppel Dock, hot and sweaty, he was parched. He quickly went to the nearest bar and ordered himself a pint of ice-cold beer. That went down in two long, gorgeous gulps. He wiped his lips with the back of his hand, ordered a refill and sat down on a long-legged stool. Ignoring the other drinkers, he thought back to the recent past. Having got his visa, he had flown to Singapore the week before, staying in a small hotel in Beras Basah Road, not far from the Chinese comrade, Lee Soong, a fluent English speaker, who had been a member of the post-war British Military Administration's Singapore Advisory Council as well as on the Town Committee of the Communist Party of Malaya, MCP. He had been to Prague the year before as a member of the World Federation of Democratic Youth and was a skilled operator.

Sharkey had paid a protocol visit to the new Secretary General of the MCP, Chin Peng. Nothing substantial was discussed and an invitation was given to the Australian to attend the MCP's 4th Plenary Session on his return from Calcutta.

Thinking about what had happened to date and well into his third pint, Sharkey had not realised that the gangways had been withdrawn with the thick hawsers unwound from the bollards. Neither did the withering blast of her deep-throated horn make any impression on him as the SS *Rajula* slowly made her way out to sea, bound for Rangoon and Calcutta, nor did it register when the boat slowed down prior to letting the pilot off.

'You Lawrence Sharkey?' A drawling, upper-class, English

voice intruded into his thoughts.

Sharkey looked around and saw a middle-aged Englishman in white uniform. 'Yeah, what of it?' was his surly answer.

'Just come to warn you to keep your bloody Commy nonsense to yourself. You're not the sort of person we like in this part of the world or on board. Understand?'

'And who the eff are you, for God's sake? An effing Pom dressed in fancy white.'

'Never you mind who I am. Just remember what I have told you. And Commy bastards like you don't have a God, which proves that you're just a wind bag like the rest of them.'

With that the Englishman turned abruptly and left. Sharkey only realised that he was the pilot when, sinking his beer in a furious rage, he went and looked over the railings and saw his unwanted Pom stepping into a small speedboat and going back to the harbour.

Cursing under his breath, he wondered how many of the drinkers at the bar had heard the exchange. It made him even more determined for the Conference to be a success and he spent much of the rest of the voyage rehearsing his script, my 'battle plan' as he called it.

At Rangoon he took a rickshaw around the town, although it was against his gut instinct to sit in a two-wheel vehicle pulled by a bare-footed human. He was appalled by the poverty and squalor: it was his first visit there and, talking to his table mates at meals, he was told that Calcutta was even worse.

Once the boat had docked at Calcutta and the medical and immigration officials had interviewed each passenger, it was, thankfully, time to disembark. He was about to head off the boat when a voice said, 'Excuse me, Sahib. Are you Mr Sharkey?'

He spun round on hearing his name and saw a man with a slight 'outward' squint, heavily hirsute with a pockmarked puffy face. His speech was a bit difficult to understand and the Australian soon saw why – the man's moustache covered a hair lip.

'Yes, I am Lance Sharkey but I'm not a sahib. I'm a prole.'

His questioner grinned. 'That is our goal, all to be prole,' and extended his hand. 'I have come to meet you and escort you to your accommodation for the Youth Congress. My name is Vikas Bugga, a proud Bengali, trooper not snooper.'

Calcutta! It soured Sharkey's soul as he gazed around: how sordid it looked and how horrible it smelt from close quarters. He stared in fascinated horror at the crowds of teeming humanity, ever milling, scantily dressed and depressingly poor, either volubly gesticulating in strident tones or dejectedly silent, avoiding eye contact wherever possible. The turbans, the beards, the dhotis, the shirts outside the trousers, the pyjamas by day were as he had expected and didn't much offend him. What did, though, were the blind, the beggars, the wheedling children, the laden women, the old and rheumy-eyed, the young but prematurely shrivelled, everywhere eddying and churning in kaleidoscopic patterns in the hot, sticky, fetid air, the scavenging dogs and the bare-ribbed horses pulling over-loaded tongas. He felt many eyes were on him – a white man with an Indian travelling by tonga – huge precocious eyes of children, tormented yet at the same time covetous, and, from a distance, tender, forlorn and velvety eyes of girls glancing at him. The raucous black crows and skeletal cows wandering in the streets with an air of indifference were the only living creatures seemingly unaffected by the heat, the clamour and the squalor. Even so, life throbbed and swirled despite everything wearing an aura of dilapidation.

Sitting together, Vikas and Lance talked. 'Our Plenum will be held in the same place as the Youth Conference.'

'I have to leave the day after the Plenum finishes. That is the Indian government's stipulation on my visa being granted,' [5] Sharkey lamented, wishing he could have a cold beer.

'In that case, what I'll do is to see if there is a boat steaming out Singapore-way on that particular day, isn't it? We have a couple of days before the Conference starts on the 19th. It lasts till the 25th.'

'Good on yer,' was all Sharkey managed to say as he wiped his sweaty forehead. 'For crying out loud, what have the Brits done for Calcutta in all the years they have been here? Look at it: never seen such a mess.'

'I agree, I agree, Mr Sharkey. But there were so many refugees when partition created East Pakistan. But the population increased more when many thousands arrived as penniless refugees from the famines during the war. And the place deteriorated even more because of the terrible killings last year.'

Sharkey nodded his understanding. He knew that the underlying problems of poverty had been there for centuries.

'I have booked you into the Garuda Hotel in a modest room.

---

5 This is a historical fact.

It is just off Koletola Street, to the north of Bow Bazaar. The Asian delegates are also there.'

Sharkey stifled a yawn. The names meant nothing to him, so he said nothing. Bugga took his silence as interest and went prattling on, 'and the Conference and the Plenum will be held in the same large hall, already booked in Wellesley – he was a great British General from Great Britain, ha, ha – Street, off Park Street, near Chowringhee, not far from the Christian cemetery.'

'Chum, that's where I'll be soon although I am a practising atheist. I don't have a map and the names mean nothing to me – yet,' he added, realising he had to soften what might be taken as a snub.

'Here we are,' the Bengali called out a few minutes later as the tonga came to a halt. 'The Garuda Hotel. This is where we're booked. Bring your kit with you and come inside.'

A bare-headed man in a suit and tie came out to meet them. Sharkey noticed his beak-like nose and strange, jutting mouth with a thin upper and a thick lower lip which protruded beyond a sullen, bony jaw, a rugged, ugly face but it had a pleasant smile. He called out, 'Welcome, welcome to you,' and told the tonga walla he'd pay him directly and walked over to Sharkey. 'You must be Mr Sharkey. I am Mr Dutt.' His voice was well modulated. They shook hands. 'Excuse me being booted and suited but not hatted or spatted but I have to play a part. You are sensible to be casual.'

He could tell from the dull look in the Australian's eyes that the allusion to 'spats' was lost on him.

Sharkey wiped his brow. *Could I do with an ice-cold beer or even two while I'm about it? It's that hot!* By mid-March Calcutta had started to heat up during the day.

'Tell you what, Mr Dutt,' said Sharkey, armpits of his shirt dark and damp. 'I don't know about you but I could do with, in fact, desperately need, a glass of ice-cold beer I'm that thirsty.'

'Then your luck's out, my friend, I fear. Everywhere in Bengal, in the whole of India come to that, except in registered places, is dry. Nothing hard and no beer. Sorry,' waggling his head.

Sharkey just couldn't believe his ears. 'You're not joking, are you?' he asked hopefully.

'No, indeed I am not.' Mr Dutt saw a look of anguish on the Australian's face. 'You'll have to be content with a cup of tea or a squash while you're here but if you book in at the Great Eastern Hotel as a foreigner, you can drink all you want with a doctor's certificate as a certified alcoholic,' *and may your Christian God, if you as a dedicated Communist even have one, have mercy on your liver as well as on your soul.*

While Sharkey was booking in, Mr Bugga espied Padamsing Rai coming down the stairs. With him was an odd, elemental, narrow-shouldered, long-necked Chinese man, slightly stooped with a worried look on his deeply pockmarked face that had a mouth as thin and cruel as a well-healed knife wound. Padamsing brought him over and introduced him, nameless, merely as a guest of Lee Soong. Although his English was good, he had few words to say. When he spoke, his voice sounded like fingernails being drawn down a blackboard. No one had any idea he was a member of the Chinese Security Service, the *Kwok Ka On Chuin Bo*.

The representative of the MGB had contacted the senior member of each group individually, given him to understand that there would be a channel for future work between the pair of them. No details were yet ready but, after the conference was over, each one was assured that, even without his knowing of it, contact, two-way if necessary, would be established over the coming months. Code names would be issued and used. The impression given was that each person was the only one to be contacted. However, in case of that one becoming a casualty, a stand-by would have to be detailed. Although it would probably be impossible to keep all this an absolute secret, if and when its existence became known, it would add to the mystique of an unplaced mystery. Not said was that the location of the Soviet controller would only ever be made known to a strictly limited group of the already indoctrinated and then its real task would always be disguised as, for instance, a normal Soviet consulate.

Soviet planning, though strict, was often shoddy. In this case the representative from Malaya was not told about such an arrangement but, in the manner of such secrets, vague details leaked out over the coming years. The Soviet planners, all in fact Russian, emphasised that the one common thread running through all the colonial powers, including the Japanese in the late war, but not quite so much in the case of the British, was thinking that they were superior in almost every aspect than the people over whom they ruled. It was ironic that the Russians themselves were probably the most 'racist' of all.

The conference programme included sessions for those already fighting their colonial masters, the Indonesians and Indo-Chinese, who would be asked to address the meeting. Language had become a bigger, much bigger, problem that had been considered initially when planning the conference. Stupidly, or perhaps arrogantly, the Russian advisors had presumed that the language would be either English or Hindi, quite forgetting that delegates from Indo-China would not know English but French and, likewise, those from the Dutch colony wouldn't know either but, presumably, Dutch. Getting an interpreter for both languages had been a problem but had been overcome by finding, after great difficulty, one of each language in Calcutta – but the expense!

The two delegates from the Dutch colony were splutteringly annoyed when their country of origin was put on the list of delegates as 'Dutch East Indies'. As soon as the war had finished in August 1945 the commander of the Nippon forces in the area, the 16th Army, Major General Nagano, on orders from Tokyo, had ordered that the occupying troops hand the country back to the inhabitants as the Republic of Indonesia. None of the conference planners had realised this, so hackles had unwittingly been ruffled. The journey to Calcutta had been fraught as well as being difficult to arrange and both delegates, Akbar Salleh and Atmaji Anugerah, felt that their presence had been taken too lightly.

'Which one of the Indonesian delegates would like to address the meeting?'

Atmaji Anugerah put his hand up and walked to the rostrum. He was a tall man with a mean face and a wispy black beard, hard eyes and, in all, a commanding presence. The interpreter joined him.

'Comrades, I come from Java. From what I have heard so far, I am inclined to think that the organisers of this conference have never been in as difficult a struggle as we have, since during the war and until now' he began. There was a stir of interest and of uneasiness in the hall. Hadn't they all suffered, indeed from childhood, by dominating colonial masters? What was this man getting at? 'The Dutch regarded us natives as their permanent servants. They came and most of them spent their whole lives in our country. I gather that, here in India, the British came to work then mostly returned to their home country and in Indo-China most French likewise. Bad though they were, they were never the arrogant, inflexible and often cruel masters as the Dutch were, or tried to be, over us, making money for themselves with never a thought for us.'

Heads in the audience nodded. Whether or not the Dutch were worse or just as bad as the English or the French was not to be argued, they had all suffered in one way or another: that those who had not suffered in any way but who had prospered were, obviously, not in the lecture hall, nor would have been invited to the conference in the first place.

Atmaji Anugerah went on with his talk: 'The Dutch army in Java surrendered to the Nippons,' a name strange to the others, 'after only nine days fighting so useless were they. We Indonesians suffered under the Nippons but they made our youth, I among them, into a Fatherland Defence Force and we were known as *Pemuda* – Youths – by the Nippons and Indonesians alike. We went into action by ourselves. We were formed into battalions and companies, and armed, drilled, exercised by the Nippons and then went into action on our own. Yes, we worked as an army. We *were* the army. All the Dutch people that the Nippons had interned when they invaded in 1942 were kept in their camps on a short diet with purposely limited medical supplies. This pleased us considerably as it was their turn to suffer.' He stopped talking and his eyes took on a look that told his listeners that his mind was back in his home country, gloating. After a significant pause he pulled himself back from infinity and continued. 'One day, in the August of 1945, we discovered that a 4-man recce group, with one of them being from the nearest village and who had escaped in 1942, had been brought to our shores in a submarine. They were landed not far from my village, a place called Subah, about halfway between Semarang and Batavia, now known as Jakarta. We were told that in Batavia there were signs saying "The Nippons must go. We are hungry". We had no idea the recce group had come until one small detail gave their presence away. The man who had left Java in 1942 went to a farmer who was working in his fields and offered him some money for information.

'He also brought some food, including palm oil, with him. We were short of food and the farmer took the stranger to his nearby shack and, with the palm oil, cooked a meal with the food he had been given none had eaten for a few years: *tempeh*, deep-fried, fermented soya beans and *bakwan*, vegetable fritters. Even *krupuk udang*, prawn crackers. Where the man from the submarine had brought the uncooked stuff from the farmer never found out and knew better than to ask.

'The money he gave to the farmer was not rupiahs that had come into circulation under the Nippons but a brand new, crisp guilder, one with palm trees and mountains with the head of the Dutch queen, Wilhelmina, on one side and on the other the crest of the Nederlandsch-Indische Handelsbank, something we had not seen since pre-war. That just shows you can't be too careful in every aspect, however small, that comes your way.

'Without thinking anything of it, the farmer took the pre-war money to the market to buy some paraffin but the shop keeper, who was a sympathiser of ours, asked him how he got it, so unusual was it, so suspicious was he. The farmer told him. Why should he hide it as the man who gave it to him said he had been born in the village but had moved out when still a boy? The shop keeper handed the note to the Nippons. Why? As it was so unusual, he would have been closely asked about how he got it if it had been found in his possession. He dared not keep it. It was dangerous as it had to mean something not allowed. The Nippons ordered us Pemudas to search and yes, our whole battalion, hunted for them and after two days we found two of them, killed one and captured the other.' A thrill went through his audience as his voice slid along each nerve in his listeners' bodies. This was an exciting story, showing resolved, tenacity and courage.

'The prisoner told us about the submarine and we learnt they were Australians. Why so few? To look for friends, which could only mean more invaders were coming. The Nippons were worried. But before the invaders came the two atomic bombs were dropped on Japan and the war ended. That meant the Nippons had to go back to their country but nobody knew quite when.'

He looked around, seeing how his audience was taking his talk, sensing they were with him. He scratched an itch in his nose and continued.

'The Nippons had let us fly our red and white national flag since September 1944. They were stern. They had two types of punishments, for "combat insurgency", or as they called it *genchi shobun,* on-the-spot-punishment, and *genju shobun*, punishment by law. They handed the defence of the country over to us and at the same time we became the Republic of Indonesia. The Dutch internees were still kept in their camps. They didn't concern us. However, the leader of the 4-man groups came to visit the Nippons and us also, claiming that he had come to let the Dutch prisoners free.' He shook his head. 'In no way did we allow it. We did not apprehend the one remaining Australian because it was now peace time and he was not Dutch. We were in charge and some of the Nippons took our side and some took the Australian's. That meant battles between them and us and, curse them, rival groups and us, that left so many dead we couldn't count them, not that it mattered, the more the better because anyone not wanting to fight properly for his own country was better dead. The battle for men's souls, often invisible, is always relentless.' These sombre words affected everyone listening.

'The Nippons who taught us most were the Kempeitai, the military police you could call them.' Yes, everybody in the room knew all about the dreaded Kempeitai, the Nippons' special service for political surveillance. 'They were not under the command of any officer in Java as they were directly under their own boss in Tokyo. The man in charge of our lot was like the Indonesian *dalang* puppet master. They knew what they wanted and how to get it. Because the imperialists were still in internment camps and could not get out, some of the wasters of our society began to live in a way that was disgraceful. The lieutenant in charge of the Kempeitai cleared out all the rubbish, the opium users, the whores, the swindlers and such like. Killed them all. There was no trouble after that. That taught us what to do to the Dutch people in the prison camps. Kill them, either by letting them starve, letting them have no medicines or shooting them.

'The Australian came to see us and begged us to help the prisoners, especially the women and children. No, never. That way they would never come back to take over our country.'

'What about weapons and transport?' someone asked him.

Atmaji Anugerah laughed derisively. 'We used Japanese armoured vehicles, small arms weapons, artillery and tanks.'

'Your Pemudas could manage all that by yourselves?' asked almost disbelievingly.

That brought Atmaji Anugerah down to earth. He shook his head. 'No, not to start with. But we had some older people who had been in the Dutch army and some of the Nippons helped us. The civilians were afraid of us and obeyed us instantly, but only when we were united. We did have another way of dealing with those who came silently to ravish our women.' Again this drew everyone's attention and the speaker's self-confidence returned. 'I'll tell you about one incident, in brief: a man, just a poor farmer, who wanted to kill two Nippons, Kempeitai they were, who had barged into his house and had started to rape his daughter. Near his house was some jungle. Even though it was dark, he had to take his revenge, there and then. He groped his way to where lengths of young bamboo and bundles of strip-like ties were stacked ready for thatching work. Feeling for a bamboo the right length and thickness, pushing quietly with his blade rather than chopping, he trimmed the slender end to a sharp point. It was only a short distance from his house where he knew an alert sentry would be sitting while the Nippons were doing their worst to his daughter. The wind was gusting from the south, carrying away any slight noise. Taking half a dozen of the ties, carrying his impromptu spear butt-forward, the angry father set off on the most difficult stage of his task so far: getting through to the top end of the timber path unheard and unseen.'

By now his listeners were agog. Would the man he successful?

'Traversing the undergrowth silently took nearly half an hour, and on reaching his chosen spot just short of the clearing, grey light was showing. There wasn't much time, but at least he could see to work.

'Among secondary thickets stood saplings up to a dozen feet tall, strong and whippy, perfect for his purpose. Choosing one growing an arm's length in from the path he tied his rope round it as high as he could reach, hauled it back with all his strength and secured it to a stump, using a slip-knot with a long trailing end. Next he lashed the butt of his spear to the sapling at chest height, resting the point in a loop of bamboo strip hung from a small tree by the path, to guide it forward and slightly down. Placing a fern frond on the path as a natural-looking mark, he led the trailing rope back and squatted to wait – till in the strengthening light a problem became frighteningly apparent. Even at walking speed a fraction of a second early or late and his spear would miss, split-second timing was crucial. Desperately he looked about: how on earth could he induce the lead man to slow down, even pause, opposite the spear? Faint vibrations trembled from two sets of feet padding confidently on the path, a voice grunted something, another replied. The rapists were leaving the house. His daughter had stopped screaming. He could just hear her moaning. He darted out, dropped his old, faded hat some yards beyond the fern frond and dashed back again, heart pounding so heavily he feared they must surely hear the drumbeats in his chest. Crêpe-soled boots padded closer, clothing brushed against lantana stems with tiny tearing sounds, the first figure loomed – and stopped. It was the elder of the two, shot gun tucked under his right arm, his companion a yard behind. Cropped head thrust forward as he studied the hat, the front man took a single cautious pace forward, paused, took another, and his trousered leg obscured the mark. The girl's father pulled gently on the rope.'

The narrator could now feel the intensity of the audience's interest.

'*Swish-thump!* The sapling sprang quivering upright.

'The second Nippon jerked back – then leapt to help the man transfixed in front of him. He was struggling to prise him free when the father emerged from behind and his parang blow split his head open.'

The audience cheered and clapped.

'Stuck fast, the wounded Nippon crouched leaning to the right, both hands gripping the haft pierced deep into his side. As the ravished girl's father moved round him, he raised his eyes and again he felt a clutch of dread: so might a neck-pinioned cobra, tail lashing but head held rigid, fix him with just such a deadly stare – then cold rage took over. The girl's father showed the wounded Nippon the parang blade, blood-stained. The eyes looked down at it then back up at him, crinkling a moment as if puzzled and taking deliberate aim chopped off the Nippon's right hand. Grip gone he sagged, and the father began to hack at him, gasping great sobs as he swung the heavy blade at arms and shoulder and neck and face till all that remained was a gory trunk still with the spear in it.

'So, that is how an ordinary farmer got his revenge by taking action when he could.'

The speaker, hoarse from talking, took a drink of water.

'But you say you were still fighting.'

'We were short of people. In late 1943 more than ten thousand men from Java were taken to Borneo. They were expendable. Village headmen were responsible for providing men for *romusha*, forced labour. I was told that 36 million people were employed on defence work. But who can count that many? Certainly, young strong men were at a premium for the Pemuda.'

'After all that what happened?' the questioner persisted. 'You went off on a tangent.'

'The Indian Army arrived from Malaya and attacked us with aircraft, naval gunfire, artillery and infantry attacks. A truce was called but we broke it. Dutch troops arrived and the worst were their Shock Troops, *Depot Speciale Troepen,* under a fiend named Raymond Westerling.'[6]

6 That detail and many others, especially of the Indonesian's discourse, can be confirmed in between pages 778 and 838 of *Blood and Ruins, The Great Imperial War, 1931-1945*, by Richard Overy, ISBN 978-0-723-

A question, spoken in French, came from the back of the room. 'What lessons have you for us?'

The French interpreter answered 'Who are you? What country do you come from?'

'Vo Nguyen Minh from French Indo-China.'

Atmaji Anugerah stared at the questioner, contemplatively. The rest of the audience waited for an answer, an answer that could help them. 'Kill every Frenchman you can, as well as any native who supports them, without regret, without remorse and without regard to anyone else.'

After that had been translated a huge collective breath of air whooshed out of everybody's mouth and hands were clapped. Vu Heng Lau held everybody's attention as he commented on that stark advice. 'That for us is not so easy, try hard though we do. Like you the Japanese gave us our independence at the end of the war but the French did not accept it. So we have been fighting them, causing many casualties but also taking them ourselves. We have one advantage you do not. We can have our planning HQ just over the border in China, while you are on an island so have nowhere to hide, unless you have some jungles, which I don't know about.'

Atmaji Anugerah looked at him, saying nothing, wrongly taking it as a veiled criticism.

'Like you Indonesians, we, too, were hungry. Perhaps up to three million people up north in Tonkin died of hunger in the last year of the war. I say "perhaps" because who can count as

---

99562-6. The name Westerling was well known to your author.

high as that?' The speaker broke off to let that sink in, then in a despairingly toneless voice continued, 'You say kill all Europeans, especially Dutch civilians and the Dutch army. In our case the French colonial army has a minority of Frenchmen: there are Indo-Chinese as well as a whole lot of Africans from Algeria, Tunis, Chad and I don't know where else. They only joined the French colonial army to feed themselves and their families. They are not our real enemies. Killing such people cannot help us after we have driven the Frenchmen out. Likewise, we didn't have any Japanese equipment to use so we employ guerrilla tactics: we keep off the roads which the French army use, disappear when they attack us and attack them when they are least expecting us. We have three types of soldier: main forces, regional forces and village guerrillas. These last are farmers by day and militants by night, uncountable hundreds all over the country. As Chairman Mao has it, the civilian population is the water we military fish swim in. From what you have said, this is the opposite from what you have tried to do and are still doing. He has written in a book of his Thoughts. In it he warns governments which have such fighters, communist fighters, in their country, "don't curse the people, they have thick skins; don't fight them because when you move in they move out: don't kill them, they become heroes: improve the lot of the people."'

It was a long speech, heartily applauded, making real sense compared to the abstract and dry lectures the Communist lecturers had given. It took longer than normal having to use two interpreters.

'And what, for example, do the regional forces do?' The

question came from the other Indonesian, Akbar Salleh, who was short, lean, strong and tough. The sinews of his neck were like a coiled spring.

'I'll give you an example of what sort of work they do that the French know nothing about. They dig tunnels where they and, sometimes, main force soldiers hide. The tunnels are most cleverly hidden. If the village is near a river the entrance is under water by the river bank. Those who enter hold their breath, go under the water and wriggle through a hole going upwards, above the water level. From there they climb into a trench complex. When making such hidey-holes the spoil is thrown into the water. Where there is no water, a similar entrance is made in the wall of a well, again under the water. Although the spoil is harder to get rid of, of course, but we have never been found out.'

The listeners pondered what original thinking and hard work had gone into such successful hiding places.

At the rostrum the Indonesian flushed and looked as though he could have battered the man from Indo-China for making him look as acting in a less formidable way and against much that the conference instructors had taught so far. He gesticulated angrily and was just about to give a response when the Indian in charge of the whole business took over.

'Thank you both for your fascinating contributions to our knowledge. We all have our own answers for our own country. What works in one need not work in another. Thank you both very much indeed.'

The interpreters passed on the message and the Indian clapped his hands, indicating to the rest of the audience to do likewise.

Thus, in its way, some sort of peace was restored.

The representative from Malaya saw that their problem was different because the Japanese had not announced Malaya's independence, or, if they had, he had not heard about it nor had the MCP, try hard though it did, harp on it as, so it seemed, those other two countries had.

In the event, at the end, Sharkey's speech, billed as the 'star turn', was an anti-climax, almost a flop. Flushed, sweating and gesticulating wildly, it went on for too long as the interpreters found his Australian accent awkward, so difficult to comprehend. He started off by offending the organisers by saying that the programme had been poorly thought out. Quoting Soviet doctrine was not enough. It was too high-flown. He gave an example by quoting: *Surprise is the greatest factor in war. There are two kinds, tactical and strategic. Tactical surprise is an operational art. A skilled unit commander can generally achieve it. Strategic surprise is attained at the political level.* That was the focus for a higher-level course: here was for basic work such as had been heard from Indonesia and Indo-China. He supposed most of the listeners had, till then, probably only ever held a catapult in their hands, a humiliating remark that left no one untouched. They saw the brash and uncouth Australian as a politician and not a guerrilla operator so was not worth listening to. When he asked if anyone had any questions for him, only one man put his hand up.

A young man stood up. 'I am a Nepali from Darjeeling and my name is Padamsing Rai. My question is: can Mr Sharkey see any contradiction in the Chinese proposals and teaching compared with their Soviet counterparts?'

The Australian thought for a moment. 'No, Marx and Lenin are the bedrock of them both. Why should there be any difference?'

'Because I have read that the Soviets try to impose their will on the countries of Europe, and even India, from the top downwards whereas the Chinese think that, once the masses know what is wanted and are converted, Communism will spread upwards. I want to know because I intend to work on the Gurkha soldiers in the British Army in Malaya to make them Communists so that the British will get rid of them, in other words, start from the bottom. Is the bottom really the correct tipping point for my work to succeed or is the top? But I can't start at the top.'

The question flummoxed the Australian who gave a general answer that showed he could not think at a basic tactical level. He lamely suggested to 'play it by ear', not looking all that pleased, especially when some in the audience started tittering.

Padamsing thanked him dutifully and sat down, looking as pleased as a thirsty cat is with a saucer of milk.

Early June 1948, North Malaya: Chen Fan Tek, the tall, gangling Hakka grocer with a long, thin face, had opened a grocery shop in Taiping after being a guerrilla in the Malayan Races Liberation Army (MRLA) during the Japanese occupation. It was late one night when he heard a rhythmic tapping on the side door. He was a light sleeper, unlike his wife who only woke up during a heavy thunder storm. The tapping was insistent and a nearby dog started barking. He recognised it as a code but even so he took a short stick and went to see if it was whom he feared it might be.

He had become accustomed to such visits even though the war had been over these last three years. He opened the door and, yes, it was the man he had feared it might be.

His visitor, a short, squat man, with a jagged scar down one cheek, went inside uninvited and demanded brandy. 'You have made a successful job of your shop. I suppose you want to stay here.' He spoke disdainfully as though not wishing to be contradicted.

'Yes, I do. I had enough discomfort during the war, roughing it in the jungle. I want to stay here and earn sufficient money for my family to have an easier life than I had when young.'

His visitor shook his head. 'No, you can't stay here. The Party wants you back. I have come to fetch you.' He gave his ultimatum in a flat tone of voice, with no subtlety shown and no refusal denied.

'No thanks. I've told you, I've had enough.'

The visitor grinned maliciously. 'Do you want your two teenage daughters used by our hungry comrades?'

Chen Fan Tek shuddered. 'It's your choice,' he was told.

The visitor finished off his drink. 'I'll come back tomorrow to have your answer,' he said abruptly, got up and left.

Chen Fan Tek had no more sleep that night. The next day he talked with his wife and when the visitor came back later, he had another drink before the two of them left together.

The many rubber estates all over Malaya, remote and separated from other estates, meant that the manager with his wife and probably a small family were exposed so were prime targets for the MCP's guerrillas in their campaign of damaging the economy by intimidating the plantation staffs. Not only the Europeans but the Tamil labour force also was frightened by rumours of Communist aggression to be taken against them who, hoping that by not being Chinese, they would not be a target.

Everton Estate was located about one third of the way along the road between Kuala Kubu Bharu and Tanjong Malim. The red laterite estate road ran through many acres of tall, slender rubber trees before reaching a sign, Manager's Bungalow, Everton Estate. It was a white-painted, two-storeyed building, standing alone, with high, sloping roofs of dark red tiles, built on a small knoll, which got what breeze there was, and surrounded by spacious lawns and colourful shrubs.

Below the bungalow were the servants' quarters and a little farther off was the 'heart' of the concern, the latex-collecting sheds where sheet rubber was made and dried before being taken away for processing. Tapping the rubber trees started in the dawn twilight as sap rises most easily in the early morning.

During the day the manager, a tall, energetic, dark-haired Welshman named Peter Jones, would inspect some fields, visit the factory and go to his office to deal with the inevitable paperwork. By three o'clock the tappers would have returned to the factory with the latex they had spent the morning tapping and later collected in buckets. The routine only varied if a 'field' had to be hewn down and replanted.

One day Peter Jones had to go out for a meeting. He told his wife he'd be back for a late lunch so not to wait for him. Kissing her good bye he got into his vehicle and drove himself off.

Because Chen Fan Tek had not immediately wanted to rejoin the MRLA guerrillas, he was under suspicion. In that he and two others who also feared retribution unless they succeeded with something that the Party would approve of, they decided, if possible, to do more than recce Everton Estate to see how much damage they could do. He knew from his grocery days that there was a European manager, his wife and small child. The three guerrillas felt that even if they only killed the manager they would no longer fear retribution from the Party.

On their recce the three men had seen the car drive away with Peter Jones being unaccompanied. 'It will be easier to ambush and kill him when the car comes back rather than force our way into the house and kill the Europeans and any staff who come to try and save them,' the Hakka told his two companions.

They mulled that over, nodded and one of them added a rider. 'We will gain more merit if we kill them all at the house but some of the workers could see us and follow-up will be quick. If we are caught we'll be strung up, that's for sure. Better think of somewhere else.'

'I know the very place,' said the third man. 'A corner on the estate road where we can ambush him and easily make our escape into the jungle. That way we won't be tracked, if at all, for several hours by when we'll be safe.'

And that is what they decided to do. They went to where the road went round a bend that was easily ambushed, hid to one side and waited till they heard the car approaching then slowing down. The three of them left their hiding place, glad to get away from the voracious mosquitoes, and stood in the middle of the narrow road, held up their hands to slow the vehicle down.

The vehicle slowed to a stop. The manager, furious with what he saw, stepped out of the vehicle and was immediately shot and killed. The guerrillas left the car as it was, engine still running and made their escape. When, by half past 3, her husband had not returned, his distraught wife rang the office to see if there was any news. As she was listening to an answer two breathless Chinese tradesmen delivering some grocery goods to the bungalow, came hurrying up on foot with the fatal news. They would have come quicker if the estate road had not been blocked.

So many similar and worse incidents of unease, unrest and military action had been happening in Malaya since World War Two, that the High Commissioner declared an Emergency on Thursday 17th of June in the north and Friday 18th in the south, to try and contain further serious trouble by the MRLA against the civil population. The killing of European planters and other unfortunates, the slashing of rubber trees, the burning of taxis and the ambushing of railway trains plus many other outrages had to be stopped. The 'Active Phase', as it was then known, of Communist Revolutionary Warfare that had erupted, had taken many by surprise although unease, unrest and military action were not confined to Malaya ...

... clouds come out now as we cross the first mountain range at four thousand feet after leaving Tonkin. The plane, a box car, begins to rock, both pilots check the controls and the navigator goes from one side of the cockpit to the other, trying to get a

visual bearing. In the cargo hold the four French riggers have been busy getting loads ready to drop. A strong buzzer sounds: five minutes off target.

Two riggers go to the edge of the cargo hold and start unfastening chains which hold the load in place. They have no parachutes as it was felt that if they fell out with six tons of ammunition there would be no time for the chutes to open. Why waste good parachutes? The load has to be unlashed as the plane goes down into its final approach run, but should it hit air turbulence at this precise moment much of the load might fall out prematurely. Yet, a steady approach gives the enemy a good chance to zero in whatever anti-aircraft guns he may have.

The plane goes into a shallow dive and, exactly over the Dropping Zone, sharply noses upward. Warned by buzzer, two of the riggers jump up and push the load out of the plane with a roar of clanging metal and whooshing static lines. Watching, the riggers see the parachutes have opened. Then all four riggers, lying flat, pull the chutes' static lines back into the plane, against the strength of the slipstream.

Then it happens: a slight tremor on the left wing, and some holes appear in it. Communist anti-aircraft-fire. Simultaneously two fighters swoop in and suddenly a big black billow opens behind them – napalm, jellied gasoline. The village burns furiously. The two fighters swooped down in turn and rake the area with machine guns ... neither the pilots of the fighters or the box car know whether that village was a Communist one or not ...

... whatever tactical victories the French won, and there

were some, the tide of history was against them and eventually their empire crumbled during the 'Octave of Easter', 1954. The political base of the colonial government was not strong enough to prevail and the people of France were in no mood for any more wars so far away when nearer to home Algeria was seen as a greater and more important problem. From 1954 onwards the political base of the Americans was even less strong than it had been under the French and most unbiased people saw the eventual end long before the Americans did.

In Malaya the political base of the British was strong. Even when planters phoned in with reports of guerrillas,[7] initially tired police officers who had spent the war as captives, were 'sniffy' of those who had escaped and come back after the war. Police morale was low, and many casualties were caused by the guerrillas, some because there were no armoured-plated lorries to convey the police jungle squads as well as insufficient training for a quickly expanding police force. British battalions were full of national servicemen whose interest in Malaya was minimal. It looked to the MCP that victory could not be all that far away. And yet ... and yet ...

Even though in the early days, members of the MCP Politburo saw the sluggish reaction of Gurkha troops as a factor in favour of a quick victory, it was misguided, albeit not to start with. It was known that units had arrived from India ludicrously under

---

7 It is a historical fact that when, in late December 1948, the Director of Operations was asked what his reaction was when planters told him of guerrilla activity, he answered 'take off the last two figures of their total, divide by two and take necessary action.' When that became known he retired for health reasons.

strength, thanks to the subversive campaign organised and carried out by agents in India. For the first two years many of the older Gurkha soldiers referred to the guerrillas as 'Congress'. Other agents in Malaya had reported that the Emergency was declared before the recruits who had been hurriedly enlisted to bring units up to strength were even halfway through their basic training. One example was that when the first lot of recruits were deployed in action their weapon training standards were so low – some had yet to fire their rifles on the range – and so dangerous to their own side rather than to the guerrillas, that when on sentry duty they fixed bayonets rather than loaded their rifles. Those officers who had fought in Burma felt that the maximum period of jungle operations should be three days at the very longest. In other words, Gurkhas were not seen as any serious threat. There was no proper kit: rice often had to be cooked in split bamboo, heavy leather boots were worn, wireless sets were so heavy they had to be carried on stretchers, helicopters and air-drops were unknown.

Certainly the British were ill-prepared for the outbreak of hostilities and the guerrillas held the initiative. The problem in the 12th Gurkhas was exacerbated by both battalions being made into Gunners with an influx of officers who knew nothing of jungle work or of Gurkhas. After some painful setbacks (and for 12 GR the withdrawal of Gunner officers with and then becoming infantry once more) all Gurkha battalions quickly regained their old standards as experience, combined with better training, made them a more feared adversaries than the CT – Communist Terrorists, the name the Government had invented to get away from the word 'bandit' which the Communists used for Nationalist Chinese soldiers – had thought likely or possible.

By 1952, even with nobody realising that the tide had started to turn against the MRLA, even though no tipping point in the government's favour had yet been reached – or would it ever be? asked the pessimists – however hard and bravely so few guerrillas fought against so many, better armed than were they, with air and sea assets that only the Security Forces had. Not only that, but the colonial government was stronger than its French or Dutch equivalent and, among its armed forces, there were initially six then later eight battalions of Gurkhas (the extra two being brought over from Hong Kong). The tenacity and skills of these remarkable men who spent the whole of the time in the jungle, as opposed to British battalions who only spent one tour in Malaya, were instrumental in eventually defeating the Communists, the only time ever on territory of their own choosing.[8]

It must not be presumed that either side in the bitter and bloody struggle was to be seen in isolation. Despite difficulties in communications, events were followed critically by a shielded and hidden shadowy organisation of such secrecy yet so potent that its tentacles reached everywhere the controllers felt they were needed. Only the tiniest handful of the hierarchy of the Communist world knew of it or even in which country it was based. Rumours placed it in India, in north Burma, in south China and even as far away as Russia. Certainly none of the non-Communist world had any idea of its existence. Any of its manifestations were put down

---

8 In the Dofar province of Oman, Communists were beaten by British troops, with the Sultan's explicit support (1970-1975).

to local factors of labour unrest in one form or another, no one ever guessing that controlling tentacles were the cause of the disturbances.

Its existence, revelation and demise came about in a completely unexpected manner, not as the result of any Special Branch intelligence effort or one of its members reneging on his oath of secrecy, but because of an officer of the 1st Battalion of the 12th Gurkha Rifles, (1/12 GR), happened to stumble across it …

This officer was a Captain Jason Percival Vere Rance: for some the cloister and the bell, for others the camp and the bugle. This latter was for Rance, a soldier to his fingertips. He was about six feet tall, with a taut, lean body and the indefinable air of a natural commander. With fair hair, penetrating blue eyes, his features were almost hawk-like and stern. He showed his pleasure with a wonderful open smile. He was a brilliant linguist and had proved to be an outstanding company commander, an exceptionally talented jungle operator, good with the men, dedicated and hard-working who, if he could get his administrative and staff training as good as his tactics, could go far, but his background was unusual – 'broken the mould' some of his seniors grumbled. He had been born in Kuala Lumpur, his father had been 'something', never asked what, tax official it was hinted, so probably not really a gentleman, and, from what he had guessed, had married 'beneath him'. Mrs Rance's background was most certainly unusual, although Jason never spoke about either parent: as a young woman she had been a ventriloquist who helped her father run a Punch-and-Judy show. She made sure that her son could master that unusual art and make different voices. Quite why, other than for party tricks, she never told him: possibly it was vanity and possibly so that her own gifts need not be lost after her death. As a young boy he had adopted his father's Chinese co-worker's son as a brother and became bilingual in Chinese, as well as having a good working knowledge of written Chinese characters, and was fluent in Malay. He kept quiet about his Chinese language ability, almost as though he was, well, not exactly ashamed of it – why should he be? – but more to keep it as a 'secret weapon'. He made company and battalion parties a roaring success by being a ventriloquist: he had a dummy which he sat on his knee and the absurd conversations in Nepali and English brought the house down every time he did it. One of his acts involved a highly coloured model krait which added to his performance.

In guerrilla jungle warfare at company level such empathy with his soldiers was essential in getting positive results, maintaining high morale and keeping casualties to an absolute minimum. His Commanding Officers could not make up their minds about him: some accepted him by judging from results his company produced, accepted his unusual characteristics, his being unconventional, his being unorthodox: others found it difficult to accept one who 'would not have been commissioned pre-war'. In the Brigade of Gurkhas, unlike in a large corps, seniors who belittled juniors were hard to hide from ... but with his men behind him, Captain Rance was hard to find fault with.

2

Saturday 4 August 1951, south of Labis, Johor, Malaya: The noise of the telephone by the side of the Major's bed in the small hours was like a buzzing bee in a drunken dream that did not make sense. It went on and on until it woke him. He had had a couple too many night caps before he went to bed and was hazier than normal. He groped his way to turn on the light, picked up the phone and, crossly, said who he was before asking who the hell was at the other end at this time of night? He inwardly cursed as his head was aching.

'It's Peter from Police HQ. I have a red-hot tip for you. A large party of guerrillas has come into your operational area. I think your whole company is in base and we have no police jungle squads anywhere near. I recommend you move now and catch them at dawn. I'll give you their grid reference.'

'Wait a sec for me to pick up a piece of paper and a pencil.' The man on the other end heard a rustle of paper. 'Go ahead. I'm ready.'

The line was not good and the grid reference that came across was misheard so wrongly written down. It was not read back so the mistake was not noticed.

The Major, a tall, burly man of florid countenance and no

unnecessary words, staggered out of his room and, at the top of his voice, shouted out in Nepali 'Stand to, stand to. Line sentry, wake up everybody, tell them to fetch their weapons and the normal amount of ammunition from the armoury and fall in when ready. Tell my "O" Group to be in my office as soon as possible. Alert the drivers for all transport to be ready to move out.'

He dressed quickly, put on his equipment and his orderly brought him his weapon, a rifle, and fifty rounds of ammo as he reached his office. He looked at the map, found the grid reference and the nearest mile stone to it as his 'O' Group came in. He told them to sit down and briefed them on the intended operation and the order of march. 'Once we are there, I'll give further orders. No time for any tea.' Before writing out a short message for the rear link signaller to send to Battalion HQ and detailing the company clerk and the office runner as escorts for the vehicles when they were empty, he stressed that their tailboards had to be lowered with no noise at all. 'Sidelights only when you see my headlights go off.'

Well within the hour the company was moving south along the Ayer Panas road, fully expectant. When, in the front of the leading truck, the Major saw that the relevant mile stone for debussing was near, he told the driver to switch off his headlights. On seeing the next milestone, he told the driver to halt. The other vehicles drew up behind. The drivers slowly lowered the tailboards with no noise, the men debussed and fell in by the side of the road. The 'O' Group reported to the OC.

'It is still too dark to go and look for the daku. We will go into the rubber estate on this side of the road and lie up till dawn.

When we move forwards towards the swamp on the far side of the rubber 4 Platoon will be left, 5 right and 6 with me as reserve with Company HQ. Fire on sight!' Platoon commanders moved to give their orders and the company moved into the rubber to lie up.

Dawn was misty. The Major gave the sign to advance; the lighter it got the farther apart the men moved. Bunching is never a good idea.

A guerrilla sentry, who had left his post and moved over to a clump of bushes to relieve nature, was on his way back to where the guerrillas had spent the night when a soldier spotted him. The Gurkha fired, killed him. On the noise of the shot, the occupants of the guerrilla camp, as yet unseen by the soldiers, were ordered forward and advanced to counter their so-far-unseen aggressors. The Gurkhas saw them as they came into view and four more of them were killed. Their return fire went wide. The Gurkhas killed two more. The rest of the guerrillas were seen disappearing towards the swamp on the edge of the rubber estate. As the troops charged after them, one managed to waylay a soldier and slash him to death with a parang before escaping. He was the only Gurkha casualty.

In the ensuing follow up a total of thirty-five guerrillas were killed or captured. The company went back to the road taking the captured guerrillas with them. Luckily a police vehicle passed which was stopped and told to go back to their police station and bring back a squad of men to collect the corpses.

The company returned to Labis and had a late meal after cleaning weapons. Battalion HQ was rung up with the good news and congratulations were the order of the day. The dead Gurkha's corpse was sent to Seremban for proper obsequies. The rest of the day was free, and the Major threw a great party that night. He was overjoyed to be awarded the DSO in the next Honours and Awards List, the only company commander to get that level of bravery award during the whole Emergency.[9]

Wednesday 8 August 1951: somewhere in the Cameron Highlands, north Malaya: The camp of the MCP Politburo and its attendant staff was cleverly sited in deep hilly jungle, difficult to see from the air or be approached without alerting the sentries. Under the thick jungle canopy it was on flat ground totally cleared of its undergrowth.

The camp was high enough to be cool by day and chilly at nights, especially after it had been raining, which it did, heavily, almost every day. It was closely guarded by chosen units of the MRLA. A couple of the few light machine guns that the MRLA had either captured or kept from the war years were tactically sited with rifle positions around the perimeter. Camp sentries alerted the inmates by low whistles. Some distance below were guerrilla outposts responsible for patrolling and engaging any approaching Security Forces, their aim being to draw them away from the main camp before engaging them decisively.

Water was never a difficulty as there was a spring at the back of the camp and a stream flowed along one edge of it. Rations, though, were a constant problem and a complicated and

---

9 That is an outline of the official history quoted in the preface.

tenuous supply trail had been put into operation. Fresh meat was sometimes available – routine patrols were not allowed to shoot for food but traps were set for deer, porcupine and jungle pig. Cooking, always strictly controlled because of smoke problems, was done in a confined area near the spring, with any excess smoke drifting away above the stream until it dispersed rather than rise above the tree canopy. On one side was a cave for stores, rice, flour, a few clothes and sleeping material for any important visitor, as well as a small workshop where arms could be mended. There was enough space for a rudimentary game of volley ball to be played of an evening. Limbs grew stiff sitting around camp all day. Outside patrols were kept to a minimum to avoid leaving tell-tale signs. An evacuation plan was practiced once a month. It had not yet been used in action.

The guerrillas' huts, made of waterproof palm thatch, were almost invisible from the air: strict orders had been given, and were always as strictly carried out, for fresh leaves to be put on the roofs as soon as the old ones became the slightest different in colour. This was necessary to keep the camp from being spotted by pilots and air photography, both constant dangers. Always tidy and clean, huts were built on low bamboo-slatted platforms six inches above the ground as protection both against insects and any possible flash flooding. The senior men slept in hammocks. Strung on poles, they too had leafy camouflage on top. Men had light-weight blankets. There were no mosquitoes or midges. In front of each guerrilla's sleeping place was his pack, always ready with what was needed if an immediate evacuation were ever ordered. Personal weapons were carried at all times: at night they were as close to the owner's body as would a wife have been. Guerrillas wore khaki shirt and trousers, puttees and canvas shoes – easy for leeches to cluster round each ankle – and a round, small-peaked khaki hat with a red star, cloth or enamel.

There was a separate part of the camp for the wireless set. Provision of and charging batteries were never easy. For the charging, a bicycle frame, complete with the pedals, was linked to the battery and prolonged pedalling charged it.

There had been an air of unease, if not of apprehension, among senior party members for the past couple of months and a Politburo meeting had been called. The nub of the worry was the sense of affairs not going as well as they might or as they had been. There was a suspicion that some of the set-backs, especially in the south of the country, might just be because of a treacherous insider working for the Security Forces. It was therefore decided that a small and senior group of members, suitably escorted, should go on a fact-finding tour, dangerous but necessary. The leader of the group was to be Comrade Ah Fat. He was, in fact, a police 'mole' of the highest ability: no one had ever had any reason to suspect him. He was well built and solid, with fluid movements. His eyes were always alert, never missing a trick, even though his peripheral gaze was not easy to follow. He looked a tad glum, was round of face, with ears close to his head: in some circles they had given him the nickname of *P'ing Yee*, Flat Ears. He stood about five and a half feet high. He had a habit of rubbing the palms of his hands together when thinking. Normally taciturn, he could be vivacious if to remain silent would have been suspicious or when he did not have to act his part so could be natural. He was well educated and spoke excellent English. However, for safety's sake, he kept that skill a closely guarded secret lest his 'other' role be jeopardised. Whenever he did speak English in front of other Chinese, it was only of middle-school standard.

The composition of the search team had just been voted when the comrade in charge of the camp defence reported that a courier and his escort had arrived and was asking for an audience with the Secretary General, Chin Peng.

'Did he give his name and have you vetted him?'

'Yes, he is Comrade Xi Zhan Yang.'

Comrade XI was as loyal a member of the party as one could find and the Secretary General relied fully on him, being his personal courier. He was based in Kuala Lumpur and had a delicate woman contact in Police HQ who gave him information never divulged to unauthorised people. 'Send him to me immediately.'

Xi, who also used an alias of Ah Ho, had a squat face, lined and careworn as an old map, and tiny nostrils which made him look like a frog. He had a slightly reedy, hooting voice. Sending his escort to report to the soldiers' part of the camp, he was told to go to where the Politburo was meeting. He looked dead beat as any long walk through the jungle, always being ready to take evasive action to hide from any military activity, was always fraught and something none of the Politburo had done since during the Japanese war. It was immensely tiring. He was welcomed and asked what his report was and 'can it wait as we are having a session?'

Xi shook his head. 'It is opportune that I talk to you all. There are two major points I think every comrade should learn about immediately.'

Sipping a hot drink, he gave the outlines of his first report which were ominous: thirty-five comrades had been killed or captured south of Labis in Johor by a strong patrol of *Goo K'a bing*, Gurkha soldiers, under the command of an imperialist *gwai lo*, foreigner. The dead included Yap Piow, the commander of No. 7 Company and Ng Chen, second-in-command of the Killer Squad. A most serious loss.

'That, Comrades, is the outline and I have a detailed written report.' He rummaged in his backpack and handed it over.

'I hope your second report is not as gloomy as the first one,' said Lee An Tung, the Head of the Central Propaganda Department. He had a dry, hot-eyed, dark, 'chiselled' face and whose clipped grey hair had the carbonised iridescence of coke. He was a squat, pugnacious-looking, slightly balding man with a perpetual frown and a worried look on his face whenever he spoke.

'No, Comrade. It is vague but, I believe, accurate. There is a *gwai lo* army officer in a Gurkha battalion who wants to join our organisation ...' There was such an intake of breath from his audience that his words were drowned. '... who is a secret card-carrying party member.' He paused and looked around him. All faces showed utter surprise.

'Do you know any other details? That is much too vague even to make outline plans on,' the Secretary General said, doubt in his voice.

The courier made a moue and pulled back his shoulders. He was tired and hungry. If he had known any more details, he would have given them. Hiding any irritation, he said, 'I personally have no first-hand knowledge but the weight of rumours says he is stationed in Seremban and wants to join us as soon as you can allow him. Once permission is given the local contacts can arrange his disappearance. After that it is up to you, Comrades.' He waved his hands at the others and stifled a sneeze as he did.

Even the Secretary General saw that Xi needed a rest so he thanked him, as did the others, told him to go and have a meal, a wash, a sleep and they would meet on the morrow, having read his report.

Chin Peng, who had a large mouth, perfect even teeth, eyes, when animated, that grew round and eyebrows that rose about an inch and a half, now merely frowned and said, 'That first report is extremely serious. We have never before lost so many at one time. It is a far cry from what we had expected from the Gurkhas a couple of years back.' The comrades' glum faces showed that they agreed with him.

'As for the second report, we cannot, must not, dismiss it. Comrade Ah Fat and your team will keep your ears open when you are in the Seremban area and check that such a man really does exist. If he does, you must try to vet his credentials before reporting back to us. Only then can we decide on his future.'

All agreed. At that stage that seemed the best method of finding out about him.

'Now, what can we do about trying to remedy the military situation, especially in Johor, and recover the initiative? Think about it and later on today we'll have another session.'

On re-assembling, the Secretary General asked 'Has anyone any ideas, any possible solution to the military problem outlined earlier on? The real point is, is it a one-off fluke or a permanent trend?'

Comrade Lee An Tung, well known for his accurate analyses, said, 'Comrades, yes, I have an idea that, fluke or trend, could result in events moving back to being in our favour. Let me dilate.' He glanced around and began. 'When we started our military campaign we had successes almost every time we engaged the imperialists as we knew we would. Now that is less and less the case. Instead of being warned of enemy movement as well as being given food and rations by our reliable civilian comrades,' he was referring to the many 'squatters', Chinese families living on unregistered plots of land on the jungle fringes, known as the Min Yuen, the Masses Movement, 'our active comrades have had to move deep into the jungle to grow their own food, their original sources now having dried up.' He was referring to what was known as the 'Briggs Plan'. This was when Lieutenant General Sir Harold Briggs, recalled from pension, ordered all squatters be re-settled in 'New Villages', so cutting off the guerrillas from any contact with them. This was not quite the surprise it was intended to be as an unscrupulous reporter found out about it and published it before the prescribed date but, apart from a few guerrillas hiding in squatter areas managing to escape, no one else was prematurely alerted.

'There are now many more *Goo K'a bing*, Gurkha soldiers, than there were in the beginning' Comrade Lee continued, 'and they are much better trained than they were to start with. It seems we misjudged their potential. British troops are noisier by far so much easier to deal with, either by ambushing them or avoiding them while the Malay Regiment's two battalions operate in areas of less importance.' He wondered how his listeners were reacting to what he was saying so looked round, saw they were interested and, from the look on their faces, still wondering what he was aiming at. 'If the *Goo K'a bing* carry on like this it will take us much longer than we had first thought to win and make the country the Democratic Republic of Malaya.' He spread out his arms and made a gesture almost of despair. 'So maybe, drat it, the civilian population will become disillusioned with us and ... I dare not say it out loud.' His audience looked at him, not daring to believe that any disloyal and unParty-like idea would be mentioned or ever accepted. But ... but no one interrupted him and he went on, 'what we must do is to get the *Goo K'a bing* away from Malaya. Then win we will.'

A pregnant hush descended as his listeners mulled over such a revolutionary and, on the surface, impossible proposal.

The Secretary General blinked, gulped – he was not a man for radical solutions to any problem – and said, 'Comrade, that is certainly an attractive, attentive and original thought but, sadly, unachievable. However, knowing you would not have mentioned it without believing in it, how do you plan to achieve it?' Unconscientiously he shook his head in despondence.

'Comrade Secretary General, I agree it sounds impossible but, given time, we can make it work. Listen! We need to persuade the British government that the Gurkhas are untrustworthy and so must be disbanded ... no, wait ... and if not quite that, get our

Indian comrades to persuade them not to return from leave and, at the same time, cause enough trouble in Borneo, especially in Sarawak, which I believe does not have any proper army, so get any remaining Gurkhas sent there from Malaya' and his voice trailed off as he let his suggestion of a Gurkha-free Malaya sink in. It was greeted with gasps of surprise and head-shaking of disbelief.

The Secretary General broke the silence that had descended as each listener pondered this seemingly impossible proposal. 'But how … how can you, or anyone else come to that, organise such a plan for any success?'

'No, of course there can be no guarantee of success, there never can be, but I really do believe it can be done but it will take time to accomplish. I can get it started. First I want to "feel the pulse" so to speak. There needs to be a kind of recce for the basis of this and there are two people I know whom we can make use of for this task.'

'And who are they?' queried Chin Peng in a dubious tone of voice, not liking to appear in ignorance.

'To start off he is Comrade Xi Zhan Yang and others whom he will persuade to be useful.'

'And how do you expect to use him?' the Secretary General asked, a touch acidly.

'To get any Gurkhas over to Borneo Comrade Xi can contact our comrades in Singapore who, quite how I personally don't know, can contact our Borneo comrades to make plans for serious disruption of normal life sufficiently to get the Gurkhas over from Malaya. The man to arrange for this to happen is Sim Ting Ong,

Secretary General of the Sarawak United People's Party, who lives in Kuching. He will be contacted by comrades going there by boat from Singapore. The man to contact in Singapore is Chen Geng, he has the same name as a general in the People's Liberation Army which he is secretly proud of. He has an office in Pedder Street. Wait.' He took a note book out of his pocket, searched for and found what he was looking for and continued, 'at number 47. His work there is in a normal trading concern so it is safe to ask for him by name. That is the outline for that part of my plan. For the other, the "disillusion" part shall I call it, do you remember what Comrade Lee Soong told us when he came back from that meeting in Calcutta in early 1948?'

'Remind us, remind us,' was chorused.

'That a renegade Nepali from the Darjeeling branch of the All-India Gorkha League' – he used the English words, even pronouncing the 'r' – 'with some comrades, has enlisted in the army and is, I believe, in Singapore. He was at one time in Seremban. I have learnt that his name is Padamsing Rai of the 12th Gurkha Rifles. He is the senior renegade to have been infiltrated. To start with he was a clerk in their first battalion. He is a well-educated man, far more so than the average Gurkha soldier and I have heard that he is now instructing Gurkhas in an army educational school in Singapore, an ideal place to disseminate our philosophy. He and any others like him could indeed be the catalyst we need for gradually influencing Gurkha soldiers to leave the army and behave in a mutinous fashion till they get home. As you probably know he will have visited one or more of the three rubber estates in Negri Sembilan that have a Nepali workforce to make contact with them. He will have great influence there as I believe he has relations among them.' Again he looked at the other comrades. 'Do you agree with me so far?'

'We approve, we approve,' was shrilled with applause.

Comrade Lee An Tung continued. 'Once we have made contact with him and heard how the renegades plan to work, we will plan how best we can help them. I don't see how we can fail but fail we must not. Getting the Gurkhas away from Malaya, east and north, so preventing them from winning, will be the *juin jit dim*, the "turning point" for our victory. Let "Turning Point" be our operational codeword.'

Sitting quietly at one side was the non-voting member of the Politburo, Ah Fat. He listened carefully, saying nothing. He knew that 'tipping' rather than 'turning' was the English equivalent to what was meant in Chinese and also that while 'turning point' was not necessarily irrevocable 'tipping point' was, even if 'history *turned* on a very small point'. In his mind's eye he saw that his secret work in the south of the country would be his personal Operation Tipping Point to thwart such plans. He had no conception of how he could achieve such a task. *It won't be me if I can't* he thought. *The art will be to recognise the chance when it comes rather than bank on it beforehand.* A thought struck him: *they have not considered stopping Gurkha recruiting!*

In due course Comrade Ah Fat and his team moved off southwards in their quest for possible leaks. There was no given time for their return as there was no point in skimping such an important job, was there?

Friday 12 September 1952, Seremban, Negri Sembilan, Malaya:
After thirty months of continuous jungle operations a period of six weeks 're-training' was decreed for 1/12 GR by Higher Authority. Men were tired and needed refreshing and re-training, so all companies withdrew into their permanent base camp. This not only included certain aspects of modern warfare and weapon classification on the range but also involved a drill competition, inter-company soccer and basket-ball matches making the overall winner the Champion Company. When it was over and before the battalion re-deployed, it was decided to have a 'Mess Night', the time-honoured mystical communion of a communal meal undertaken according to strict protocol handed down over many military generations. However, it so happened that the battalion was caught up in an operation code-named Janus,[10] caused by the renegade British officer Hinlea, trying to abscond to the guerrillas. The ensuing attempt to capture him – successful, to everyone's relief and satisfaction – had meant that the Mess Night had had to be postponed. The following week would see the battalion deployed once more on operations so this Friday was the only day it could be arranged.

Tropical mess kit had not yet been introduced so officers wore 'Penguin Order', black trousers edged with black ribbon, white shirts, black bow ties and a green cummerbund. On the long ebony Mess table silver and crystal floated and a row of candlesticks seemed to march in stepless union. In the middle was the centrepiece of two silver cannon, opposite which sat the

---

10 See *Operation Janus*.

Commanding Officer, the 'Karnel Saheb', father of the battalion, whose word was law and who represented, in person, the Queen. The meal was over by half past eight, the table cleared and dusted down. Only three glasses remained in front of each person, one for each of the individual preference of drink for the loyal toast. At the top of the table sat the President and at the other end the Vice President; from either end three decanters, port, Madeira and whisky, were religiously started on their left-hand journey to the other end, to be passed on by each officer after filling his glass. They only left the surface of the table when raised to pour out their precious contents, otherwise they were slid from person to person to finish up at the opposite end from where they had started.

The buzz of chatter stilled, resurged, then died down at a knock on the table with a gavel. All eyes turned to the President, Major O'Neal, the Second-in-Command, a pre-war regular, now standing up, glass of port in his right hand, blinking with the nervous tic caused from having been a prisoner in Japanese hands for over three years, to propose the loyal toast. 'Mr Vice, the Queen.' 'Queen' still sounded strange after so many years of hearing 'King' since August 1947 and 'King Emperor' for so many years in India beforehand.

The Gurkha Mess Sergeant stood rigidly to attention behind his chair.

Major O'Neal, sad-faced, balding and wrinkled, was now burnt out. From the earliest days of his service he tried hard to get to know his men, speaking their language 'well enough' although not as fluently as some of the wartime commissioned officers spoke it. To him the soldiers were 'the little men': he had been accepted by them because he was acceptable, an English saheb in the same mould as they, their fathers and their forefathers had known British officers for nearly a century and a half. Over those many years of soldierly comradeship, in war and peace, a most remarkable bond of trust and friendship, loyalty and devotion, had been acquired and developed, seemingly unending.

At the other end of the table the Vice President, Captain Rance, now stood up, clutching his glass of port in his right hand. He personally had been instrumental to the success of Operation Janus. Before joining 1/12 GR he had served in Burma with 4/1 GR. He had been engulfed by the war and, like so many others of a similar age, had quickly become older than his years. With his linguistic ability, nimble brain and tactical flair, he got the best out of the soldiers. He had a sense of humour and was slow to show anger even when he felt it, to say nothing of the gift of always appearing cheerful. Initially the Gurkha officers of 1/12 GR, finding him of a different calibre from the staider pre-war regulars, had not quite known how to react to him but they accepted him quickly enough once they found he was genuine, tolerant, reliable, firm, just and fully understood them. He was, in fact, the quintessential regimental officer, yet his obvious ease with the soldiers had drawn caustic comments, mostly behind his back, from the elder generation of British officer who either envied his ability or just did not understand it. *Bad for discipline* some muttered but they were, in fact, gravely wrong.

'Gentlemen, the Queen.'

In answer to those sonorous words of the toast, everybody

stood up, as one, clasping their filled glass in their right hand, scowling sternly as they faced their front, their turn to intone this semi-mystic litany:

'The Queen,'

As glasses clattered back onto the table, the field officers added their privileged amen, 'God bless her!'

Seated once more, from either end of the table the three decanters were once again religiously started on their left-hand journey to the other end and glasses were refilled. Cigars were cut and lit; snuff was sniffed. Then, pleasantly relaxed, Major O'Neal leant back in his chair, head slightly turned, and the Mess Sergeant bent forward to hear what was to be said although he knew the order would be for the pipers and drummers to come and play. At his sign through the open door at the end of the room there was a drone and squeal as the pipers, bags full, started piping. Seven Gurkhas, four pipers and three drummers, two tenor and one base in his leopard-skin apron, dressed in rifle-green jackets with miniature medals peeping through and trews, black leather belts and Highland pattern shoes with white spats, entered the room and what little talk there was dried up. In step, they moved, with slightly swaggering gait, round the table, pipes squealing and drums thumping. They moved with a striking dignity in their bearing and how they comported themselves, erect bodies, in step with slightly swinging gait, brown faces inscrutable and medals aglint. They circled the table twice before the lead piper, the Pipe Major, who carried the Commanding Officer's personal banner, embroidered with his family crest, swayed gently as a signal for a change of tune. After two more circuits they halted behind the

Colonel's chair, turned towards the table and continued playing.

Some officers nodded their head in time to the tune, some strummed on the table and a few sat stock-still. The Commanding Officer, Lieutenant Colonel Robert Williams, caught the eye of Captain Jason Rance, who met his senior's gaze unflinchingly. *Of all my officers*, thought the Colonel, *that young man will either go the furthest or be the most disappointed. He is brave, clever and has a wonderful rapport with the soldiers who respond to him in an unusually out-going way. As a linguist he has fully made his mark and his razor-sharp brain with almost total recall are all hallmarks of potential. Very different from when I was a young officer*, he mused, drawing on his cigar and watching the pipers and drummers march out.

Right hands beat acclaim on the table and cries of 'shabash', well done, ended when the seven men played themselves out of the room. The Pipe Major came back by himself, marched at the quick, rifle-regiment pace, to just behind the Colonel's chair, halted, turned inwards and saluted. The Colonel stood up, took the quaich of neat whisky from the silver salver held ready by the Mess Sergeant and handed it to the Pipe Major.

'Well done, Pipe Major. You played well. Drink this with our special thanks.'

The Pipe Major took the quaich with both hands, raised it to the level of his mouth and gave the formal toast, '*Tagra rahau.*' May you remain strong.

'*Tagra rahau,*' answered the officers in a base rumble, words neither formulaic nor perfunctory; they expressed everyone's wish at this most exacting of times. The Pipe Major drained the contents in one, gave the empty quaich to the Mess Sergeant, saluted, turned to his right and marched away to more applause.

Outside, out of sight and out of hearing, the drummers and the other pipers were also drinking their tipple.

Rance, meanwhile, unaware that the Colonel was still studying him, had turned to his neighbour and was engrossed in conversation. *Can he read my thoughts?* Colonel Williams asked himself. *Highly successful or disappointed: he can turn from a smiling, equitable person to one of intense action with a hard bright flame burning inside him.*

The Pipe Major came back, playing a solo lament and, that finished, marched out of the room and, as he stopped playing, there was a short silence before the table was hit harder and the shouts of applause came louder than before. Having left his pipes outside he quick marched back again for another toast: 'May you remain strong'. Again the answer. Again the applause as he marched out.

Then the last toast of the evening: 'Mr Vice! The Regiment!'

'Gentlemen! The Regiment!'

Post-dinner drinks with conversation followed until the CO left. As no one could leave before him, everybody left quickly afterwards.

Tuesday 16 September 1952, Port Dickson, Negri Sembilan, Malaya: It was the end of recruit training for the Second Battalion of the Malay Regiment. It had been a stressful, rushed period as there were many more recruits to be trained than in the previous year. The majority of officers were British, seconded from their regiments in the British Army. As a colonial regiment this was accepted but the officers were not long-term incumbents as were British officers in Gurkha infantry units. They served for three-years on secondment only, so maintaining tip-top standards was always a great challenge. They were worried that the time for successful training had not been long enough for a really good result at the final inspection.

The inspecting officer at the field exercises, first at section level, followed by a platoon attack against the 'enemy', members of the First Battalion, and finally a company attack was none other than the High Commissioner-cum-Director of Operations, General Sir Gerald Templer himself. The General had heard a British officer give out orders in Malay, had heard others speak to the soldiers and, in general, was not all that impressed with their linguistic standards.

That evening there was a battalion meal, officers and soldiers eating in the same place, a different ceremony from the Gurkha Mess Night, but a significant bond of union nevertheless. The officers wore mess kit, white monkey jackets, white shirts, bow ties, miniature medals and green trousers with a broad yellow stripe. Because the soldiers wore their hats all evening so did the officers, a dark green velvet *songkok* with the addition of a single gold band. The General, looking superb in his mess kit, with his many orders on his chest, flanked by the CO, entered the dining hall. The Malay RSM ordered the men to stand to attention, drew himself up to his full height, saluted the General and 'barked' '*Selamat petang, Tuan*', Good evening, sir. '*Askar Melayu yang kedua, boleh makan, Tuan?*' can the men of the Second Battalion eat, sir?

The CO asked the General's permission for the meal to begin. 'Yes.'

The CO thanked the RSM. '*Terima kasih, makan-la*', thank you, you may eat. The RSM turned to the men and said one word. '*Makan!*' In a flash the men, four hundred of them, sat down, all smiles and attacked their food, mutton or chicken curry and rice, with various side eats. Drinks were iced orange juice or rose water.

Next morning, after his second cup of tea at breakfast in the CO's quarter, Templer said to his host, 'shall we go into your office and talk matters over before I fly off?' There was a note of bluntness in his voice that those who knew his plain speaking would have noticed. The CO, new to the General, didn't notice it.

'I was not altogether impressed yesterday. Oh, the men certainly tried hard but they were not sharp enough. I thought that some of your British officers were slack. Listening to their Malay, not that I'm a linguist, I felt that they should have been better. When did the new batch of recruits enlist?'

'Sir, it should have been in April but that was the fasting month so they came in May when they were still not as strong as they should have been.'

'But that's all of four months ago. Surely that's long enough to get your men up to scratch.'

The CO looked glum and kept silent.

'I've been hard on every department in Malaya that I think has been slack. I think you, maybe not personally, but British officers and NCOs have been.'

The CO looked glummer and still kept silent.

'I will extend your training period by one month. You were due to go to Kota Bharu. I'll have to get some other unit for that period. And when you show your faces there I want more than usually good results.'

Before the CO could answer, the General's ADC came in. 'Sir, your helicopter is due to take off when you are ready. All the kit is loaded.'

The General stood up, thanked the CO for putting him and his ADC up for the night, and left. As the CO heard the 'chopper' fly away he wondered if his own chances would also fly away. He shook his head, sighed heavily and called his Adjutant.

Tuesday 16 September 1952, Seremban: The camp that 1/12 GR occupied was, except for one two-storey building used as the Mess, a collection of single-storied wooden huts. Only in the offices were there fans. Turned on any speed more than slow, people found themselves like one-armed wallpaper hangers in their battle to keep cool and get their paperwork done. The CO's office was no different. A conference had been called and after the officers had assembled, the CO looked round at them standing by their chairs. The Second-in-Command saluted and said, 'Sir, we are all present and correct.'

The CO said, 'Sit down, Gentlemen. Smoke if you wish to.' He never did nor ever had.

Clothes rustled and chairs creaked as they settled down. Only two officers lit up. 'I expect you can all guess why we are here, why I have called you.' A slight Scottish burr was heard when he spoke English and Nepali. The look on everyone's face, stern and unsmiling, showed that they knew why they had been summoned. This was the first time the battalion had had a chance of being addressed by the CO since their return from Operation Janus, mounted to try and capture Captain Hinlea who had secretly left to join the guerrillas. The operation had only been the total success it was because of some brilliant detective work by Captain Jason Rance, who, by using his Chinese language skills, had discovered his destination, till then unknown, and equally brilliant work when he and a 4-man team, with superb tracking and fieldcraft skills, had successfully caught up with the absconding group taking him to the Central Committee of the MCP, a few week's hazardous journey away in north Malaya. After a fierce fire fight Hinlea and several guerrillas had been killed. Those remaining had surrendered to Rance, saying they were ready to serve under him against other guerrillas if he so wished them to. The forward elements of the guerrilla escort group, clearing the way for Hinlea and his escort, had been ambushed by the main part of the battalion farther on. In all it was an operation perfectly carried out.

'I will proceed.' The CO looked the very image of a pre-war regular, which he was. Precise, economical movements revealed his soldierly bearing. Six feet tall, ramrod straight, square-shouldered and flat-stomached, he carried no spare flesh. He had an austere face with compelling eyes, thick dark eyebrows, black curly hair, a high forehead, a straight Roman nose and a clipped, trim moustache. He used half-moon specs for reading. He had served with distinction in Burma during the war. He had a way with Gurkhas that the younger officers envied which belied his outwardly severe looks, today made more severe by the recent trauma the battalion had undergone, though he tried not to show it. 'The battalion, as all of us know, has recently suffered a severe disgrace, luckily only known about in a very small circle, by the late Captain Hinlea trying to defect to the Communists. Our Gurkhas are, I gather from the Gurkha Major saheb, devastated by the loss of the battalion's good name and cannot understand how any British officer could behave as a traitor or, probably, why he was ever commissioned.'

Yes, his officers knew all that, felt it deeply and were at one with wishing to regain their good name and wanting their reputation for integrity being even higher than it had been before.

'There is a Gurkha proverb that says one man's bad behaviour outpoints one hundred good men's efforts. You have probably come across it.' A few of the more senior officers nodded their agreement. 'I have been warned not to talk about what has happened. Disposal of the bodies has been left to the discretion of Special Branch. Hinlea, who professed no religion, has had his corpse buried in the Christian cemetery below our camp, without any battalion parade, only because the local padre insisted it be. He said some prayers for the "lost" soul.' The look on the CO's face showed his antipathy but he had realised that, really, there was no other choice of his final destination, with or without prayers.

'What I want to tell you is that that incident will in no way, I say again, in no way, be referred to ever again. I won't say "it never happened" as it obviously did but it has ceased to exist. What I do want to say again is that Captain Rance and his successful team have saved the army and the regiment from a great and soul-searing disgrace. They incurred danger beyond the dictates of duty but under no circumstances can this become public knowledge. A thick, dark, heavy curtain has to be drawn over these recent events, never to be pulled back. Those orders come from the very top.'

He paused, as though making up his mind, plucking at the lobe of one ear as he did. 'I shouldn't really tell you what my senior officer told me but, only within these four walls, I will: I asked the Brigadier if he'd support bravery awards for all five operators but,' and here he faltered slightly, 'he refused, point blank. Rather pompously, I thought, he said "the Army, like the Royal Academy, desires docility in her children and even originality has to be stereotyped." I want to thank Captain Rance in front of you all. Stand up, Jason.'

Lieutenant Colonel Williams, commissioned from Sandhurst pre-war, had mixed ideas about Captain Rance, commissioned from the Indian Military Academy in Dehra Dun. *Wouldn't have been commissioned pre-war* he had felt. He had come to the conclusion that his parents were not quite top drawer, so that was automatically a bad mark against their son, good officer though he might be. The Colonel had already spoken to him and his team in his house. Then Jason had been told 'Your empathy with the men is as irrefutable as the shorthand of the Recording Angel. You have the indispensable virtues of humour, humility and honesty but sadly, in this instance, the only official and curtailed record of it will be on your confidential Record of Service. Apart from wearing enemy uniform which is strictly forbidden under one of the Geneva Conventions, (he and his men had done this for camouflage as they were so heavily out-numbered) the only law you have broken is the Law of Averages.'

Jason remembered that as he stood up and was applauded by his brother officers. He felt and looked slightly embarrassed. He noticed that the CO had a tiny flash of levity in his eyes that did not quite suit the solemnity of the occasion.

'Before my last point I wish to let you know that I have already personally congratulated the four men involved with Captain Rance. Now the next series of brigade operations will be to try and find the places on the ground where guerrilla escorts taking Hinlea to the main Communist HQ were to have handed him over to the next escort group and to try and find and eliminate the deep jungle "gardens" the guerrillas are growing to supplement their rations. The less they are able to eat the easier it will be to eliminate them. Special Branch, with its secret, what shall I call them? ... connections will do, have a feeling that, by and large, the MCP has started to lose their overall military initiative.

There was a pause, then 'Monday 2 October will be the day you will move out. Any questions?'

'Sir,' OC C Company put his hand up. 'Is there any way of us knowing how exactly Captain Rance managed to be so successful?'

'Yes. He will be writing an operational report both for battalion records and higher formations.' He looked at Rance. 'Rance, make sure you include more intimate details than for a normal operation report. No hurry but as soon and as full as practicable. Tactics only, "my group:" and "the guerrilla group", no mention of Hinlea, only what you and your team did and how you did it.'

'I'll certainly include all relevant, even non-tactical details, sir,' Jason said but even so there were certain points he could not put on paper, his 'brother', Ah Fat, the same age as was he and who he knew as *P'ing Yee*, Flat Ears, and who knew him as *Shandung P'aau*, Shandong (Eastern hills) Cannon, because of his sturdiness. They had known each other since they were young and they had played together whenever they could and later, during school holidays, camping in the jungle where they tracked each other: fieldcraft! It was during his boyhood years that Jason's ability to work with Asians was implanted by gaining an extra dimension of communication by understanding something not said: a hint, a gesture, a reaction, a glance, a shrug, even an unexpected silence, all of which had formed an unnoticed sediment at the back of his mind, always there to be used unconscientiously. Jason, an only child, had loved the fun of frolicking about with his Chinese friend and having even more fun with a language that Mrs Rance, his mother, never could get her tongue around. He had never lost tonal accuracy from those childhood days and his knowledge, both of spoken and written Chinese, as well as an almost as good a comprehension of spoken Malay, was something he hardly ever mentioned. His father had told him that seeming not to understand what Chinese people were talking about could possibly give him a life-saving advantage.

Ah Fat had spent the wartime years with the guerrillas fighting against the Japanese. His father had advised him to stay with them, although both father and son hated the Communists – the Something-for-Nothing Brigade, Communism being one of the biggest confidence tricks ever played when conventions were far more rooted than morality – and work against them from the inside. So successful had his ploy been that he had been fully accepted by the Central Committee as a non-voting member of the Politburo. Such a closely guarded secret could never, never be bandied abroad so would not be in his report.

The two men had met when Ah Fat had visited the Negri Sembilan Regional Committee's location on a fact-finding task and a messenger from the Yam Yam dance hall in Seremban had arrived with news about Hinlea wishing to join the MCP. This had allowed Ah Fat to go to Seremban where, happily and completely unexpectedly, the two of them had met up. The very last time they had met was when Jason saved his friend's life the night before Hinlea and the other guerrillas were killed.

Monday 29 September 1952, somewhere in the Cameron Highlands: Ah Fat, tired and looking drawn after his long and dangerous journey from the south of the country, reached the Central Committee camp. Having washed and changed into clean clothing, he reported to the General Secretary, who expressed surprise at not seeing the expected *gwai lo*.

'You're later than we thought you'd be. Why so slow and where is the new comrade? We were all expecting you and him before now. Why is he not with you?' he asked, almost churlishly.

Ah Fat felt piqued and unappreciated yet he must never allow his real job to be discovered. Even so, a considerate word would have been welcomed. A commander who had any 'feel' for how his men had fared would have seen how exhausted his subordinate looked and that tense expression on his face, so asked about the journey. In fact it had been more hazardous than usual and he would not have been successful if he had not remembered what he had learnt when fighting against the Japanese, how to hide in water, head hidden, breathing through a small tube of cane bamboo. He always kept what he termed his 'secret weapon' with him, a 2-foot-long tube of 'pithless' cane bamboo in case he was ever caught by a stream deep enough to hide unseen with his head under water. He had used it once successfully during the war and it had saved his life. It was also of talismanic value to him.

It had been of vital use again when his leading scout brought news of a British platoon ten to fifteen minutes distance off coming their way. They were walking along the side of a narrow river, one that had cane bamboo and rushes on both banks. Ah Fat turned round suddenly and jolted the ankle he had already twisted. He tried to follow his men who were quickly moving away uphill but it was too painful. He called softly to one of his gunmen, 'I've messed up my ankle. Take my pack with you and my pistol and ammunition. I'll have to hide in the water. Come back and help me after the *gwai lo* have gone.' *Thank goodness I've my secret weapon with me.*

The gunman took the pack, pistol and ammunition and disappeared into the jungle, automatically erasing traces where he and the others had moved. *We will have to engage the enemy if they discover him,* he decided.

Ah Fat felt for his tube from where he always carried it, on a string round his neck, but it was not there. *Where can I have dropped it?* he thought miserably. *I must have something else or I'm done for.* He quickly cut off a small piece of cane bamboo, useless with the pith still in it. He ground his teeth in frustration. *Don't panic!* Looking round he spied an aloe plant at the water's edge. Aloes stood higher than a man and had tall, fleshy, spiny-toothed leaves. He limped over to it, hastily took a knife out of his pocket and cut a long thorn off. With this he scratched out the pith in the piece of cane bamboo so making it hollow enough to breathe through. He worked fast, with deft movements, hoping against hope that he could hide before the enemy soldiers appeared.

In front of him was an outsize spider's web, with the huge, hairy, black creature in the centre in the process of bundling up a fly. Ducking under the web so as not to break it, leg paining him so making movement cumbersome, he slowly turned round and, facing the way the enemy troops were coming towards him, stepped on a large stone and deliberately walked backwards into the water. He rubbed his footprints off the stone and splashed some water on it. He saw that there was one footprint he could not properly erase. He bent down, splayed his fingers and made it look like a tiger's paw mark. He took another couple of paces backwards, making his way towards another aloe plant. Then, putting the piece of bamboo into his mouth as a breathing tube, silently lay down under the water, holding his nose.

He was only just in time.

His companions hiding in a glade saw the British soldiers. An Asian, with heavily tattooed arms, pointed to the ground.

The guerrillas did not know that he was an Iban tracker from Sarawak and that Ibans were attached to British troops who were not skilled in tracking. 'Our comrade has been seen,' the senior guerrilla said. 'Get ready to save him.' He saw the tattooed man bend down as though investigating, stand up and point to the large spider's web.

The troops took no notice as they moved on past it. They probably didn't even notice it!

The guerrillas up on the slope breathed a communal sigh of relief when they saw which way the British troops had gone. After judging five minutes, Ah Fat slowly, slowly lifted his head out of the water, looked around and seeing nobody, stood up, taking deep breaths of air with joy. His comrades hurried back down to the track to help him out of the water.

They hid in a secluded spot while Ah Fat changed out of his wet clothes into dry ones and rested his ankle. Half an hour later, revived, 'On our way now,' he said, getting up. They moved on as fast as his damaged ankle allowed.

The Iban tracker's mind nagged at him. *What was it I might have missed?* He thought back and played the scene over in his mind and minutely visualised the pug mark once more. *Got it! Two points: there was no tiger smell and, he inwardly cursed, the tiger's pug mark was as though the animal was moving backwards. Tigers don't move backwards* ... Ibans are mercurial people. He inwardly shrank at admitting his error and losing face. He decided not to say anything about it and, anyway, his English was not really up to explaining it. *Good luck to the clever man who made that mark: he deserved to get away with it!*

… yes, it had been a difficult journey but back to the present.

Ah Fat looked straight at his questioner, feigning sadness and dismay – *tradecraft!* – licked his lips and shook his head. Time to disseminate: he decided not to mention anything about escaping from the British soldiers. 'Oh, Comrade Secretary General, let me give you the bad news straightaway: something went so very wrong. All our group, except me, were ambushed. The *gwai lo* comrade was killed as were all the other comrades, including Comrade Lau Beng, the Regional Committee Commissar. It was only by the grace of Lenin that I was saved by having surprisingly contacted another comradely group when I and my own escort went to shoot a deer for food. I took them to one side so that the group with the new comrade could continue without their knowledge. It was then that the disaster occurred. I stayed back only long enough to find out details of any casualties then moved on with my own escort. So thankful to be alive and back with you, can hardly be said forcibly enough. I humbly apologise.'

'I am disappointed …'

Ah Fat interrupted. 'Comrade Secretary General I have already apologised …'

He was rudely cut off. 'I am not blaming you to the extent that it will be detrimental to your character, so don't worry. It was just that I wanted some first-hand knowledge about the morale of the Security Forces, especially of the Gurkhas …' His voice tailed off and he stared into the distance. 'I'll have to call a Politburo meeting first thing tomorrow,' he muttered to himself.

The Politburo met as ordained and Ah Fat was made to give

chapter and verse about his search for leaks – nothing found – and the now-dead *gwai lo*. After a gloomy shaking of heads and tut-tutting, Lee An Tung said, 'Comrades, of course I, too, am disappointed. We had all hoped to get his leaving the army for us to embarrass the imperialists, lower their morale so greatly help us in our struggle. That makes my next suggestion even more important.' He looked round at his audience who gazed at him with rapt attention.

'Comrade Secretary General, let me be frank. May I ask your permission for this to be a closed session without any written records being made and no recriminations to what anybody says after I have made my points?'

'Comrade, I have always trusted you. Yes, I agree but even so let's put it to the vote.'

Comrade Lee An Tung was known for his accurate analyses so the motion was passed with no one objecting. The Head of the Central Propaganda Department leant back, turned slowly and looked at Ah Fat. 'Comrades, however loyal this comrade is, and we all know there is none more loyal, he knows his way about in places where his presence is not queried, unlike the rest of us. I therefore feel we must use him to the very limit of his undoubted abilities. With our permission let us do something unprecedented as our situation is so serious.'

He paused dramatically and, palms turned inwards, raised his hands as if invoking some sort of blessing. 'Let us get him to arrange a strike from inside the imperialist ranks even if unsuccessful as well as also sending him on an out-of-country reconnaissance to exert pressure from outside.'

The effect was one of stunned silence, people looking from one to another, none wanting to be the first to make any comment.

'Before any of us can comment on this revolutionary idea give us details. What, in point of fact, are you suggesting?' Chin Peng asked, in a surprised tone of voice, rather wishing it were he who had thought of the idea if it turned out a good one.

'I would want him to go and see our comrades in Singapore and ...' once more he broke off. 'That renegade Nepali from Darjeeling who I hear has enlisted with some like-minded comrades, is probably still in Singapore. He, or rather they, could well be the medium we need to turn the balance against the British in our favour. So, he is the one we need to find and learn his plans.'

What a wonderful idea, everybody thought. It made good sense to strike from the inside. Smiles wreathed all faces and congratulations were given. Then the Secretary General put the question to Ah Fat. 'Comrade, that would not be too much for a man of your ability, would it? Our future will be in your hands.'

The others looked expectantly at him. Po-faced but rejoicing inside – *yes, it will! Tradecraft, tradecraft* he muttered inwardly – and with an expression of deep concentration, he slowly answered. 'Comrades, I am ready to do anything for the Party, as you must already know, I and my most trusted escort. But this task is different from many others I have undertaken as it may turn out to be more wide-ranging than you are expecting it to be. Also, there can be no guarantee of success ...'

He was interrupted by the Secretary General who, placatingly, said, 'Comrade, of course you can't guarantee that, nor do we demand anything that in any way will be dangerous to your hidden party membership. If you find your only way of making an escape, you will sacrifice your most trusted escort, Wong Ming, your Bear.' He was referring to the one-time military commander of the Negri Sembilan Regional Committee, and, although none of the Politburo knew it, now a friend of Captain Rance. He was a short, almost square man, and powerfully built – he looked like a bear so his nickname was *Hung Lo*, Bear.

Ah Fat's expression did not change but mentally he said to himself that that would never happen. Before he could make any further comment Comrade Lee An Tung said, 'even if you can't contact the renegade Gurkha, let me explain my other idea the out-of-country recce. I propose that you undertake a task to ensure success which is vital to our eventual victory. I believe that the situation is potentially so serious that what I have just told you to do is child's play compared with this second proposal.'

Ah Fat tensed, his hands unconsciously coming together and chafing each other, thinking hard. *I must not show any doubt on my face, only conviction.*

The Secretary General turned to Comrade Lee An Tung and asked him for details, 'which I will put to the vote after we have heard them for approval or otherwise.'

'Reports I have received are that there is a secret headquarters that has links with all major communist parties in Southeast Asia, most probably in Calcutta.' All eyes were fixed on him as he continued 'I have learnt that the contact is where in one of two Chinatowns. One is in Tangra, known as Tangra Chinatown, in the east of the city. The other, Tiretta Bazaar, usually known as Old Chinatown, is in central Calcutta. Both communities are leatherworkers. They are Hakkas. Among them is the link to this secret HQ, an MGB set-up, somewhere in Calcutta.'

A frisson of excitement was palpable in everybody and showed on their faces, eager and shining. *What research had been done to know all that!* They all knew that MGB meant the Soviet Ministry of State Security but they did not know the Russian translation.

An aeroplane was heard off to a flank. The noise of the throbbing engine upset them and no one spoke till it was heard no longer.

The plan and its background continued to be unfolded. 'We know of course that such HQs are always located outside the area of operations. In our case it is not in KL but here. Likewise, I know that operations against the Americans were conducted from somewhere in Africa. And as I have just said, Calcutta is my best guess where the Soviet MGB has this intensely secret office. Comrade Ah Fat will go there for confirmation and for our news to spread to Kathmandu for "alternative treatment" as the doctor might put it, just in case the renegade Gurkha cannot help. There is no need for him to go any farther than Calcutta. He will be doing a job in a way no one else can, possibly even needing a change of persona. He will travel with a boat of the Indo-China Steam Navigation Co. Ltd., registered in Hong Kong, either on the SS *Eastern Queen* or the SS *Princess of the Orient*. They ply from Hong Kong to Calcutta and back, calling at Singapore and Rangoon. The pursers have been groomed to "help" people like him so he is not, I say again not, to travel on a British-India boat even if it means waiting a while because, were he to, he would not have the pursers as a link to Chinatown.'

That was a lot to digest and it would be foolish openly to jump at the chance. A show of reluctance was needed so Ah Fat kept silent for a couple of minutes as though contemplating the scale of his task.

'Comrade Ah Fat,' the Secretary General again queried, 'are you prepared to undertake this difficult, dangerous and daunting task for the Party? Are you up to it?' The question was sharp and pointed, asked with a hint of menace.

Ah Fat wanted to ask the three senior men, whom he had never seen voluntarily face danger, if they would go on such a mission but naturally that was entirely out of the question. 'Of course, I'll most certainly try my best because I won't know if I am up to it unless and until I do try,' he answered, making direct eye contact with his questioner. 'Even if I can contact the renegade soldier or any of his type you still want me to go to Calcutta, don't you? If so, the administrative details for that will need to be completed in a way that brings no suspicion to my real aim. I have a passport but I will need a visa, money for a ticket and, so that I won't have to wait too long, a fixed date. And, yes, a sure berth on the boat.'

Lee An Tung said, 'Money we can deal with here, certainly enough to keep you going until you get to Singapore where our man is Chen Geng. He will fix currency and visa details for you. I repeat: his office is at 47 Pedder Street. As his work is normal trade it is safe to ask for him by name.'

And with that Ah Fat said he was satisfied. The Politburo voted on it unanimously.

Tuesday 30 September 1952, Singapore: Acting Sergeant Padamsing Rai had done very nicely, thank you. After his recruit training, where he had shone, he was posted to 1/12 GR as a clerk. He had asked for and been granted local leave and had visited Bhutan Estate, one of the three with a Nepalese workforce, and had found a Kamal Rai with whom he discovered he shared a great-grandfather, a firm enough bond for 'board and lodging' to be offered. Kamal was in his mid-twenties, immensely strong, with deep-set eyes that flashed dangerously when he was annoyed and a face that had a calm look, although there was an air of subtlety about it. He had been educated at King George V's School in Seremban where the medium of instruction was English, and his teachers had regarded him as a scholar. He had operated against the Japanese during the war. He had found the visit difficult because his visitor kept on asking for 'comrades' to help try, quite how was not revealed, to make Gurkha soldiers react badly against their British officers. Such talk was completely foreign to him, against all he held dear. Now remembering the good relations he had forged with Captain Rance,[11] he was in no way receptive to Padamsing's attempted bullying and unwanted insinuations. This led to threats and bad feelings. Kamal did not make any mention of his dealings with Captain Rance but, to keep matters more friendly, said he'd do what he could and let his distant relative know what he'd achieved on the next visit. *By then I'll have thought up something to keep him quiet and me safe.* Padamsing saw Kamal was too strong to bully so 'nagging'

---

11 See *Operation Blowpipe*.

would have to do instead.

When educational facilities for Gurkhas were established in 1949 Padamsing was sent as an instructor to the Army School of Education (Gurkhas) in Singapore as an acting sergeant, a most unusually quick promotion. He thought he had made some converts for the 'cause' although he knew that such work was strictly forbidden. However, his inner proclivity demanded man-to-man release, practically unknown in village life. Both proclivity and persuasion were suspected by Gurkha hillmen students who only gave an impression of having been persuaded by his political oratory – something foreign to them – but who in reality ignored his blandishments and totally rejected his tendency. There was also a British sergeant instructor at the school who had the same 'appetite': neither knew that they were under observation by the suspicious British OC.

The renegade Gurkha had been called to the office telephone, identified himself and an unknown voice speaking good but accented English had said, 'You don't know me. You must meet me at' and the voice slowly pronounced the inappropriately named Balmoral Inn in Ulu Pandan 'next Saturday at around four o'clock.'

'Why?' asked bluntly.

In a lowered voice, 'Party orders'

'Who's calling?' the Gurkha had asked, caught off balance.

'We haven't met. Just call me Ah Ho' and the line went dead.

Padam was thrilled. He got his out pass and arrived early. He sat at the bar and ordered a beer. As he waited, he thought back to the day he had been inducted to be a Communist agent. He recalled how he had asked 'Lance' Sharkey a question he could not answer at that Calcutta meeting so did not notice when a Chinese man entered, looked around and joined him. Lost in reverie, he was jolted awake. He was not to know that he was Xi Zhan Yang, the secret courier based in Kuala Lumpur. 'I am Ah Ho, the man who called you on the phone. No need to ask how I knew you or your number. We are smart. I have been sent to contact you so let's go and talk in that empty corner not at the bar. Don't act suspiciously.' He ordered two beers and away they went to the back of the room.

Padamsing was agog. *Action!* After a minimum of small talk, the Chinese man said, 'the Politburo wants to know how many men you have converted, in what battalions they are serving, their addresses in Nepal or the Darjeeling area and who, among the staff, are suspicious of your activities.'

The Gurkha gulped in astonishment. 'Comrade Ah Ho, I have not gone into so much detail as that.'

'Tell me why not. You are under strict orders.'

'It would be too suspicious to go about it that way. I am preparing the basic yeast of indiscipline which will only ferment when men get back to their units. But nothing positive can or will happen until a tipping point is reached and that cannot be for quite a while yet.'

'Too slow. Much too slow.' Xi Zhan Yang's briefing had been given at third-hand and had acquired a degree of urgency that had not been planned. 'I'll be back within three weeks' – the original time given had been six months – 'and you'll give me the answer then. Take down my phone number: after three rings ring off.

Ring again. After two more rings, ring off. Then ring again.' He glared menacingly at the Gurkha, finished off his beer, stood up, glared once more and left.

The Gurkha gawped.

Saturday 4 October 1952, Soviet Consulate, Alipore Park Road, Calcutta: The Soviets were on friendly terms with the Indians, both with anti-British governments, admittedly for different reasons, and so the array of aerials on the roof of the main building of the consulate, in plain sight for anyone who took any notice of them, was taken by the authorities as normal. What only the MGB 'Rezident', a man who called himself Leonid Pavlovich Sobolev and who spoke fluent but guttural English, knew was that it was the centre of a web of contacts consisting of all the Communist parties in southeast Asia, some of which could be contacted directly, others which needed a 'cut-out'. The situation on the mainland of China was still so confused that he had no contact there but for Hong Kong there was a method of contact, albeit slow and infrequent, that the Rezident relied on: oral messages carried by the pursers on two ships, SS *Eastern Queen* and SS *Princess of the Orient*, both operated by the Indo-China Steam Navigation Co. Ltd. to the Tangra cut-out.

Chinese linguists were a rarity in the USSR and Hindi speakers also were few and far between. When the first post-war visit of a Soviet leader to India took place fewer than a dozen Hindi linguists were to be found in the whole of the country. Now the only Chinese contacts easily available to the Rezident were in the Hakka community in Tangra Chinatown. The one Indian that the

Rezident trusted and used as a link was a Vikas Bugga.

Sobolev, whose one unusual habit was wiping his nose on any curtain as he passed it, was enjoying an after-lunch brandy when he was contacted by an obsequious underling telling him that a visitor had come to see him.

'What, now, when I'm relaxing on a Saturday? Without any warning?' he grumbled. 'Send him away.'

The messenger said that he had tried to but the man was insistent. '"I am only here for a short time. I must see my Big Brother," was what he said.'

'Big Brother' was the secret code used by the Rezident when he made any call, never from his office phone, to an executive. To get a message from Big Brother meant it had to be obeyed without any questions at all.

'Did he give a name?'

'Yes, I found it difficult to remember so I asked him to write it down.' The underling pulled out a slip of paper and read, hesitantly, 'Vikas Bugga.'

Blast him. He's about the only Indian I can't send away. For all their talk of collective humanity, Russians were inborn racists, within and without the Soviet Union.

'Send him in, now.'

Almost in no time Mr Bugga came bouncing in. 'I am sorry to come in without warning but I did not know until yesterday that I would be able to have time to come and see you.'

'Don't apologise,' said the Rezident graciously. 'Sit down and have a glass of brandy and tell me what I can do for you, or better, what you can do for me.'

'You can do nothing for me except put me to bed if I get drunk as a skunk. But for you, I need to tell you I have had two letters from the Nepali contact who is working on our side making converts in the British Army Gurkhas in Malaya. I knew him before he enlisted when he was in Darjeeling.'

The Rezident held his hand up to stem the flow. He was trying to place just what this garrulous man was talking about. *Got it!* 'This is about trying to get the Gurkhas out of Malaya and back to Nepal, isn't it?'

His visitor nodded.

'Go ahead.'

'In his last letter to me he said that he hoped he would have enough people being against the British to make the British authorities in the War Office in London want to disband, if not all of the Gurkhas, at least a battalion before very long.'

'Now that is good news. Let us toast to it.'

They toasted, then the Rezident asked if there was any timeframe.

'You mean when do I think that will happen?'

'Yes, that is what I do mean.'

'Of course I can't say but it could be sooner than later.'

After some small talk Vikas Bugga took his leave, promising to keep close contact and, if possible, to give prior warning of his next visit. He gave the Rezident an emergency phone number. 'Say my eldest son wants to talk to me.'

The Rezident smiled to himself. Business had not been all that successful for a while. A boatload of anti-government, mutinying Gurkhas penetrating Nepal and the Darjeeling area should be good for promotion prospects. In view of possibly being made ambassador somewhere he toasted silently with another brandy.

Monday 6 October 1952, on board SS *Eastern Queen*, Hong Kong: Captain Lam Wai Lim, skipper of the vessel that belonged to the Indo-China Steam Navigation Co. Ltd., was a seasoned mariner who loved the sea as much as he loved his family, which was saying a lot. A squat, affable man with a round, honest-looking face, receding hair and sparkling eyes, he had a happy knack of getting on with people. He had not all that long to wait for his pension to which he was looking forward. He knew his ship intimately, having been five years with her: she was not so big, about 500 feet long, with her beam of 65 feet, a speed of 16 knots and fitting 2192 passengers, including those in cabins. He never had to look at the book to quote all its specifications, so well did he know them.

He had just received notice for the following month about a curious cargo and he called his purser, Law Chu Hoi, to his cabin. 'Sit down. I have something unusual to tell you.'

The purser, a thin rake of a man, balding with a pock-marked face, sat down, wondering what it was. He was always 'alert': he was a dedicated Communist under the strictest disguise, always abusing them if ever asked his opinion of them. If anyone in Hong Kong knew his true job as a courier for the Party, he would be banished to the mainland, instantly, or rather irrevocably, after detailed investigation.

'Next month we have a boatload of Gurkha troops, the majority to be picked up in Singapore and a few from Penang. We will, in any case, stop for shipping some cargo at Rangoon before disembarking the soldiers and their families in Calcutta and bringing a returning leave party back to Penang and Singapore.'

'This is unusual. A first timer. Normally the British India Line people take them, don't they?'

'So I believe but it's us this time.'

'Hm, I wonder why. About how many troops will there be?'

'All told, single men and families, probably not more than 1400 but you will have to plan for, say, fifty more. Gurkha rations are basically rice and pulse. Some are faddy about our delicious pork and won't eat it but meat can be goat, sheep or poultry but never beef.'

'There will be plenty of room for them.'

'Yes, there will. We will have our normal October run first and be in time for the soldiers.'

The skipper dismissed his purser who wondered if trooping Gurkhas would result in anything unusual.

Monday 6 October 1952, Seremban: The operation ordered after re-training had been due to last for three weeks but Higher Authority had found another target. The move out to the operational area had been given for 1000 hours on the Monday. At half past nine an office runner breathlessly went to A Company office and found the men being checked before they moved off. He gave the OC a salute, meticulously returned, and told him that the CO wanted him in the office, *at once*. Jason sighed. *What now?* he asked himself, telling his 2 ic to take over and finish off checking the men.

By then he had written his report on how he had managed to be successful on Operation Janus. All his jungle knowledge was based on how he and his friend Ah Fat had tracked each other in the jungles near Sepang when they were schoolboys on holiday. His skills were enhanced by learning jungle warfare at the Indian Military Academy in Dehra Dun prior going to war in Burma where he was made the Recce Platoon commander and outshone any previous commander in what he did and what he taught his men. Now in Malaya it didn't matter whether the operation was patrolling, ambushing, surrounding an enemy camp or, simply, making an overnight base camp: success depended on movement being as invisible as possible to any enemy. It never occurred to him to say that for success in the jungle a 'change of mental gear' was needed as it was, by then, second nature to him.

One point he had made was 'for the hunter a misplaced footprint merely meant a lost contact; for the hunted death or capture'. He wondered whether to add 'I know because I have been both' but decided against it lest he be accused of being flamboyant or merely showing off by exaggerating what he had done in Burma during the war. At the end he added 'and don't forget, the best way to escape from an elephant is to run downhill.'

Somewhere in the report was a note that a proper patrol was, virtually, a moving ambush. Not in the report but stressed to his company on briefings was 'to look where you're going', that time when a platoon had been moving up to a river towards the enemy on the other side of the water, who were in greater strength than they were but who had not spotted them. Their old camp on the Gurkhas' side of the river was now empty and the platoon commander was unsure whether he could cross the river and attack the present enemy camp without taking casualties. Moving into position one man, not looking where he was going, fell up to his knees into a guerrilla latrine. He smelt so badly the other soldiers moved away from him, non-tactically. He went forward to the river to clean up and his companions thought he was going to charge the enemy by himself. They dashed after him, did not see him washing himself behind a rock, crossed the river and routed the guerrillas, killing some of them before the others escaped.

But where was the man who had fallen into the latrine? No one could see him and he was feared missing – captured or killed? Going back across the river they were relieved to see him still getting clean.

'Look where you're going. Next time it might be up to the knees, having fallen in head first, so you won't be so lucky.'

He also included the incident that gave him the most satisfaction: that was when he wanted to overhear a conversation in the guerrilla camp when there was no method of getting near enough without being seen. He had cut an arum leaf where it came out of the mud and, putting it in front of him as a shield, squirmed to the top of a bank, within earshot. He overheard all that was being said, thereby letting him achieve success in preventing the renegade officer from escaping. He was startled when two guerrillas came over to where the leaf was for a piss. They actually aimed at the leaf which gave a humming noise back. Neither realised that the leaf was out of place: no arum leaf was ever found at the top of a bank in the dry.

It was while he was writing his report that he realised why the CO had given him that strange look when he was told to stand up: he had met his wife arranging some flowers in the Mess and had addressed her by her Christian name as was the custom. She had turned angrily upon him and hissed 'don't you call me by my enemy's name' and turned back on him, mumbling to herself.

Jason had crept away, realising he had used the name of the Second-in-Command's wife.

At the CO's office he found out why he had been sent for. 'Your plans are changed. I have just had a personal phone call from the Director of Operations himself, apologising for the short notice but I have to send one rifle company to Kota Bharu for operations under 1 Malay Brigade and I've chosen you. Do you know where it is?'

'Yes, sir, I do but I have never been there.' He remembered being slightly shocked when told that there was a 'Beach of Passionate Love' in the area.

'You will go to Gemas where the East Coast line leaves the main north-south line in Brigade transport and from there by rail on the Blowpipe Express. Movements Branch will organise your return similarly. You will be based in Kota Bharu until the 23rd of this month. You will not be extended as you will need to send men on the leave party that is about a month away. Normally, of course, it is earlier than now as we try to get our men to enjoy Dashera at home but, for some unknown reason, it's later this year. And I might as well tell you now, more as a reward for doing so well on Janus as for any other reason, I am detailing you as OC

Troops on board as it is our battalion's turn to provide someone for the job.'

Jason grinned. 'Thank you, sir. I'll like that. Both ways? There and back?'

The Colonel nodded. 'I hear that the East Coast line is dangerous. Just in case take one of the medical corporals with you, with a pack, complete with morphine and stitching needle and thread. Can't be too careful.'

'If it'll be as bad as that, thank you sir. Can you tell me my aim, sir, in Kota Bharu?'

'Your aim is to pick up any guerrilla movement is what the Director of Operations said. Nothing has been heard about them for a long time and some inquisitive patrolling might find something. The population is chiefly Malay: I gather there are few, if any, Chinese or Indians around there but you'll be briefed in such details when you get there. Maps and any transport requirements will be issued from the local HQ. The "why?" Because the Malay Regiment battalion that should have gone there has been forced to spend another month's training to let their new recruits reach the required standard. One of the things I do want you to do is search for any Gurkhas who fought in that disastrous Malayan campaign in 1942. There are rumours that some tried to escape the Japanese by going to Kelantan. Apparently after the war they stayed on there, not having been able to return to Nepal. If you can find any that would be great. Ask them if they want to return to Nepal or not. They could well have married local girls and raised a family by now so maybe they won't want to move. I also want you to phone the OC in the Gurkha school in Singapore.

He's a friend of mine. He was a prisoner of the Japanese and may be able to give you some background details. Tell him I was too busy to talk to him but give him my salaams. Any more?'

'Two points, sir. What time am I to move out and who will I liaise with if anything untoward occurs on the journey up, an ambush on the railway line for instance?'

'Yes, you won't be able to catch today's train so I've told Brigade to pick you up at noon. You'll bivouac for the night at Gemas and catch tomorrow's train. This is the answer to your second query' and he handed over a piece of paper on which the wave length to be used was written. 'You will be call sign 5 and Roger Nan Tare is the local HQ up in Kota Bharu. Sorry, I should have given you that earlier.'

Jason saluted and went back to give out his new orders.

Jason asked the battalion exchange to ring the Gurkha School in Singapore. 'I'll ring you back,' said the operator. When he was put through he asked if he was speaking to the OC.

'He is not here,' came the answer in fluent English. 'May I know who you are, sir?'

'I am Captain Rance of 1/12 GR, calling from Seremban. And you?'

'I'm Sergeant Padamsing Rai. I joined 1/12 GR after being recruited in 1948 but you won't remember me, but I remember you. Can I pass a message for you, sir? The OC won't be in for a while.'

'Sergeant, I am taking my company to Kota Bharu and my CO, Lieutenant Colonel Williams, wanted to ask your OC if he could say anything about any Gurkhas who might have settled there during or after the retreat down Malaya in 1942 rather than be taken as prisoners of war as was your OC. In any case my CO wishes to give him his salaams. Do that please. That is all I have you. Have you anything for me?'

'Do you know when you'll be back, sir?'

'Sergeant Padamsing, in three weeks or so. The autumn leave party will be leaving a week later and men have to be got ready first.'

'Thank you, sir, that is more than all.' It was only later that Jason recalled the unusual answer.

As he put the phone down, the office runner shyly asked him who it was he was talking to at the school.

'That's a strange question. It was Sergeant Padamsing Rai. Why do you ask?'

'Saheb, I am asking because Sergeant Padamsing Rai was an instructor on the education course you sent me on and he was one of two ustads who tried to convert us to being a Communist and not to come back after our next leave.'

Jason looked astonished. 'Really? Have you told anyone else?'

The runner looked uncomfortable, 'No Saheb. I haven't. He also wanted to play with me but I wouldn't let him' and the soldier, to whom nothing like that had ever happened before, looked embarrassed. 'I told him I was not a woman. Saheb, may I say something else, please?'

'Of course you may. Out with it.'

'The *gora* sergeant instructor in the school is also like that.' The soldier turned his head to one side and shed tears.

Most unusual. That's the first time I've heard of such Jason thought angrily. *I'll fix it when I get back.*

'Why have you not mentioned it to anyone, say the Gurkha Major saheb?'

'We were told that if we did it would be serious for us and our family when we went on our next leave.'

'Don't worry, *keta*, I'll look into it when I get back.'

The young man seemed relieved. He trusted his OC in every respect. They all did.

After Padamsing had replaced the phone he sat back, an idea forming in his head. *I've got my answer for Comrade Ah Ho but instead of a company in Kota Bharu I'll make it a battalion. Nobody concerned need know that it's a leave party that's going off to India by boat. I'll tell him it's my success that's getting them demobilised.* He chuckled malevolently. *I'll ring him up now.* As he reached for the phone another thought struck him, *and I'll tell him to make sure someone responsible in Kathmandu is informed otherwise it may not work.*

Comrade Xi Zhan Yang's address had been given to Ah Fat who, with the Bear, had gone to Kuala Lumpur, not only to contact him and the 'sleeper' in Police HQ but also to visit their families, a cherished but seldom achieved event. It was also a superb chance to contact his friend, Too Chee Chew, affectionately known as C C Too, a brilliant propagandist who headed the Special Branch of the Malayan Police. The two of them had known each other long enough for voices to be recognised on the phone.

On his third day there, after taking his children to school, which was a treat for them, Ah Fat tried to contact Comrade Xi but was unlucky. On contacting the woman 'mole' he learnt that Xi had already gone to Singapore but before he and the Bear moved there, he rang C C Too, without announcing himself, in English, by saying an old schoolboy joke, 'It's a good day for the race,' to which the answer, 'The human race' meant that each caller had recognise the other.

'Can I pop round this evening for a drink and, if you're feeling kind, a bite of some of our favourite dish?'

'Of course,' and C C Too put the phone down. The less said always, especially on the phone, the better.

At C C Too's house Ah Fat told him just what was happening 'up north'.

'Now that *is* interesting. "Operation Tipping Point" shows how serious they are. This is entirely new to me,' which Ah Fat thought was, for him, probably a first.

'Somehow this seems incomplete, not enough to act against and counter but most useful background knowledge. What else have you for me?'

Ah Fat went on to describe plans to go to Calcutta, that he was to collect tickets for the next voyage of the SS *Eastern Queen* whenever that happened to be.

'Who is your contact in Singapore and where is he?'

Ah Fat told him.

'Now, shall I alert my opposite number there now or wait till you come back? He's Reggie Hutton whom you know from war days. You don't know the Gurkha's name but you do his unit. I'll get Reggie to find out any details of interest and' he looked in a note book he took out a drawer in his table, 'take down his phone number.'

'Yes, you're quite right. I remember him as a thin, austere, bespectacled man, slightly balding. Clever, a good linguist,' Ah Fat said, making a note of the phone number. 'Makes sense and it could be of help.' He thought for a moment and said, 'Tell you what. Would it be possible to let him know now? He may be at home and we could have a word together.'

C C Too nodded assent and, as there was no direct dialling, asked the telephone exchange operator to connect him through to Singapore and gave the number.

After quite a while the phone rang and was straightway picked up. 'Hutton here.'

'Reggie, tighten your seat belt! I have an old friend who needs no introducing so I'll hand him over to you.'

Ah Fat took the phone and said, 'Mr Hutton have you your hat on?'

That old wartime code! 'Flat Ears! I can't believe it. How are you and how can I help you?'

'Reggie, I'd like to call in on you in a day or two. At home is best. I have your number and I'll give you a bell when I get to your part of the world.'

'That'll be great. Anything else?'

'That's all,' and he rang off, not really liking to use the phone at all.

It was time for Ah Fat to leave and, thanking his host, was driven home in Mr Too's car. On the morrow Ah Fat and his Bear moved on down to Singapore by rail.

Monday 6 October, Singapore, on board SS *Kimanis*: Xi Zhan Yang, the Communist courier, his passport marking him as Ah Ho, with a chosen comrade from the Singapore Communist Party, had boarded the vessel earlier that morning. It had all been a bit of a hurry and there had been no time for any detailed briefing. The SS *Kimanis* was bound for Labuan as was usual but, unusually, it would sail on as far as Kuching before turning back to Labuan and Singapore. It had taken the MCP, working under the guise of the shipping company that owned the boat, no time to order its voyage to be extended. The ship's captain had no idea why but he had received the urgent order on the phone, using a code word for recognition. 'I don't know if you have had any message from your sick brother in Kuching but in case you have not he told me he had difficulty in tracing you and I said I'd pass the message on.'

'No. I have heard nothing from him yet.' It was policy never to ask who was speaking when he received any call like this one, concerning 'a sick brother'.

The two men shared a cabin but, so suspicious were they, they could not be sure it was not bugged so, having put away what little luggage they had, they went to the bar and took two squashes outside onto the deck where there was no chance of their being overheard, always a risk. They sat down in deck chairs, keeping quiet when anyone passed by, and Ah Ho said, 'Sorry about the rush but it happens sometimes. You and I have to get to Kuching and meet Sim Ting Ong, Secretary General of the Sarawak United

People's Party. Do you know him?'

No, his companion had never heard either the man's name or of the party.

'It's like this. There is a most secret plot that has been put into action, but there is no need to say by whom but let's just say the highest.'

His companion was thrilled at being involved in something this big and leant forward, eyes button-bright. 'Tell me about it.'

'We have to get the Sarawak United People's Party, the SUPP, to start causing trouble around the country in such a way that the colonial government there becomes so scared it'll ask for Gurkha troops to come and quell the disquiet.'

'My! That really is something. But why Gurkhas?'

'It seems that they are doing too well in Malaya and the party wants a chance to re-organise without being constantly nibbled at by losses caused by Gurkhas. And, yes, it really is something. Sarawak is a big place with high mountains, thick jungle, wide rivers and many native tribes, each with their own language. Even the Malay they speak is different from mainland Malay, so I have heard. I gather "we" in Borneo Malay is the same as "they" on the mainland and also round the other way. But there will be no need to speak anything but our Cantonese to Sim Ting Ong so we won't get muddled up. I doubt the Malays here know that there is any difference,' and he gave a mirthless chuckle.

The hooter sounded, tugs already roped to the boat started pulling it out into midstream. The boat gave a slight lurch. 'Our journey has begun,' Xi Zhan Yang said, with a sigh. 'We can relax till we get to Kuching.'

'How long will it take, do you think?'

'I don't know. Less than ten days I expect. We'll ask the captain when we meet him.'

Monday 6 October 1952, Seremban: The CSM brought the soldiers to attention and reported that the company was ready to move. Captain Rance thanked him, told him to stand everybody at ease, then stand easy. He called his Gurkha officers to take post with their platoon. His 2 ic stood next to him.

Jason looked around him then addressed his men: 'I was called away by the Commanding saheb to be given new orders. We are not going with the rest of the battalion but have a separate task.' He could see interest on every face. *Our saheb is good enough to have special jobs to be given to us* was what passed through most men's mind. 'We are going up to the northeast corner of Malaya to a place called Kota Bharu. No Gurkha troops have been there before. Normally it is where the Malay Regiment, based in Port Dickson, operates but their new recruits need more training so we have to fill the gap. This will be a challenge to show people who don't know Gurkhas how good we are.

'Apart from being given our operational orders by the local HQ the Commanding saheb has said that we may find some Gurkhas who tried to escape from the Japanese in 1942 and stayed with civilians rather than be taken as prisoners-of-war. If we do, we'll see if they want to go back to Nepal or stay with whoever they have lived with in the last ten years.'

That caused a ripple of interest not normally seen during any OC's briefing. 'Now, we are to get there by rail from Gemas.

Brigade are sending some transport here at 1200 hours, so we can relax till then. We will have to stay the night in Gemas because today's train will have left by now,' and unconsciously he glanced at his watch as he said that.

'I don't know how many of you have travelled by train recently as normally we move by road but, unlike the line that goes up the west of the country, this East Coast line goes through country that has many more places to ambush trains and blow them up than on the other line. I have learnt that' and he searched best how to describe two 'flats', 'open platforms on wheels are put in front of the engine so if the line has been mined they will blow up rather than the engine.' He saw concentration on his men's faces as they tried to visualise what had been described. 'That means that the line will be broken so until it is repaired or another train comes down from the north, we'll have to stay where we have been ambushed and can expect to be attacked.' He turned and called out to the CQMS, 'Quartermaster ustad there is no need to issue any more rations, is there, because we are carrying five days' worth?'

'Correct, Hajur,' came the snappy reply.

'Because of the risk of an ambush, no one will take off his skeleton equipment, all will have weapons ready with those carrying rifles having one up the spout. You will only load once you have entrained, and section commanders will ensure that safety catches are on. I know this is unusual but I regard the rail journey as a kind of offensive patrol: there are few troops in the area and the guerrillas have become bold.' He looked round and noticed from the expressions of his men showed him his words were not wasted. 'The immediate action drill if we are attacked is for 1 Platoon to move to a flank at the tail end of the train as the engine might explode. I will organise covering fire to keep the enemy's heads down as much as possible. With the other platoons we will probably be in shouting range but only try to yell at me once you have been seen. The enemy will be on the upper slope and so will be able to bring down heavy fire on anyone attacking frontally so platoons will automatically get out on the opposite side from where the fire is coming. If this happens do not worry about any civilian passengers. Orders for the rest of the company will be given as soon as I see how the situation is developing. But never forget, here, or in Burma or anywhere else come to that, where there is an attack, those last few yards always seem the longest!'

He waited a while for the men to digest what he had said. They had been together long enough to know how to work almost effortlessly either in sub-units or as a company. 'Fall in at 1145 hours and we'll move to the main road to meet the Brigade transport. Officers, fall out, Major ba, dismiss the parade.'

The relatively short road journey to Gemas passed without incident. Men debussed outside the station. Rance thanked the British drivers and sent the transport back. He told the 2 ic to let the men relax in a corner of the station yard while he went to find the station master to confirm that space in the morrow's train had been reserved for them and to ask for any nearby place to spend the night. He found him in his office, an elderly, rotund and pleasant-faced Tamil and introduced himself. Yes, there would be a separate carriage for his company tomorrow he was told, at the back end of the train. Rance then asked if there was anywhere nearby where his men could spend the night and cook up their rations. 'I'll get a porter to show you a nice place, isn't it,' the Station Master said. 'An empty shed near the goods wagons. Toilets are nearby. Have you fuel, if not I can arrange firewood.'

'Station master sahib, that is a most kind thought which we all appreciate as it is a long way to go to find and cut firewood for ourselves.' Also it would mean that the men's solid fuel cookers need not be used.

A porter was called, and Jason led him out to where his men were and handed him over to the CSM. Later on he went back to the station master for a chat. He asked him how long he had been working on the railway, how much guerrilla activity was there on the line and anything he should know when moving up?

'Oh sir, how can I know what those dreadful men will do to our Blowpipe Express. They have ambushed it a few times but blowing up the line is not good. Luckily, since the first time, no engine has been badly damaged as the flats in front took the force of the explosion. Put your trust in God, sir, he is a most reliable fellow.'

Jason asked him about his family. Yes, he was a grandfather now with six little ones. 'And you sir?'

'Oh, Station master sahib. I am an army officer so could not operate in the jungle happily if I knew I had a family liable to be attacked. My job would suffer.'

'Sir, you are thinking highly and deeply.'

Jason looked at the man quizzically. 'Exactly how?' he asked. The Tamil tried to explain himself. 'When I say "highly" I mean "highly" and when I say "deeply" I mean "deeply", isn't it' he sagely observed.

'It is,' said Jason and asked him if there were any stops along the line long enough for his men to cook their morning meal and the Station Master shook his head. 'No sir, at some of the stations it might be possible to buy a snack and a glass of tea but I don't really know what happens in those stations up the line. I have never been to them. The only halt of more than a few minutes is in Kuala Lipis where the up and the down trains pass, otherwise it is a single line.'

Jason thanked him and went back to his men as it was time for his evening meal and to see where his batman had arranged for him to sleep having declined the station master's kind invitation to spend the night with him and his family. Nobody told him, why should they? that a Chinese had entered into their sleeping space carrying a tray of *mi* and, in bazaar Malay, asked the Gurkhas if they wanted to buy a dish of the stuff. A few of them did. As they paid their money over he asked them where they were going and he was told that they were going up the line to Kota Bharu on the morrow. Having learnt that, he lost no time in leaving the building.

Jason called his 'O' Group and told them about the lack of time to cook during the train ride so it was decided to get up at four o'clock and cook the meal along with the morning tea. The meal would be carried in the men's mess tins so, with full water bottles, there should be no difficulty about eating on the journey.

With that they settled down for the night as comfortably heads covered with towels against the mosquitoes that whined around their ears.

3

Monday 6 October 1952, Alipore Park Road, Calcutta: The Rezident's private phone rang. He picked it up but before he could say anything the voice at the other end said, 'Hello, this is your younger brother speaking.' Leonid Pavlovich Sobolev instantly became alert – more than usual because he recognised the Chinese-accented English so knew it was an overseas call. No one who monitored such conversations secretly could ever guess any inner meaning from what was said. International calls were not common and were expensive; one that went on too long was suspicious.

'Yes, I recognise your voice. Is all well with you and your family?'

'Yes, all is well I am glad to say. I have a friend who has a relation not on the phone but can be contacted by you. I need to talk to him. It should not take too long for you to call him.'

'Be more specific. I am not a mind reader,' came the gruff reply.

'He is a Mr Tangra and a Law Chu Hoi has a message for him about a' – he coughed drily – 'sick relative.' The dry cough merely meant 'don't take this literally'.

The Rezident stiffened on hearing the first name. It was, in fact, not a man's name but the code word for either of the two agents who worked in the one of the Chinatowns in Calcutta. These were peopled by Hakka Chinese who worked in tanneries and had done so for longer than anyone could remember. About three hundred and fifty tanneries had been built over many years on marshy and reclaimed low-lying land. Part of their output was made-to-order shoes. Either of them, a Wong Kek Fui or a Chen Kim Fung, was his link for information coming from any Hong Kong source and although Hak Wa speakers were a rarity in India they were common in Singapore and Hong Kong so it was not as secure a language as might be thought even for short messages to be passed.

As for the second name, the Rezident immediately recognised it as that of the purser of the SS *Eastern Queen*, one of his two secret contacts who kept him informed of any crucial Hong Kong or Singapore news.

'Can you ring back in an hour's time? No make it an hour and a half.'

'Yes, I can. I'll book a call as soon as I have rung off and pay for five minutes' worth.'

The connection was cut and Leonid Pavlovich Sobolev leant back in his chair. *It isn't anything to do with the Borneo visit, surely?* He had been kept up to date about that and could think of no other reason for a call from Singapore. His blood tingled expectantly.

It was two hours before the phone rang again and the Rezident picked it up, annoyed with himself to see his hand trembling slightly. In English the caller said, 'I want to speak to Mr Tangra.' The phone was handed to Wong Kek Fui who was waiting expectantly and, in Hak Wa, said, yes, he was listening.

'On his next visit Law Chu Hoi will be bringing a battalion of *Loi Pok Yi* who have joined us and are being sent back from Malaya as no longer wanted. Tell Big Brother to get the news to our man in the wooden temple and him to spread it.'

Just to make sure Wong Kek Fui repeated it.

'Yes, correct' and the line went dead.

'What was that about?" the Rezident asked.

His Hakka agent who spoke basic English and understood it if it was spoken slowly enough, looked glum as he repeated the message slowly. 'A battalion of Gurkhas have changed sides and joined us, and you must get the news to our man in the wooden temple.'

The Russian nodded with evident satisfaction. 'Good but what and where is the wooden temple, I wonder? Is it one of yours' – he nearly said, 'heathen ones' but quickly decided not to – 'in Tangra?'

'Sir, we don't have any wooden temples in Tangra so it must be somewhere else.'

The Rezident tried not to appear angry at such an obvious comment. 'No, in that case it wouldn't refer to Tangra but the rest of the message is clear, isn't it?'

The Hakka nodded, was thanked and dismissed with a fistful of small notes as a retainer. Alone once more the Russian considered the message. *Gurkhas. Nepal. Wooden temple. Who could explain that? Vikas Bugga is the only man I know who can.*

He looked at his watch. By then it was close on seven o'clock and his man should be home by now. He got out his note book, found the number he wanted and rang it from his special phone.

'Your luck is in so let's begin,' came the cheery voice from the other end without introducing himself. 'I was just about to go out so what's all this about? Don't shout or be so rash as to ask me for any cash.'

The Russian shook his head at the unexpected effervescence and gave the word Bugga knew him by when phoning. 'I have a question for your son' – 'Son', the code word used for an emergency. 'Talking about Gurkhas what does wooden temple imply?'

'Oh my goodness gracious mee, is that an emergencee?'

'It may be for me. Can you tell me – or if not, who can?'

'Yes, it is the English translation of Kathmandu.'

'Kathmandu? What do you mean?'

'Kathmandu is the capital of Nepal.' *By Lenin, you really are ignorant* Vikas Bugga thought.

'Thank you. I'll let you get drunk as a skunk when you next visit me.' The conversation ended abruptly, leaving Vikas Bugga shaking his head in wonderment at what the Soviets thought was so urgent and the Rezident's ignorance.

Tuesday 7 October 1952, on the East Coast railway: A quarter of an hour before the train was due to leave Gemas, the men of A Company, 1/12 GR, were marched to the station and shown the separate coach put on at the rear especially for them and no one else. In they got. Nobody knew that the *mi* seller of the previous evening had contacted the train's assistant guard who, in turn, had put a call through to someone in Kuala Lipis, just short of halfway up the line. He, in turn, managed to get a message to a group of five guerrillas who lived 'in plain sight' in a *kampong* just farther on who moved off early the next morning. Had anyone been there to see them walking up the track, they would have taken them for workmen carrying their tools. About five miles up the line, overlooked by a steep jungle-covered slope, they moved round a bend which trains had to slow down for. Three of them opened their tool kits and set to work while the other two stayed as sentries on either end of the target area.

Back in Gemas the guard blew his whistle, waved his flag and the train moved off. The men settled down, some started talking, some looked out of the window at the countryside, the same as ever though subtly different, yet others nodded off with the train's movement making them sleepy. Some people wondered why such movement did this to Gurkhas: it was because when small they were rocked to sleep in hammocks strung up on the veranda of their house so any similar movement in later life almost automatically sent them to sleep.

Monotony overtook them, only relieved when they were told when to eat. At Kuala Lipis the down and the up trains passed each other. The next stop up the line was at Gua Musang, not that the soldiers knew anything about it and, even had they, it would have meant nothing to them.

Well before the trains had passed each other at Kuala Lipis the 'workmen' had deployed on the high ground overlooking the target bend. They had laid a mine affixed to a tie which they planned to explode remotely, derail the engine, open fire on and kill the Gurkhas and any other passengers. They had unearthed a light machine gun and four rifles to fire on the train when it halted. They knew what time to expect the train and heard it puffing before they saw it coming round the start of the bend. The guerrilla commander held up his arm, looked through the trees and when the train had reached the spot he had chosen to explode the mine, dropped it sharply but slightly prematurely. The satisfyingly loud bang did not damage the engine as planned but both 'flats' were thrown into the air, which broke the link with the engine and slid off the track down the far bank. The engine's bogey wheels were derailed and the train came to an abrupt halt. Even though the speed was slow the front passenger coaches buckled and crunched against each other as machine gun and rifle fire broke out.

The end carriage with the Gurkhas was not hit but some men were jolted onto the floor. 1 Platoon Commander, Gurkha Lieutenant Pahalsing Gurung, immediately stood up, carbine in hand and shouted, 'Follow me. Leave your big packs here.' He was an impressive man, slim and wiry. He had a long nose, flared nostrils, a prominent chin and a thick moustache. The first door he tried to open was somehow jammed so he told the man nearest the far door to try and open it. It opened easily and the men lowered themselves onto the ground, instinctively moving their weapon's safety catch to 'fire'. They were hidden from the guerrillas who continued firing at the train, causing four civilian fatalities. 1 Platoon moved down the bank and, crab-wise, shuffled back the way the train had come, slipping awkwardly on the slope. Fifty yards farther on the Lieutenant saw they were shielded by the bend so moved up and over the railway tracks into the jungle. As they moved up the steep slope they could hear covering fire for them.

At the same time Rance sent 2 Platoon up the line, out of sight until well round the bend and enter the jungle to take up a position to the guerrillas' rear to ambush them if they ran away from 1 Platoon's attack. 'Watch your firing, Saheb,' Jason called out. 'Only aimed shots at the daku.' The last thing he wanted was what was known as 'blue-on-blue'.

2 Platoon Commander raised his arm in acknowledgement and moved smartly off, along the bank out of sight of the enemy. Company HQ and 3 Platoon were already engaging the guerrillas with prophylactic fire from between the gaps of the carriages to prevent any attack on the train. This spoiled the guerrillas' aim and they shot high. Jason was tempted to fire his 2-inch mortar well over behind the guerrillas to catch them if they ran away but he heard the Gurkhas' battle cry 'Ayo Gurkhali chaaaaarge' echoing down from the hill which meant that 1 Platoon was engaging the guerrillas so he desisted. Then came a shout of 'Cease fire'.

Up on the position five guerrillas lay on the ground, three of them dead. One of the soldiers went to look at the corpses: the less badly wounded guerrilla waited till the Gurkha had his back to him then jumped up and violently slashed at him with a parang, seriously wounding him. The struck man screamed as he fell, senseless, to the ground. The Gurkha next to him wasted no time in killing the attacker with his khukri. That left one guerrilla wounded who was immediately tied up with a toggle rope that each soldier carried.

Jason heard the scream. *A wounded man: whose?* He called the medical corporal and they dashed off uphill. They found the severely injured soldier and the medical corporal examined his wound, deeming it safe to administer morphine. 'I'll clean him up and then I'll give him some morphine, Saheb. When he's fully unconscious I'll stitch him up.'

'Yes, do that. Also look at the wounded daku. We will have to evacuate both of them.' He blessed the CO's foresight to take a medic with him.

Just in case the train was still a target of any other guerrillas he told the 2 ic to send out patrols and to select a position for an overnight camp. He detailed the signaller to try and establish communications with Kota Bharu while he went back down the hill to talk to the Tamil guard, whom he found sitting shivering in the guard's van, overwhelmed. Frightened passengers were milling about listlessly, some with blood on their face scratched by bits of flying glass. 'There are four dead men in the front coach', one cried out.

'Guard, what are your standing orders in case of an attack like this with dead and wounded passengers?' he asked. 'Surely you have some first aid kit for those with blood on their face? Why not use it?'

'Oh sir, this is the second time this has happened to me,' the guard wailed, as the engine driver and his stoker, both shaken but unhurt, joined them having heard the 'Cease fire' shout.

Jason commiserated and firmly but kindly asked his questions again.

The engine driver interrupted and said, 'the engine has been derailed and the one recovery crane is in Gemas. We won't be able to move for at least two days.'

The guard came to his senses. 'Take the mobile train telephone, hook it to the wire beside the track and contact Kuala Lipis station.' He turned to his assistant and snarled, 'Help the wounded passengers.'

'I'll give you a Gurkha escort to go down the line to where there's a ladder up the pole to put the phone on. Once you have done that please let me know if your phone is working or not. While you are doing that I will go back up the hill and try and contact Kota Bharu.'

'But if the telephone line has been cut, sir, what am I to do? I can't mend it myself.'

The guard had been badly shaken so Jason tried to placate him. 'In any case as soon as the people in the next station realise that the up-train is delayed I am sure they will send someone to look and see why. In any case the noise of the battle will have been heard and reported.'

'Saheb, I have made contact,' called the signaller as his company commander came into sight. Jason breathed a sigh of relief. Before he had time to take the headset and talk to Brigade in Kota Bharu, he was told that the wounded guerrilla had died. *So that makes it five out of five.*

Jason put on a head set and said, 'Roger Nan Tare, Sunray 5 on set, over.'

'Sunray minor here. Send sitrep, over.'

'5 …' and Jason explained what had happened and the current situation. He also explained he had no map so did not know anything more than the last station they had passed through was Kuala Lipis.

'5. Roger. We will phone Kuala Lipis station and order trolleys to be sent up as soon as possible. The authorities there will provide an escort and take away passengers and the guerrilla corpses. We will warn the hospital to stand by for your wounded man and the police station for the five corpses to be recognised. A train will come and pick you and other passengers up sometime tomorrow. Roger so far, over?'

'5. Roger. I am self-contained but cannot look after the civilians. Confirm, over.'

The upshot was that the Police Field Force would succour the civilians and leave the troops alone.

The 2 ic had chosen a suitable camp site a little way off from where the incident had occurred, knowing that the men were not happy sleeping near where men had been killed. He had also detailed the CSM to get a stretcher made of branches and stretched poncho capes and take the wounded soldier carefully down to the guard's van.

The wounded man, dulled by the morphine and parang slash carefully stitched up, was put on the stretcher then oh so carefully carried down the steep slope and made comfortable in the guard's van. The poncho was washed from its blood stains in a nearby stream and taken back up to the camp. Meanwhile Jason wrote a message for Battalion HQ, telling them about the incident and his contact with HQ 1 Malay Brigade.

The search patrols returned with the news that they had found a weapon cache, with some rifles and much ammunition. Jason was highly delighted. It was too late to do anything so he decided to tell the trolleys' escort commander about the cache. The weapons and ammo would be guarded until the morrow when a responsible party should be sent to collect them.

By then the five dead men had been carried down to the train, an unpleasant but necessary task. They were laid by the track without any covering, there not being any available, along with the dead civilians which their scared peers could not take their eyes off such a grim sight until three trolleys arrived. There was a Chinese doctor on one and Jason told him the exact amount of morphine administered to the wounded Gurkha. The doctor said it was clear that it would take some time before he was fit enough to be moved back down to Seremban. The civilians also went back to Kuala Lipis and it was after dark when the five stiffs reached the police station.

Jason told the man in charge of the trolleys to send up some men on the morrow to collect the cache. There would be plenty of time before a train from Kelantan came to pick them up.

During the small hours the sentry lost his bearing as he moved round the camp. He stepped a couple of paces beyond the perimeter and, steadying himself as he looked around, he inadvertently leant against an elephant's leg, which he took to be a tree. He found his rifle trying to move upwards by itself so he pulled it down abruptly. The next thing he knew was that he was flying through the air and even the renowned Gurkha phlegm was unable to suppress a loud yell of surprised pain when he landed in a thorn bush. The camp immediately stood to, found the disorientated sentry, relieved him and the medical orderly took his thorns out. It was only the next morning when the sentry was shown a pile of fresh elephant dung that he changed his story from being attacked by the soul of one of the dead guerrillas to an as-frightening-but-more-prosaic elephant.

About midday a train from Kota Bharu came to take them and the civilian passengers on the remainder of their journey. No one relaxed until they were out of jungle-girt ground in case of another ambush.

Tuesday 7 – Thursday 23 October 1952, Kelantan: Looking out of their carriage windows at the flat countryside, the men saw that Kelantan was different from what they were used to operating in, flatter, more open and, somehow, greener. It did not seem likely that guerrillas could operate in such terrain and, to the observant, everyone seemed to be a Malay, with no Chinese or Indians. The train reached Tumpat station in the late afternoon. Jason saw a Malay captain peering about so went up to him and saluted. 'I am OC A Company, 1/12 Gurkha Rifles. Captain Rance. I am sorry to be late,' he said with a genuine smile as he introduced himself and saluted the Malay.

'I am Captain Yusof Ali, on the staff of 1 Malay Brigade HQ here,' the Malay officer answered, in turn saluting. They shook hands. He was a small, dapper man, with a wide chest and long arms. His face was young-looking and his gaze often seemed to wander into a world of its own. 'Welcome. This is the first time we've had Gurkhas under command, normally only Malay troops are. 3 Malay are here, firing their annual range classification and guarding some royal rowing races.'

He continued too quickly for Jason to find out more on such an intriguing and unusual military task by adding 'they are due to move back to Port Dickson at the end of the week. There is transport outside to take you to your lines. I'll go with you then take you to 1 Brigade HQ and meet the Deputy Commander, a Colonel, who is standing in for the Brigadier who is on leave. I'm sorry you had trouble on your way up and had a man wounded. But you managed to kill all five of them, didn't you?' He spoke in English.

Jason nodded and answered in the same language, 'It was all a bit unexpected but I have a good bunch of lads.' He called his Gurkha officers over.

Rance's Gurkha officers all spoke some Malay so that was the language Rance used to introduce them. Captain Ali was visibly pleased with this courtesy so seldom offered by a Mat Salleh. The company was ready to move off and went out through the station onto the main road. As far north as this the sun set later and rose earlier than it did nearer the Equator. They were driven away some little distance out of the town to a camp, Rance being given a ride in Captain Ali's staff car. The accommodation was huts with *atap* roofs. After debussing the Malay captain looked at his watch. 'Can we leave now, please, it's getting late, it takes a bit of time to get to HQ and I don't like keeping my boss waiting.'

'2 ic saheb. Carry on as you think fit. I have to go to Brigade HQ.'

At the HQ Jason was introduced to the Colonel, also a Malay, who gave him a quick briefing on the current situation. Not much was happening, not much had happened and, with any luck, not much would happen. 'We are in a quiet area here, Captain Rance, and long may it remain so. The population is more religious than in other parts of the country and so is not at all interested in Communism.'

'What tasks have you for me sir?' Rance asked as he went to a large map on the wall. 'As we are on the border with Thailand is there any likelihood of incursions or any such activity?'

'No, none whatever.' Captain Ali made as to say something and the Colonel said, 'We will allot you some transport and I'd like you to tour the area, show your faces, so to speak, let the villagers see the Gurkhas and, yes, you can go up to the border. Is that all?'

'Three more points, sir: mandatory opening times for sitreps, issue of maps and, a surprise question, do you know of any Gurkha soldiers who settled around here after escaping from the Japanese in 1942?'

The Colonel glanced at his watch, said to his Staff Captain, 'Get my vehicle ready' and turning to Jason said, 'Captain Ali will answer the first two questions and you can stop at any police station you pass and ask about the last question, provided you have contacted the Officer in charge of the Police District, the OCPD, concerned first.'

Jason heard his car drive up. 'Good night,' the Colonel said as he abruptly left. Jason found himself saluting nobody. *You've never saluted a blank file before, have you?* he asked himself.

From his more detailed operational briefing on the following morning Jason found that apart from guarding food stocks and the occasional police check on any suspicious stranger, the situation was almost normal, certainly compared with farther south. Guerrilla activity had not been reported for about six months and then only on the fringes of the southern operational boundary. The nearest point of danger, in Jason's mind, was on the Thai border. It was so quiet that any unarmed guerrilla courier from the south, wearing plain clothes, could pass as a normal civilian and so not be suspected of any nefarious activity, even though here, surely, was too far to the east for routine contact with southern Thai guerrillas. From his briefing it seemed that troops did not make deep jungle recces. Jason wondered why: *no perceived threat? No particular inclination?*

Jason thanked the Brigade Major who had been briefing him and said, 'Unless you have any objections, what I'd like to do, certainly for the first week, is to rotate my platoons, one or two at a time, for a couple of days in any areas you'd like me to look at to get used to the place. For myself I'd like to borrow a Jeep and visit police stations, especially ones near the international border. As I mentioned yesterday I have been given a non-operational task by my CO, namely to see if there are any remnants of the Gurkhas from the 1942 campaign –what a disaster! – as well as feel the pulse of events.' That was agreed to, provided he met the OCPD, first. Most police officers of that rank and above were British. That was acceptable to the military authorities. Jason returned to his lines, devised a programme for the first week and left the 2 ic to work on it while he went to meet the OCPD. On his way there he was fascinated to see the royal canoes practising rowing for the up-coming festival. He did not know when it took place or what it was all about. *I must ask the OCPD.*

When he reached the office he was amazed and delighted to see the incumbent was none other than Rodney Mole, the 3-inch Mortar Officer he had worked alongside when he was serving in 4/1 GR in Burma. He was a tall, lean man with a sharp, narrow face, nose a little out of shape – he had played rugger at school – and had a sensitive mouth.

Rodney was equally surprised to see who had come to visit him. 'Well, who would have thought we'd meet up here?' he asked joyously. 'And, pray, what can I do for you? Have a seat while you tell me all about it.'

Jason explained that his company was 'standing in' until the incoming Malay Regiment troops were ready. He explained how he intended to operate and then mentioned about his search for any wartime Gurkhas who might still be in the area. Rodney was entirely sympathetic with that and suggested if dates worked out, he'd like to accompany Jason.

'And now it's your turn to tell me about you,' said Jason, smiling broadly. He knew that Rodney was a man of upright character who saw the best in people even if there was not much to see in the first place.

'I was infiltrated into Malaya by submarine at the end of 1944 and found I so liked the Malays I wanted to return and work with them after I learnt that the peacetime army didn't want me,' he told Jason. 'I applied for and was accepted by the Malay police and here I am, really happy although, as in any job, it has its ups and downs. Luckily for me mine are mostly ups.'

They visited most of the police stations under Rodney's jurisdiction in police transport. In every one, the occupants were amazed at Jason's fluency and pronunciation compared with other Europeans. Jason, in turn, found that in some police stations the Malay language spoken was different from that he had grown up with. He had not been warned that there was a difference. He always started off by telling them that his troops' task was purely military and then went on to mention any missing *orang Gurkha* who might have hidden from the Japanese in the last war. He never got an affirmative answer, but the looks they gave each other when he broached the topic troubled him. *Do they know something?* he wondered *or is it that Gurkhas mean nothing to them?*

When they had completed their tour Jason thanked Rodney, who asked him to pop in and take 'pot luck' any time he felt like it.

'Why not now, Rodney, there's time for a quick cuppa.'

'Or for a cold beer,' smiled the OCPD. 'Come along. I'd like to show you my garden. My driver will run you back to your lines.'

The two men sat on the veranda, Jason with his cup of tea and Rodney with a fresh lime. And indeed Jason had seldom seen such a profusion of colour: white, pink and red hibiscus; beds of red cannas; pink oleander bushes; frangipani trees; purple morning glory; deep violet bougainvillea and others he didn't recognise.

'Rodney, this is wonderful,' he breathed. 'You can't have done it all yourself but it is obvious that you have looked after it with green fingers.'

As Jason rose to go it was dusk: he thanked his old friend and said it was the perfect way to end a perfect day. 'You'll have to visit us before we go,' he said on parting.

After his platoons had returned from their patrols, all of which took place in the western part of the state, Jason debriefed them to find out what they had found – which was nothing! He fretted that there really didn't seem much point in their coming here all the way from Seremban. In an unusually gloomy frame of mind when he went to brief HQ on his 'no news' report he unwittingly spoke in faultless Malay to the Colonel who was astonished and complimented him. 'Where did you learn to speak our language so well?' he asked and was amazed to learn Jason's background. Jason could see he seemed to regard him in a better light than before as he was, if not politer than he had been, less abrupt. *As I have noticed so many times, the way to a person's heart is from the tongue through the ear!*

'Sir, I have been studying the map and see that a road runs along the frontier. Have you had any incursions from the Malays living in Thailand? I can't image that any Thais would infiltrate unless a blind eye is turned when they come shopping?' He knew that during the late war the Japanese had incorporated this part of Malaya into southern Thailand.

The Colonel was struck by the idea. 'I had not thought of that before. With your knowledge of Malay it might be a good idea to leave a rear party in your camp and you to take the three platoons to search the border, not to cross it, mind you, to see what evidence, if any, you can find.'

'How long for, sir?'

'Say, a week. Or a bit longer if you like. You are about half way through your stay here, aren't you?'

'May I suggest I start with ten days' rations and dump them so there'll only be a need for one fresh rations re-supply? I'll take a central point and patrol north for the first five days and the south for the last part.'

'The Malay Colonel bit his lip in thought. 'Yes, I'll go along with that. Plan something and let me know. But no, I repeat no crossing the border.'

'I fully understand, sir' Jason said and, having saluted his senior, went back to his lines. There he studied his map and saw a hilly area, Bukit Bunga, Flower Hill, near the border. It seemed the obvious place to use as a base for movement north and south. There was a road near it for easy re-supply. Leaving a small rear party back in camp, transport took the rest of his company as far as the village of Rantau Panjang, a stone's throw from the Thai border, and on down to as near Bukit Bunga as vehicles could get. They debussed, sent the vehicles back and moved west into the jungle, seeing the boundary markers from time to time. They set up a patrol base and for the first two days platoons patrolled in both directions.

On Day three, Jason had this report: 'As we lay in ambush we saw a herd of bison, Saheb, porcupine and wild boar. We looked down a glade into Thai territory and saw a trap big enough for boar.'

'And yet no human tracks?' Jason asked.

'Not on this side, Saheb.'

Jason sat still, contemplating this. He had been briefed that there were Malays on both sides of the border but everyone knew that they never ate pork meat. He turned to the man who had mentioned the trap. 'Are you sure that the trap could not be for porcupines?'

The man looked perplexed then grinned. 'No Saheb, not sure, but to make sure why don't we ambush it to find out?'

'We have three days before we need go back to the road to collect our fresh rations and only a carrying party need go for them so yes, let's do that.' They got ready to move and the patrol leader who had seen the trap led the way and, on the morrow about noon, two men were seen approaching it. Jason, who was a few yards in the rear, was called forward. He saw the men, took his binoculars out of their case and closely studied them. *Surely not! Look like Gurkhas but can't be so, or can it?*

'Ustad,' he said to the NCO next to him. 'Look through these and tell me what you think.'

The NCO studied the two men, drew in his breath sharply and said, 'Saheb, can't be but they look like us.'

'Yes, that's what I thought. Tell you what, let's go and talk to them. It's a gamble and we've been told not to go over the border but if we're careful, it can't matter. Ustad, you and two others follow me. The rest cover us and only fire if we seem in danger of being fired on.'

The three men stepped over the border which they recognised by one of the intermittent boundary stones, moved to within fifty yards of the two men and Jason said, 'Ustad, we must not frighten them. They still can't see us. Tell you what, sing a song, loudly, so they'll hear it. Sing the one we sang as we left our depots in India when we went on draft to the war' and he softly sang the chorus:

'The leaves of the trees are green at the top,

We're on our way, on our way to the war.'

'Yes, I know it' and as loudly as possible he sang it.

The effect was one of unbelievable shock to the two men. They stared, open-mouthed, in the direction of the song, turned to one another with grins almost from ear to ear and joined in. The song came to the end of the verse and Jason, moving forward, called to them in Nepali. 'Oho, Old Men, we have come to talk to you. Stay where you are. I am a British saheb and we are a Gurkha patrol so no harm can come to you.'

They moved up to the two men who, as they neared, stared dumbfounded, as though hardly able to believe it was not a dream. Both of them had wrinkled faces, with induced, furtive expressions, cross-hatched and fine wrinkles in the corners of their eye sockets, gnarled hands and threadbare clothes. They were older than their years and had the furtive air of one worried lest he be accused of trespassing.

The elder said, jerkingly, as if not sure he was really awake, 'Saheb, have you come to fetch us?'

'We have come to look for you,' Jason said with a pang of pity – pity, which is more promiscuous than lust. 'We can take you back to Malaya then send you back to Nepal if you so wish. What battalion were you with?'

'2/2 GR. We were together. Our company commander was Captain Williams.'

'It is he, now our Commanding saheb, who sent us to try and find you.'

The two men, still recovering from the shock, merely shook their heads in wonder at what Fate had decreed so suddenly and unexpectedly.

Jason said, 'When did you last eat?'

'Yesterday. We are hungry but nothing has come into our trap.'

'Come back with us. We are quite close. We'll cook you a meal and give you a drink of rum and you can tell us all about it.'

They were unsure if that was wise.

'If you can't trust a British saheb, who can you?' asked the NCO rhetorically. 'Come, we promise you there is no trap. Why should there be?'

They moved back to their night stop and cooked a meal for the two men. While it was cooking a brew of tea was prepared and the smile of delight on both faces was a wonder to see. 'Tea, like this?' one of them said and, on his fingers, started counting the years. 'Ten years,' and a tear of joy rolled down his cheek.

After their meal and a swig of rum, Jason asked them their story. Yes, they had tried to escape from the Japanese and, as there was no hope of returning, had settled in a Malay village on the Thai side of the border, married and raised a family. The elder looking said, 'We each have a wife and family. The girls' parents only allowed that if we ...' and he became embarrassed as he was ashamed to say 'circumcised' according to Malay rites.

'Would you like to return to Nepal?'

'Oh Saheb.' It was obvious they were on the horns of a

dilemma. Jason made a quick decision. He took out his note book and wrote the battalion's address and phone number and gave it to them. 'Let's not decide now. If ever you want to go, send us a letter or if you get the chance to phone here is the number. Best to cross over into Kelantan as it is the same country rather than try from Thailand. In any case we'll be here for a few more days.'

The man took the note, put it in his pocket and sat still.

'You probably don't have a job, do you, otherwise how do you earn your living?'

And then a long story came out: in essence they were now helping make a camp so that if any guerrillas from Malaya wanted to come and hide in it it would be ready for them. It was being dug with defence posts in a sizable area and would indeed be strong.

'How far is it from here?'

'A long day's walk not carrying a big pack.'

It was then Jason's turn to sit still and ponder.

'How many villages and military posts are there between here and your camp?'

Of course there were both but not many of either. The two men knew the area like the proverbial backs of their hands. It was hilly country and there were ways to get there without meeting anybody.

The two soldiers with Jason listened. *Where is this leading? The Saheb is always one to take a chance.*

'Will you take us there in a way nobody will see us and help us back?' Jason asked.

'How can you help us if we do? If we are found out we will

be drastically punished.'

'I only have very little Malay currency on me and no Thai baht. Finance is difficult. Help? As I said before, if you want to go back to Nepal I will help you all I can.'

'We'll take you and bring you back. We can talk about the future after we are back here.'

Back in the patrol base Gurkha Lieutenant Pahalsing Gurung took the OC's batman, Rifleman Kulbahadur Limbu, to one side and said, 'The OC saheb has, in my view, most rashly decided to go in uniform, armed, and only to take some hard tack, biscuits, bars of issue chocolate and tea to drink from his compo rations; with three men, two unarmed. It is a great risk.'

Kulbahadur Limbu was a tall, paler than normal lad, broad-shouldered, upright and strong who almost glided rather than walked. He was the battalion's expert tracker.

'What if you don't come back, Saheb?' someone asked Jason who answered with a smile 'I've had no bad dreams recently. I'll be back alright. I have my lucky krait with me.'

Pahalsing continued quietly talking to Kulbahadur. '*Keta*, we know the saheb will not stop at anything once he has made his mind up. However, he always has our interests at heart' and he looked at the batman with gimlet-like eyes. 'He is your personal responsibility and if he does not come back, in your next incarnation you will be a dung beetle,' to which there was no answer save a nod of the head.

Around the same time considerable activity continued elsewhere in Malaya. The Royal Australian Air Force had bombed Chin

Peng's camp and only just missed killing the entire Politburo. The decision to move north into Thailand was not taken until late 1952 but detailed reconnaissances for a new camp had already been made. To the east of the eventual camp site elements of the Kuomintang Army, known to the Communists as 'bandits', the same name originally given to the guerrillas in Malaya. – hence the name of 'Communist Terrorists'– would periodically visit. The Kuomintang soldiers were no military threat as such, only an armed nuisance: they had strayed south from the 'Golden Triangle', the opium-growing area where Burma, Laos and Thailand meet. They wore 'puffy' brown peaked hats, some of which still had the wreathed badge of the Chinese National Army in them.[12]

After a drink of tea and an early meal Jason's group set off at dawn with the greys of the sky turning to rose. They had a brew at midday. As they rested they were momentarily startled by the staccato drilling of two woodpeckers on a tree trunk for insects and a monkey high in the trees above them beating on the branches with sticks. By travelling light and walking fast, it was late afternoon when they came across an area that had been cleared of some trees and certainly been worked on but it was in such a non-tactical site Jason could not believe that it was a possible military base. He queried it with the elder of the two wartime men who looked blank.

'Saheb, there are two camp sites. This is only the first one. The other is much too far to reach in the time we have.'

---

12 Both incidents are described in Chapter 10, *My Side of History*, Chin Peng.

'Have you seen Chinese soldiers working here?' Jason demanded, feeling frustrated that his journey might well have been in vain.

'Yes, a group did come and look around.'

'And what happened then?' – *if anything. Yet there must have been a reason for the work done here.*

'Other people came, some Thais and a few Chinese, with saws and axes to work on the foundations of the camp.'

Then Jason saw that even if initially the area might have been chosen as a military base it was now a logging area so there was nothing for them to do but to go back. In a way it was a disappointment but, being rational, it saved a lot of bother by it not being occupied by any military force. They moved to an empty hut they had seen on their way in to spend the night.

'Let's doss down here. We're all tired enough' Jason said. There was not a lot of choice, anyway.

Kulbahadur grinned. 'We've been in more dangerous places before so why not?'

They opened up their hard tack, cooked a brew of tea and, before settling down for the night, talked amongst themselves as only soldiers can. They then settled down, covering their face against the many mosquitoes as comfortably as they could and drifted off to sleep.

Sometime later they were woken by a dog barking. They sat up and, in the dark, Jason and Kulbahadur grabbed their weapon, their lives in the tip of the index finger of their right hand. Spiders of alarm ran a web over their skin. They saw a torch light flashed and heard Chinese voices. 'Ah, here's a place we can spend the rest of the night. What a god-forsaken place this is. Nothing worth taking.'

'No, and I expect there are no women either.'

'You *ham saap kwai*. Can't you ever take your mind off horizontal refreshment?' asked the other man with jovial affection. The four men in the hut froze. 'Shh,' whispered Jason. 'Leave this to me.' Later, thinking over how he reacted, he gave himself full marks. In a shrill falsetto, in Chinese he squawked 'No women, did you say? How could you forget me? So, you have come at last? How long have I been waiting for a really *ham saap kwai* to satisfy me?'

There was a yelp from outside, a silence then, 'Are you real?'

'Come and find out for yourself. But first tell me who you are. You don't sound as if you come from the south and your unveiled instincts are not those of a decent comrade. You are not bandits, *fei toh,* are you?'

'Them? *Kung fei*, Communist bandits? We spit on that kind of person. We are Nationalists, never *kung fei*.'

This time it was Jason who was surprised. This was the last complication he wanted, cursing himself as being too foolhardy. *I must get rid of them but how?*

Still using his falsetto and giggling, he said, 'I'll give you a test before you can have me. Are you afraid of snakes?' getting his krait out his pocket as he said it.

'Snakes? I can hear you moving around. What are you doing? Waiting for our short snakes?'

'Taking off my knickers for you. But before I allow you to uncoil your snakes, shine your light at the door of the hut.'

As he did so Jason threw his dummy krait on the ground so it could be seen and hissed loudly as he did.

There was a joint yelp as the intruders ran away as fast as they could. 'Kulé, get that snake back quickly. Up, you others, and we will have to move out and hide some distance away. They may come back.'

They got out and moved off a hundred yards or so and sat with their backs to some trees. Not long afterwards they heard people returning to the hut. Three rifle shots were fired, the hut was set on fire and the prowlers made off.

Shortly afterwards there was a horrific cloudburst and there was nothing to do but sit, get wet through and shiver violently. When it was light they started on their way back. They passed through some marshy ground with a salt lick they had noticed on their way in when there were no animals – but now! A herd of almost black, great wild bison – bulls, cows and calves – the bulls enormously horned and dangerous, standing six feet at their shoulders and nine feet long from nose to tail – were grazing. [13] In Malaya Jason knew them as *seladang*. Pawing the ground as they smelt men from about two hundred yards away, two bulls charged at the four men. '*Gaur,*' Kulbahadur yelled.

Sprinting to some nearby teak trees with sturdy liana vines strong enough to bear their weight, they clambered up, just high enough to be out of reach of the angry animals' horns.

'Saheb, we've won out again,' said Kulbahadur approvingly between pants of breath as the two bulls angrily pawed the

---

13 The whole area became the Hala Bala Wild Life Sanctuary in 1996.

ground below.

Jason smiled back. 'I have come across pink-coloured buffaloes that dislike Europeans' smell but don't seem to mind Nepalis'. I have had to escape from them but these creatures! Is it the same with them or is it their mating season I wonder?' There was no answer from the others who merely made themselves more comfortable as they got their breath back again. 'We'll have to wait a while for these animals to leave us alone,' which they did about twenty minutes later.

Jason looked at his watch. 'Time to move. We must hurry. Top gear all the way. No need to take any security precautions now so no need to keep quiet.'

It started to rain heavily and, making best time, they reached their patrol base just before last light, soaked to the skin, hungry and dead tired – but at least they were safe.

Gurkha Lieutenant Pahalsing Gurung welcomed them effusively. He had been on tenterhooks since they had left. 'Saheb, there's not much tactically to report,' said Jason tiredly. 'I'll tell you what happened after a good night's sleep.'

'Hunchha Hajur' replied the Gurkha officer then, to Kulbahadur almost under his breath, he said, 'No need now to be reborn as a dung beetle.'

They changed their clothes, lent the two wartime men some spare kit, made a fire of logs, got warm, dried their clothes and the two men with Kulé had a drink of rum. Jason, not liking the stuff, had a mess tin cover of tea. After their meal they had an early bed, being tired out.

The OCs briefing next morning did not take long. 'It was

hardly worth the trouble but to find Nationalist Chinese soldiers as far south is something people should know about. I'll tell them when we get back.'

His senior Platoon Commander looked at him knowingly and, with the quiver of a smile, said, 'Not if you are as wise as you normally are, Saheb.'

Jason looked at him sharply. 'Meaning what, Saheb?'

'Letting people know that you have broken all international laws by entering another country without any authority, armed and in uniform. That's trespassing, isn't it? A court-martial offence!'

'O-ho, Saheb. Sorry,' and he twisted his ears emulating being punished by a superior. 'I can say the two men we met came over the border and told us about it.'

After their meal he asked his two guides 'So, what will you do now? Have you made your minds up?'

'Can you guarantee our getting back to Nepal?'

'No, I personally can guarantee nothing but I certainly can say that my Commanding saheb will do all he can. I cannot see you being unsuccessful. And, just, just suppose, although I can't imagine it, he was unsuccessful, we could always get you back here if you wanted it. All I have to ask you is to say we found you in Rantau Panjang.'

'Of course, Saheb,' said with a smile only Hill Gurkhas are capable of.

The rest of their stay spent in that area was an anti-climax. Jason reported into HQ at the end of the time, told the Colonel that he had found two wartime Gurkhas in Rantau Panjang who had told them about strange soldiers wearing strange hats and now wanted to be taken back to Nepal and this was what he was going to do once he was back in Seremban.

The Colonel said that strange soldiers in strange hats in Thailand were the Thais' business not his and did not pursue the matter. He thanked Captain Rance and dismissed him. Before the company left Jason managed to get Rodney Mole to come and have a meal with his men, who put on an impromptu dance, much to the OCPD's delight. They next day they were away. Thankfully their return journey was without incident.

Back in Seremban Jason handed over the two wartime Gurkhas to the CO and they were almost stultified to meet him. He did not tell the CO about his journey into Thailand, he'd keep the information to himself. What he did tell him was that the unnatural proclivity of one Sergeant Padamsing Rai, a member of the battalion now instructing soldiers in the Gurkha army school, was causing distress and dishonour amongst students. There was also a British sergeant who had similar tendencies.

Jason met the wounded man who was 'line sick', recovering in barracks and excused parades until he was fully fit. 'By the time I'm back within a month you'll be good as new,' Jason told him.

The soldier smiled his thanks rather than saying anything, the way it happens in the Hills.

Matters moved surprisingly fast: before the *Eastern Queen* reached Singapore, the British sergeant working at the Gurkha school had been flown back to England and the Gurkha 'administratively discharged'. So that he could be got rid of as quickly and quietly as possible he was to be escorted back to Calcutta aboard the next ship carrying a leave party, the *Eastern Queen.*

Jason was told that an officer on the reserve was coming out for his annual 'refresher' and he would take A Company over. He turned out to be an Irishman who had served with Gurkhas in the war and had 'second sight', although certain circumstances had to pertain. He was Major James McGurk, a small, fey, sour-apple of a man, grey-skinned and shrivelled.

Wednesday 29 October 1952, Alipore Park Road, Calcutta: The Rezident had been in Calcutta long enough to have had his 'scouts' look around and find that there was a sizeable Nepalese population in the sprawling city. Some of them drove buses or taxis, others were security guards or shop keepers. A number of them had been in the army, 'seen the world' and did not want to return to Nepal and live under an undeveloped and authoritarian government, especially having served in the army of a democratic government, something their own country did not have. The most fretful and at odds with their home country were those who had been forcibly converted to Islam by marauding bands of Muslims in the two years before partition in 1947 and, despite repeated requests to be re-accepted by the Nepalese authorities, found themselves as permanent religious outcastes. Some of these were ripe material for Communist recruitment: one in particular had found work in the Nepalese consulate in Sterendale Road so had a direct line to Kathmandu.

Over the weekend this man was contacted and ordered to

report to the Soviet consulate. He was told about the coded phone call from Singapore by Chen Geng, of course no details of names being given. On the following Monday a letter explaining about the next boatload of Calcutta–bound Gurkhas being a mutinying battalion of now-Communist Gurkhas sent back to Nepal on disbandment, was slipped into the weekly diplomatic bag to Kathmandu. The message– the Rezident never asked how it was sent – reached King Tribhuvan, who the previous August had overthrown the Rana regime that had ruled the country since 1846, and had imposed direct rule. He reacted most strongly, hating the idea of Communism. He called one of the few men he trusted, his senior General, and told him the bad news. He did not say how he got it but merely from 'unofficial sources'. 'How can we absorb so many people who will be against our Government?' he queried anxiously.

'Sarkar', said the General, using the word all royalty were addressed by, 'this is a grave problem indeed. We could ask for details from the British ambassador but as you have not received it from official sources is there just a chance of it being a malicious rumour?'

'Rumour or not, we cannot afford to take any chances.' His Majesty directed that a secret message be sent to the Nepalese consulate in Rangoon telling the Consul on no account whatsoever was he or any member of his small staff to visit that next boatload of Gurkhas passing through. However, if there was a British officer on board he could be asked for background details. The General felt it was not up to him to suggest that the Consul would surely contact some Gurkhas if he went on board to meet any British officer in charge of the draft, so remained silent.

Instructions were readied and shown to the King for approval: such was essential for everything.

Wednesday 29 October – Monday 3 November 1952, Kuching, Sarawak: The SS *Kimanis* had made a leisurely journey, stopping at Jesselton in North Borneo before sailing west along the coast to Kuching. The man calling himself Ah Ho and his friend had return tickets and, before disembarking to carry out their task, they asked the purser when the vessel was returning. They were told that they should be back by Sunday night if they wanted their berths confirmed. Just saying they'd be back wasn't good enough. The two men agreed they would be back by then. Their travel documents were in order and, having nothing to declare, they left the dock area without any hassle.

At that time the Sarawak United People's Party, SUPP, was not illegal and the two found out that the office of Sim Ting Ong, the Secretary General, was in Jalan Tan Sri Ong Kee, an out-of-the-way place not easy to find. Find it they did eventually, hot and tired, and Ah Ho knocked on the door. No answer. He looked to see if there was a bell: no. He knocked again, louder. An eye appeared at the Judas window, the two men were studied and the door was opened as far as the chain securing it allowed.

'Who are you?' a Chinese man asked, tersely.

They gave their names, adding 'We have heard a lot about Mr Sim Ting Ong and would like to meet him. We come from Singapore, where we have commercial interests.'

'I am his secretary. Stay here. He normally doesn't want to

meet strangers. I'll go and ask.' He was back in a few minutes. 'Follow me,' he said curtly, leading the way upstairs and knocking on a door. They heard a gruff command to enter. They went inside and saw an elderly, gnarled and desiccated Chinese man, seated on an upright chair behind a desk. His eyes were like extinct craters, grey, inaccessible and hard as volcanic rock.

The two men from Singapore introduced themselves and explained that, although one of them was a businessman, both had other significant interests. 'He who sent us here by boat, on which we have to return on board on Sunday, needs a report, positive or negative, about a proposition he has for you. He has heard so much good of you he hopes that he and you are *tung chi*' – equal thinkers – 'about common concerns.'

'Equal thinkers' was a term that almost invariably defined a 'comrade', nearly always a Communist one.

'Common concerns? What have you and I in common? 'The voice was like gravel on a chalkboard, the result of throat cancer surgery which had left him with a profoundly unnerving intonation and a repulsive neck scar to match. He muttered some imprecation under his breath. 'I say again, concerns about what? I am only a simple politician and not a businessman.'

'I think it will help you understand if we tell you who sent us to contact you. You may have heard of him.'

'I'm not interested but, yes, tell me his name.'

'His real name is Ong Boon Hua but he is widely known as Chin Peng and, like you, is Secretary General of a party. He is a little hazy on details but he remembers hearing, in 1946, the White Rajah, Charles Vyner Brooke handed Sarawak to Britain's

Colonial Office. There was an incident when two youths stabbed Duncan Stewart Brooke, who would have been his successor, wanting to have Sarawak independent and not under the British.' Ah Ho was delighted that the research he had done in Singapore's public library was coming in so useful. 'Chin Peng's idea is for history to try and repeat itself and Sarawak become ours, the Party's, not Britain's.'

Sim Ting Ong's expression did not change although it was obvious that he was impressed by his visitor's knowledge. He took out a key from his pocket, gave it to his secretary and told him to open the safe next to the wall behind the desk and take out a small black note book.

The secretary opened the safe, felt around inside, found what he was looking for and handed it over with the key. Sim Ting Ong opened it and turned some pages. A look of recognition passed over his face. 'And if you are bluffing?' he asked in a grunted threat.

'Test us how you like and if you don't like what we say you can hand us over to the police as trespassers.'

'You seem sincere so I'll hear what you have to say. And your purpose? There must be a reason for such a high-level executive to send you to me.'

'Comrade, there is. We have come to ask you a big, big favour which we are sure you will appreciate. We sincerely hope that after we have explained our aims there will be enough time in the next four days for you to give us your answer.'

'Tell me all.'

This Ah Ho did and, to his relief, the SUPP Secretary General nodded his approval, saying, 'Let us eat first then we'll talk of plans.' He called out to his secretary, 'Brandy and three glasses.' They talked banalities until their meal was brought in. After the plates had been taken away, Sim Ting Ong said, 'Give me an outline of what you have come to tell me.'

'It is rather a delicate subject. Initially in Malaya we all thought that those arrogant British would not have the impudence to return here after the war in which their soldiers were so inferior, though better than those drunken Australians I will admit, that they lost both Malaya and Singapore to the fascist Japanese. Even though there were some of them who stayed in the jungle with us to operate against the Japanese, none of them was anywhere as aggressive or skilled as we were. Then the mercenaries from Nepal ...'

He was interrupted. 'Who, where?'

Ah Ho chided himself. He had forgotten no Gurkhas had ever fought in Borneo so obviously they were not known about. He explained them, saying how they had in no way lived up to their fearsome reputation 'so we thought we could beat them easily. But we found they proved tougher than ever we thought and now we want to get rid of them.'

'But what is that to me?'

'I am coming to that. That is why we are here.' And he told him, in as much detail as was needed to get his points across. The idea pleased Sim Ting Ong and the upshot was that he decided to arrange a plenum for the Sunday morning to discuss it and, hopefully, to get approval – 'I can't gather them before then'. If so, they would thrash out a general plan in enough detail for the two men from Singapore to give a satisfactory report on their return. It was only during the plenum did even Sim Ting Ong come to learn that the military forces in the country, the Sarawak Rangers, did not possess any machine guns, sub or light, so could not prevail against the SUPP planned insurrection.

Sunday 9 November 1952, 25 Robinson Road, Singapore: Reggie Hutton's phone rang when it was dusk. '9928,' was the bleak answer.

'Mr Hutton have you got your hat on sir? Is it too late to come and see you? There are two of us but I don't think you know my friend.'

'Where are you calling from?'

'We have just arrived on the day train from KL and have decided to wait in the station precincts till dark before ringing you. We have yet to fix accommodation for our stay.'

Reggie thought that one out quickly. His wife was away in England and his house had a spare room. 'Look, you say you haven't booked anywhere. We haven't met for a long, long time. We'll have a lot to talk about, old times et cetera. Come and spend tonight with me.'

'Yes, we'd like that: old times and new ones also.'

'Do you know your way around Singapore?'

'Afraid not but tell me where you live and we'll come by taxi.'

'No, stay where you are, I'll come and fetch you.'

Ah Fat and his Bear stood in a shady place outside the station precincts. When an expensive car drove up and the driver got out, Ah Fat recognised his wartime friend. 'Come on. Over to the car.'

It was a joyous reunion, they had not met since during the war. Ah Fat introduced his Bear and on the way back to Reggie's place he explained the way they had joined forces. Reggie Hutton needed to know enough about him to trust him as much as he trusted Ah Fat.

'I have heard that you and Captain Rance are great friends. When did you last meet?' and that led on to a brief explanation of what had happened on Operation Janus when his friend had saved his life.

'Do you know where he is now?'

'No sir. I don't.'

They reached Reggie's place and he offered them a room and a wash. 'Freshen up before we have a meal' and went to tell the cook to make ready for two more people.

After eating they sat down for a talk and Ah Fat told his host and friend all that had happened since the killing of the thirty-five guerrillas. It took quite some time to tell. Although it was not in Reggie's territory as such it was of general background interest to him and he welcomed hearing it. He was particularly interested in Chen Geng – *that, in fact, doesn't surprise me but does confirm my suspicion* – and was fascinated to learn about the Sarawak ploy.

'Now that really is something,' he said out loud. He was a personal friend of the Commissioner General for southeast Asian colonies, whose residence, 'Bukit Serene' – known as 'Bucket Latrine' by the expats – was near Johor Bharu and who had considerable sway with the Colonial Office over such matters: looking ahead, it was that relationship and Ah Fat's briefing that put paid to any uprising in Borneo so there being no movement of Gurkhas there. Members of the SUPP were dismayed when they tried to organise risings in the main littoral towns and found that the Sarawak Constabulary were ready for them. Some SUPP members were arrested for disturbing public order and others fled. In fact it took about a decade before the SUPP became effectively anti-government once more. However, the news of trouble spread to the Iban community with a vengeance, literally, as many of them saw the proposition of an uprising as a cover to look to their own business ...

Saturday 8 November 1952 and onwards, Sarawak: ... Ibans in the Ulu Ai area of the Second Division of Sarawak were probably more fractious than any others. Except for normal family feuds and quarrels about hunting rights, Iban had no quarrel with Iban. The larger political issues of the day were normally too remote for the longhouse dwellers to be affected. When they were, however, parochial outlooks coloured all opinion so much that most Government edicts, orders, plans and ideas were greeted with vociferous antipathy or mute disdain, more likely the former. But the news for action did not come from the Government so could not be ignored.

The Ibans were known as head hunters. The habit of lopping heads off, dying out until it was rekindled during the Japanese occupation, may have been a relic of tribal strife but was now far more likely to be the result of a hen-pecked husband driven to distraction by a nagging wife or a young blood wanting to impress some deliciously nubile lass in order to wed her – both men clocking up enough points to redress an adverse balance in the 'manhood stakes'. Head hunting was often done by waylaying a small child or an old woman washing in a stream away from the rest of the crowd, in an area probably some two or even three days' walk from the predators' own longhouse. Having lopped off the head, the great thing was to get it home before relatives bent on revenge caught up with and lopped the lopper's off in retaliation.

Each time a head was topped, a joint of the fingers on the left hand, starting with the top of the little finger and working downwards then towards the thumb, was tattooed. Only a few men's score was so many heads that the back of the left hand was also tattooed. A man's personal score could thus easily be counted.

One youth, languishing in love but not having any favours given to him, resolved to find a head to show his 'intended' how much he was worth. His longhouse, twenty doors long, was situated on the junction of the rivers Sumpa and Ai, in the area of Jambu. The youth's grandfather, Empikau, was, besides being a Pengara, chief of many longhouses, a famous head hunter with nineteen tattoos, spreading to the back of his left hand. Looking at him one saw an ugly, pockmarked face, heavily tattooed, as were his arms and thighs. He was strong and a skilled hunter, cunning and cruel. From even before the war he had practised head hunting. When, during the war, lost Japanese blundered into his area the temptation was too much. One Japanese officer, weak and hungry, particularly angered him. In his rage he had broken both wrists and ankles and thrown him under the house, which was raised about ten feet off the ground on strong stilts and entered by climbing a notched pole. The wreck of the man had to move on knees and elbows, fighting with the dogs for scraps thrown down. He died within the week. His sword was Empikau's prized possession.[14]

The youth's grandfather's actions inspired him and although he knew he could never better or even equal them, he could at least start off by getting one head. For that he had to move well outside the area, even where there were no Ibans but another of Sarawak's many ethnic groups.

He went a couple of days away to Belaga, then moved upstream along a smaller river. At dusk he reached a house where he was allowed to stay the night. The house was of a different pattern from his familiar longhouse in that it was built on the ground and was not a 'long' one. Indoors, on one side were separate rooms with, at either end, a raised portion, rather like a small stage. In the middle was a board on legs and, from time to time, plates of grisly and putrefying fish, mud and river, and meat, monkey or pig, were brought by the women of the house. When hungry, people came and sat on a bench next to the board and ate as much as they wanted.

At hand on the floor were large pottery jars, knee-high, with dragon motifs, in which was either putrefying rice or tapioca. Two bamboo tubes protruded through a wooden bung in which water was poured into the neck of the jar onto the rotting matter inside. The men folk took turn and turn about at sucking the

---

14 Some years later a spittingly angry Empikau threatened to decapitate your author to make twenty with this same sword.

water through the tube and at chewing the bits of smelly stuff that were small enough to come through it.

Large gongs were banged intermittently the whole night. Singing, riddle asking and quip making; dogs yapping and snarling when thumped because they got in the way; women talking shrilly; pigs, under the house, squealing; chickens clucking and cocks crowing at various intervals; children crying and shouting all added to bedlam that lasted till dawn. That meant no chance of a chop there or even a good night's sleep.

He was a determined lad and he helped the group he had fallen in with pole and paddle upstream some three to four hours next morning. The house they went to the next night was just as noisy as the other house had been.

The following day the group was to move back to the first house. Before dusk, the lad went outside to relieve nature in the undergrowth, just out of sight of the house. As he finished, the head man's teen-age son walked up for the same purpose. As he squatted...an ideal opportunity! *Chop now* and chop he did. Carrying the bleeding head he ran off. He washed it at another stream, tied it up in some cloth he had ready, put it in a knapsack and started on his way back.

It took him two days to reach Nanga Sumpa and what a party was held on his successful return, especially when the lad told people whose head he had chopped.

A feast was held in his honour and after the meal was over, all moved out to the veranda. Liberal supplies of rice beer flowed and the men started to dance the 'hornbill dance', using much arm movement, with wing feathers of that bird draped over their shoulders, jabbing, stabbing, lunging and jerking: it lasted all night. So much was thought of the lad's work that at midnight he had the choice of which virgin would be his bride. He chose his first heartthrob and later there was more jabbing, stabbing, lunging and jerking – but without wings this time.

Meanwhile in Singapore Ah Fat went on to explain why they were there so Reggie asked, 'And your plans are …?'

'We are going to Calcutta …' and another gem was exposed by the revelation of the secret HQ, probably there. If so it was to be found. 'That is my target. I hope to get to it through Chinatown Hakkas in Calcutta. My link to them is the purser on the *Eastern Queen*' … and so it went on till almost midnight.

Next morning after breakfast Reggie asked Ah Fat what his next step was.

'I must contact Chen Geng. I can't go straight from here as he might try and check my good faith by finding out where we spent last night. I'd be ruined if he did that. I think it is better to reach him from a cheap hotel.'

'Wise, wise indeed.'

'As you once taught me, "some are wise; some are otherwise",' and both of them giggled foolishly.

Reggie took them in his car to a central place from where they would take a taxi to a cheap hotel away from the centre of the island. Before saying farewell, Reggie said, 'Wonderful to meet up again. Pop in on your way back. I'd be most grateful for anything you can tell me.' He felt that authorities in India might well be interested in anything Ah Fat found out: it would also be far easier for him to contact people there than it would be for Ah Fat to, even if such a thing were ever to enter his mind – which it never did.

They shook hands and parted for their own destinations.

Tuesday 11 November 1952, Singapore: Captain Rance went down to Singapore to the Gurkha Transit Camp where he found out that the leave details, from all eight battalions and the three corps units, would report in good time for final documentation and transport to take them to the docks. There the Movement Warrant Officer would embark them and then give Jason the paperwork. There seemed no difficulty, all plain sailing, in both senses of the word he hoped, grinning to himself. He looked forward to enjoying himself. *A free holiday and the Queen is paying for me!*

His accommodation was in the transit camp at Nee Soon, a camp built round a hollow. There was a pathway across from one side to the other but the steps were irregular, some too long for the normal stride, others too short, some too high from the last one, some too low so could be tripped over. It was British prisoners-of-war's long-lasting practical joke that kept them amused as they saw the Japanese stumble. Jason had also been told that the Japanese used British troops to build a wooden war memorial in the centre of the dip. This they did and, unknown to the Japanese, had managed to put many termites in the base so that the memorial would crumble as the insects started eating the wood.

Ah Fat had not worried that he had not been able to contact either the turncoat Gurkha or Xi Zhan Yang a.k.a. Ah Ho as he had been briefed to contact Chen Geng, whose particulars he knew already. Next morning, leaving his Bear alone, he walked towards the city. At the first book shop he reached he bought a street map of Singapore and entered a café to study it. Over a coffee he found the road he was looking for and, instinctively remembering his tradecraft – just in case – planned a circuitous route to get to his destination.

He did not fancy going by taxi but, as it was hot, he did take a bus, three buses in fact, the first two going in the wrong way. It was one o'clock when he arrived and he did not expect Chen Geng to be in his office at lunch time but, on the off chance he might be there and have no other visitors, looked for, found Pedder Street and made his way into number 47. On the second floor there was a door marked with Chen Geng's name and Ah Fat knocked on it.

No answer. He knocked again and, from behind him, a voice said, 'stay still. Don't move' and a pistol was poked into his ribs.

Ah Fat stiffened, did not turn round but merely said, 'I am looking for Comrade Cheng Geng. I am Comrade Ah Fat and I come from the Malayan Communist Party. I have been told that Comrade Xi Zhan Yang will have contacted him, or should I say you, by this time.'

The pistol was removed and its owner told him to turn round. Ah Fat did and saw a middle-aged, rotund man with laughter lines around his eyes and a scar over his left eyebrow. Looking at him diagonally he saw, despite all the bravado, a frightened man with a weak mouth. 'Yes, I believe that. You have the name that

I had been briefed about. I had to make sure about you. These days we can't be too careful since we found out about that evil man Lai Tek who caused us so much damage. Come inside and have a seat.'

Ah Fat had met Lai Tek but only later learnt that he was a triple agent who had almost destroyed the Malayan Communist Party's higher echelon during the war. Saying 'No offence taken, Comrade. I would have done the same,' he followed Cheng Geng inside and sat down on the seat offered.

'Had anything to eat?'

'No. A bite would go down well.'

Chen Geng lifted his phone, dialled the nearest eating house and ordered two plates of rice and *char sui,* crispy roast pork belly. As they waited he extracted a bottle of brandy and two glasses from a drawer, and poured out a couple of fingers' worth for both of them. 'Water?'

'Yes. It's a bit early for me.'

Both glasses were topped up with water from a bottle that was also tucked away in the same drawer, a toast was drunk and they exchanged small talk until their meal arrived. It was only after they had finished and the plates put outside the door for collection that business began.

Out of another drawer Chen Geng pulled out an envelope and handed it to Ah Fat. 'Inside is a ticket for a first–class cabin on the *Eastern Queen,* Singapore-Calcutta and return. There are also enough American "green backs" to cover all normal expense.'

Ah Fat breathed a sigh of relief. 'Good. I was expecting enough Party funds from my journey but only one ticket, not two?' Ah Fat queried, dubiously. *Nothing for Wang Ming?*

'Yes, a single ticket. I was never asked to book two. It's too late now to book another. The boat is full up, so I have learnt.'

'So, I'm in a first-class cabin?' queried Ah Fat, in surprise.

'Yes. I know the purser, Comrade Law Chu Hoi, who, unbeknown to the captain, is one of us. The chain from Malaya to India is made up of a few trustworthy individuals. I sent him a signal, using a form of language telling him that you needed special treatment. Your name will be your passport for comradely instructions until you reach wherever the chain comes to an end – or should I say "begins"?' he added with a smile.

A first-class cabin was unexpected but most welcome. Ah Fat did not show any surprise. All he said was 'Well, that is thoughtful of you. Thank you. I have never been on a boat before and this time of year the sea might be rough so a comfortable bunk will be welcome.'

'Good. I am glad you are pleased. Now, be on jetty number 10 at nine o'clock tomorrow morning and show this ticket as and when you are asked for it. Have you been to the Indian High Commission for your visa? No? Let me know your passport number. I'll ring the man in charge and you'll get it in no time at all. Where are you spending tonight?'

Ah Fat told him. 'Go back in my car, collect your things. On the way back drop into the Indian High Commission for your visa then come and spend the night with me.'

At the hotel he had to tell the Bear to go back to KL and stay with his family. 'I'll contact you on my way back, maybe in a month's time.' This pleased Wang Ming who, at heart, was a family man and was now unexpectedly free to enjoy an unexpected spell of home leave.

Ah Fat was momentarily surprised to see lines of Gurkha soldiers standing on the quayside waiting to embark, with a British Warrant Officer holding a clipboard standing in front of them. *Surely that's unusual?* he asked himself. *It would be too much of a coincidence if Shandung P'aau were on board also.* In fact Jason was at the back of the soldiers as Ah Fat looked around and they did not see one another. Carrying his suitcase he went on board, glad not to be in the sun waiting till the last Gurkha had gone up the gangway. Once on board he looked for and found the Purser's Office. The purser was sitting at a table, covered with lists of names. He was a thin rake of a man, balding with a pock-marked face, with deep-set eyes and thick eyebrows. The face had an air of subtlety about it, making him look dangerous. A latticed iron framework prevented anyone leaning over – there was also money in his safe so it was a necessary precaution – and Ah Fat, quietly said, 'Comrade Law Chu Hoi?'

The purser almost jumped out of his skin and instinctively looked right and left, even though he knew no one could be in the office or, since the voice was so quiet, could any passer-by have heard it.

'You must be Comrade Ah Fat.'

'Yes, I am,'

The purser looked down a list. 'You are in cabin number 1 on the port side. I'll call the cabin boy' and he pressed a button on his desk.

'Port?'

'Yes, "port" means 'left".'

'Am I sharing it or have it to myself?'

The purser smiled. 'You would only share it if you had booked to share it. You are on your own.'

'May I ask who is in cabin number 2?'

The purser looked down at his list. 'Someone who will mean nothing to you, a Captain Jason Rance, the OC Troops, going both ways, like you.'

Ah Fat pretended to look blank … *Tradecraft! But what a wonderful opportunity! We won't have been together for so long since we were schoolboys.*

Thursday 13 November 1952, Singapore Docks: Jason reached Jetty number 10 and saw a Movements Warrant Officer, Class 1, with a nominal roll standing in front of the leave party and went up to him. 'I am the OC Troops, Sergeant Major. You are going to check everybody as they embark, families and single men alike?'

'Correct, sir. My name is Mr Hutchinson,' he added frostily as only Commanding Officers were deemed eligible to call such a senior person by his rank when he spoke to him. Every one lower than a lieutenant colonel was expected to address such a person as 'Mr So-and-So'. He was a bluff, burly man, obviously competent at a certain level yet Jason had the feeling he would be easily waterlogged beyond the shallows of the commonplace.

Jason made that august warrant officer look uncomfortable as he saluted him and said, 'Mr Hutchinson, I am merely Captain Rance. Please give me details of how you are managing this task.'

Mr Hutchinson had the grace to grin ruefully. "I will call them forward, first families with the name of the head, Gurkha officers to go to their 2nd Class cabins and finally single men by units, checking them as they walk up the gangway.'

Jason nodded and in a loud voice so that all waiting to embark could hear him, repeated that in Nepali. ' ... and once you're all safely on board I'll come and see you.' He knew that his own battalion's Gurkha Major was among the leave details and called out so all could hear, 'GM Saheb, when I am ready I'll call you over the Tannoy system to come to the Purser's Office and we'll go round together.'

'Hunchha Hajur.'

'Before you go, sir, do you know that I have two members of the Corps of Military Police, Red Caps, escorting a prisoner among the men you are responsible for?' Mr Hutchinson asked.

'No, that I don't. Where and who is he?'

'Mr Hutchinson looked at his list. 'He is a rifleman, demoted from acting sergeant, from 1/12 GR and his name is Padamsing Rai.' *The man I spoke to on the phone before going to Kelantan!* He is in the detention cell in one of the buildings on this jetty. He will be in the brig on board. The two Red Caps will be responsible for exercising him each day and escorting him to and from his meals. They are also responsible for taking him the whole way to Calcutta and once there will sign him over to the civil police who will, so I've heard, escort him as far as the Gurkha Recruiting Depot in Darjeeling, I think it is. Once there he will be paid what he is due, given his release documents which won't make 'ealthy reading, I can assure you, sir, and officially dismissed,'

'I suppose I ought to go and see him and warn him to behave himself once he's on board.'

'I'll take you along once all your troops are inside.'

It took a long time to get everyone embarked, what with frightened and fractious children having to be carried on board when they could have walked. There was one little girl who was so ill she had to be taken to the sick bay rather than to her parents' cabin. Jason was assured that there was a competent ship's doctor on board.

'Captain Rance, sir. I'll take you along and show you the prisoner.' He glanced at Jason's shoulder titles. 'From your lot, sir. Bad news.'

Jason agreed that it was and most unusual in a Gurkha battalion. They went over to the cell, a pokey little room which was almost unbearably hot. The door was opened and the prisoner was ordered to stand to attention by one of the Red Caps who had been standing outside.

'Rifleman Padamsing Rai. I am Captain Rance, the OC Troops. I am responsible for you till you get to Calcutta. I don't know why you are here or what has happened to make you no longer a soldier but, until you are discharged, you are still under military discipline.'

'Rance saheb. You and I spoke on the phone some time back when you told me you were to be OC Troops and were on your way to Kelantan.'

'Yes, you must be the one. I can now remember seeing you in the battalion.'

A tear came into the Gurkha's eyes. 'Sir, there has been

a dreadful mistake. I am not guilty of any misconduct. I can't understand why I am being dismissed.' He had been surprised, shamed and shocked when he was found in the same bed as the British sergeant by two members of the Special Investigation Branch, as had the British Sergeant also been. Such behaviour was anathema to the British Army and there were government laws strictly forbidding it. To say it never occurred between consenting hill men could be wrong but it was so rare as to be taken as never happening. Rance guessed that the man's removal from the army was the result of his report and was secretly relieved to see him on his way out but surprised at the speed of such happening. As for the Gurkha himself, he had not put his untoward behaviour down to his discharge and had thought that his communist activities must have been found out and were responsible for it. *Just in case something serious happens to me I will never let on what I joined up for* he vowed to himself. *If Ah Ho finds out he could reach me back at home.*

He heard Captain Rance say 'I don't know either. Sorry, nothing about changing the decision in your being dismissed is in my hands' before he moved away.

The Movements Warrant Office said to the Military Police Corporals, 'Take him aboard and put him in the lock-up. I believe the purser knows about this. In any case, check before and, don't forget, get a signature for him when you hand him over to the Calcutta Police. The prisoner was led away and at long last Jason saw it was his turn to walk up the gangway with his suitcase.

His first impression on boarding the Chinese vessel was the strong small of cooking, something he had not noticed on other ships he had sailed in. He went to the Purser's Office and reported in. 'I am Captain Rance, OC Troops for the voyage, both ways,' he said in English.

The purser looked at him, trying to hide his dislike of all Europeans who, to him, smelt of bad meat. 'You are in cabin 2. I'll ring for the cabin boy who will take you up.'

'Thank you but I'd prefer it if he merely took my case. I must go and see if my men have settled in properly and have anything to report. If you need to talk about the prisoner you can contact me at any time.'

'I understand.' Law Chu Hoi, not used to thinking that red-haired devils had any interest in anyone but themselves, hid his surprise. 'If that is what you wish. If you need help in finding your way around the boat I'll give you someone to help you.' *It's my job to be civil …* He also gave the OC Troops details of meal timings, reporting sick and made mention of boat drill.

Jason asked the purser if he could use the Tannoy loud speaker and, reluctantly and somewhat rudely, pushed the microphone through the bars at him. He asked the Gurkha Major to come to the Purser's Office and told the deck passengers that the two of them would visit them shortly. Cabin passengers were not included but he would visit them with any ship's inspection on the morrow.

Up in cabin 1, Ah Fat, who was lying on his bunk, drowsing, not having had such an idle time for as long as he could remember, shot up, smiling, when he heard that oh so familiar voice. *I thought he'd never come!* Ah Fat understood quite a lot of Nepali, having worked with Gurkhas, so knew it would be a while before Jason reached his cabin. *I'll surprise him* he chuckled softly, *but how?*

Meanwhile someone had taken Jason's luggage to his cabin and Ah Fat heard the door open. He slipped his door open quietly but no Jason, only his baggage. *He'll be along later.*

After the GM saheb had come to the Purser's Office the two of them, along with a ship's guide, took them to the mess decks. Everyone seemed as content as they could be when herded together in a hot, sweaty and cloistered atmosphere. On each mess deck Jason told them details of meal timings and what to do if a man became ill. At the end the GM invited Jason into his cabin where his wife and three children were, all still a bit afraid of their new surroundings. In his wonderful way Jason used his ventriloquist skills to get the children shouting with laughter and their mother smiling broadly so they forget their fears. 'I'll be on my way now, GM saheb' said the OC Troops, making namasté to the mother and waving to the children, went up a deck from the 2nd Class cabins to the 1st.

As he was opening the door a pair of hands covered his eyes from behind and 'Guess who?' was whispered in his ear.

He spun round. '*P'ing Yee*. It can't be true,' but of course it was. 'What a wonderful and unexpected surprise' and they embraced warmly. Separated they looked at each other and both started talking at once. That made them made them laugh out loud. 'Flat Ears, let me have a shower and a change as I need both and then we'll have a great chat. It must be extra special for you to be on board here. I'm dying to hear all about it.'

Ah Fat said, 'I hope you don't mean that literally' but as he only said it to himself Jason was left without the implied message.

4

Thursday 13 November 1952, Nepalese Consulate, Rangoon:
The Royal Nepal Airlines Corporation's original six aircraft had
all crashed within six months of the corporation being formed.
While a new fleet with better trained pilots was being assembled,
it charted planes from the Darbanga Airways, whose pilots,
therefore, were Indians.

The pilot on today's flight from Calcutta had been told not
to engage in any conversations with his Nepali passenger who,
he saw, was 'booted and suited', with a handkerchief in his coat's
top pocket. The King of Nepal had been so worried about the
battalion of returning mutinying troops that he had written a royal
decree and sent it hot-foot by air to his consulate in Rangoon by
hand of a senior member of the royal family, a Prince. The Nepali
Consul in Calcutta was bidden to help arrange for the Cessna to
fly out of India and back again. The Prince was on no account to
give the King's message to anyone else but to the Consul himself.

With minimum fuss the pilot helped him into his seat next
to his own, fixed his seatbelt, smiled but got no reaction. He
shut the door before walking round the plane doing the required
checks before getting into his own seat. As he started the engine
he wondered if his passenger was afraid of flying as was the pilot's

father – 'Father, why don't you fly with me?' 'Because in the air where you are but on the ground here you are' – contacted the tower and was told which runway to use. After his final engine check he got permission for take-off and away they flew. The weather was fine and the flight smooth, the Cessna 170 being a 'placid' machine.

The pilot told his passenger when there was only half an hour's flying time from Rangoon. 'Contact the controller in the tower, tell him to ring the Nepalese consulate and tell the Consul personally to come and collect an important document' was the response. This the pilot duly did.

Twenty minutes later the pilot and his passenger saw the shining top of the Shwedagon Pagoda, a golden dot in the distance. Shortly before reaching it they flew over some flat ground to the west of the Irrawaddy, not for one moment knowing that on 1 May 1945 153 Gurkha Parachute Battalion had been dropped there to capture the city from the Japanese but before they could advance they were bombed by some American 'Flying Fortress' bombers and suffered some nasty casualties. By the time the Gurkhas managed to get into the city the Japanese had left without causing any damage. At the same time a rescue party had liberated British prisoners-of-war from Insein jail. Happily ignorant, the pilot called the tower, giving his call sign and asked for instructions for landing.

The Consul, Dhruba Kumar Oli, was a tall man, once handsome but now run to seed, looking older than he was, paunchy and out of sorts so apt to wheeze. When the controller had rung the consulate a clerk answered the phone and took the message. Dhruba was stunned when told about it. 'Hajur, the message stressed that you personally had to go and collect it, at once,' his clerk quickly added as he saw his master was unwilling to do as requested.

'Such a peremptory summons has never happened to me before.' It was below his dignity to act as an office runner. 'Who sent the message?'

'I didn't ask,' the clerk mumbled, 'the phone was put down the other end too quickly.' Not quite true but good enough! His personal motto was 'anything for a quiet life and my monthly pay'.

The Consul wavered. *Obey or send someone else?* On balance he decided, just this once, to swallow his pride and go himself.

'Tell my driver to get my car ready now, at once!' he called out, trying not to sound as though he was being taken advantage of and that he was still his own man. At least he had a clear conscience so there was really nothing to worry about, was there?

The Consul went to the Enquiries Desk and was shown into the private room of the airport manager. He did not recognise the Nepali already there nor knew that the handkerchief in the top pocket – he himself was 'open neck' – was one warning sign of an important man. Unfortunately he said, sharply without any of the usual courtesies, 'Well, here I am. What's all this all about? Why the hurry? Why me?' He therefore, hapless man, did not greet royalty as royalty expected to be greeted, neither using the special vocabulary that talking to royalty required nor showing due deference.

The Prince, not known for his tact and feeling that it was below his dignity to talk to a mere Consul, for once bit his tongue – *why waste words with riff-raff?* – merely frowned disdainfully and took the letter out of a bag he had round his neck. 'I am His Majesty's nephew. His Majesty has ordered you to obey this implicitly. Take it,' he said, scowling, as he handed it over at arm's length, with his left hand, showing his disdain at not being spoken to properly.

Embarrassment flooded through the Consul who now realised that the giver of the letter was a Prince of the Realm, of royal blood, who had been demeaned by a complete lack of required protocol. *Disaster!* He bowed low, making namaste, wheezing in his nervousness as he said, 'Sarkar. Jo Hukum.' This was the phrase, translated as 'whatever personal order' that was always used to royalty on being told to do anything. The Prince threw a piece of paper on the floor. 'Pick it up and sign it. It is a receipt for the letter.' *Degradation is a good punishment for such a proud nonentity!*

Quaking at this once-in-a-lifetime encounter with the royal family, the Consul bent, picked it up, signed it and tried to hand it back.

'Put it on that table,' the Prince said, indicating that taking anything from the hand of non-royalty was degrading. 'And as His Majesty's Consul – for how much longer, I wonder? – in future wear national dress.'

As the Prince turned to go he said, 'His Majesty's order is that only you and your Vice Consul will know about the contents of this letter. Only open it after you have returned. Once you have read it destroy it.'

An airport official came into the office. 'Sir, your pilot is ready for the return flight. The sky is getting heavy with cumulus cloud.'

With no more ado the Prince strode out behind the official. The Consul gulped, stared after him, misery and embarrassment engulfing him. In his car returning to the consulate, fearful that this morning's encounter would irrevocably and fatally militate against him, he tried to compose his features back to normalcy. It would never do to lose face 'downwards' as well as 'upwards' in the same day. *Who was it* he asked himself *who had said 'don't worry about the bang, fear the whimper? Yes, that has yet to come.*

In his office, with the door closed, he opened the letter. The note paper had the royal crest on it and was written in court Nepali, mostly not understandable to lesser mortals. He read that 'you are forbidden to visit the boatload of British Army Gurkhas, under any pretext whatsoever, due in on the next troop ship because they are a battalion which has, most recently in the northeast of Malaya, mutinied and demanded to be regarded as Communists. The British government has therefore disbanded it.' He was further enjoined to discover the background to 'such an unexpected conversion and to warn the Nepalese consulate in Calcutta what action was recommended to counter any agitation on the way through the town up to being finally paid off. The Throne would be informed what had been said.' Although the King had orally included the Vice Consul not to visit the troops, he had not included him in his letter.

The Consul shook his head in utter bewilderment. *How could this have happened?* he asked himself, almost tearfully.

It was ironic that neither the OC Troops nor his Chinese friend had the least inkling of any of this nor that the author of the rumour was under close arrest in the ship's brig!

Thursday 13 – Tuesday 25 November 1952, on board SS *Eastern Queen*: Apart from 'boat drill' with life jackets in case of an emergency and the daily cleaning and inspection of mess decks and cabins, routine life on board ship was simple, get up, lounge around, eat, go to bed. Jason went with the ship's inspecting officer to mess decks and cabins so was known to the wives and children, always with a kind word and a facial gimmick for the kids. There was only the worry of the sick child whose condition steadily deteriorated.

As soon as Law Chu Hoi, the purser, had completed his initial duties he called Ah Fat to his private cabin for a briefing. A Chinese going to the cabin of a Chinese in a Chinese boat caused less than any interest and no suspicion whatsoever. 'I won't ask you who your friends are as you won't ask me who are mine but there are some who know us both and know our orders. We need acknowledge nothing else' was his cryptic opening remark.

He looked at Ah Fat who nodded knowingly but said nothing.

'These are our orders. We plan to be in Calcutta for six days. During that time I will have much to do but after my work has slackened, possibly on our second day in port, you and I will go to a place called South Tangra. This is one of the two Chinatowns in Calcutta where the Hakka community work in leather tanneries.

There we will meet either Wong Kek Fui or Cheng Fan Tek, who will be your link for further contacts. Whichever is available will take you to a certain place and introduce you to a certain important person and leave you to carry out whatever orders you have already been given. I do not want to know about them as I have no need to.' He let that sink in. 'Whatever you have to do must be done before we sail if you want to travel back to Singapore with us. We simply cannot wait for you if you haven't finished by then.'

'Thank you for explaining all so clearly to me. It is heartening to have someone as efficient and calm to deal with and through' – *and I'm as good a toad-eater as the next man* Ah Fat thought to himself – 'and of course such information is my secret weapon for Party use only.'

'In that case a drop of brandy will go down well' and, going to a locker, he took out a bottle and two glasses. It was a long session, almost too long for Ah Fat who did not have a good head for liquor.

Initially, also, Jason had been busy checking the paperwork, nominal rolls by units, of the leave party and ensuring all was well with the troops and families, especially the sick girl. He also visited the prisoner, who had his own two CMP minders who felt their sea journey was really a holiday with no officious sergeants or officers to worry them. So it was only on their fourth day at sea, after leaving Penang, that Jason had enough time for a long, long session with his childhood friend, with whom till then he had had only passing pleasantries. '*P'ing Yee*, never have I been more surprised than when I found you were on the boat. There must be a most important reason for your being allowed to be away from "them" for so long.'

'Yes, *Shandung P'aau*, there is and of course I'll let you into the secret …' and out it all came, the disillusion of a quick victory so to get Gurkhas away from Malaya, to India or Sarawak but preferably the former. To this end and hearing that there was a mysterious centre that was so cleverly controlling all communist activities throughout southeast Asia and in India, at least on the eastern seaboard, probably in Calcutta, Ah Fat's task was to go there and try and find it and its operator to aid the MCP in its task. 'That shows you, Jason, just how desperately serious they are about the current situation: my journey is seen as their only hope, their "tipping point" for victory, even though my being sent is really nothing but inspired and unproven speculation.'

Jason, for once temporarily speechless with astonishment, shook his head in wonder at such a course of action both being possible and considered necessary. 'But, surely, there must be more to it than that. You can't just go to Calcutta blind.'

'You're right there. I can't and I'm not. This is where this Chinese boat comes into it. The purser is …' and the rest of the story followed. 'So you see I have guides all the way to the centre of the presumed and hoped-for spider's web, or at least that is the plan.'

Jason, wondering, on the off chance, if any of this concerned him, asked 'do you see me being involved in this in any way? I know that Dame Fortune, that most fickle lady, plans matters without consulting us but one of my mottos is "react to the unexpected" and if anything ever was unexpected, this is.'

Ah Fat looked at him, thoughtfully. 'A tall, fair-haired, blue-eyed Caucasian loitering in an Indian Chinatown? I suppose tourists or, even, European businessmen in the leather trade could visit the place, Jason. The purser and I will go there on Day 2 or 3. Yes, it would be fun for us to go together but not before I go with him. You don't speak Hak Wa but you can get by with your Cantonese. You might learn something by not speaking it! Were you to come trailing along with me and the purser you'll be so incongruous and of such suspicion that I myself will be in danger of being thought of colluding with imperialists, fascists, colonials and I don't know who else,' and he smiled ruefully.

'Yes, I think a threesome is quite out the question.' said Jason disarmingly. 'Let's "play it by ear" and see what turns up when we get there, shall we? Could be that nothing will.'

Two days out from Rangoon the sick child died. Both parents were distraught and wondered how they could take their daughter's body back to Nepal for correct obsequies to be carried out. The father, a corporal from 1/10 GR, came to see Jason with the senior Gurkha officer of his own battalion for advice.

'Taking your daughter's body all the way to Nepal may not be possible or advisable,' Jason said, 'nor do I know how the authorities in Rangoon and later on in Calcutta will accept a dead body. I have no experience of deaths at sea. Let me go and see the Captain for advice.' Yes, that was sensible. 'I'll come back with what he says and let you know.'

Jason went to see Captain Lam Wai Lim who had already been

told of the death. Unthinkingly Jason broached him in Chinese which made the elderly man flex his back muscles in surprise but, with the inherent good manners of all Chinese, reacted as though being spoken to in fluent Chinese by a *gwai lo* was something normal. Jason mentioned the need for correct obsequies and the desire of the parents not to forgo such.

'Captain Rance, my firm advice is a burial at sea. My carpenters can make a coffin which we will drape, sadly not with a Union Jack or a Nepalese flag as we hold neither, but the flag of the Steam Navigation Company. To take a dead body onto Burmese soil will result in repercussions that will be so protracted that we will have to leave you and the father of the baby behind in Rangoon. They will suspect foul play. It could take weeks. No, please try and convince the parents and their friends that my advice is almost mandatory.'

'Won't the Burmese authorities take the signature of the ship's doctor as certifying the reason for the death? They must, surely,' Jason expostulated.

'Even if they do believe it they will behave as if they don't. Anything quicker than, say, six weeks, will cost you more money than even a British captain can afford.'

Jason shook his head in weary disgust, thanked the Captain and said he would only give him a direct answer for the burial once he had spoken to the family.

He called for the parents and the senior Gurkha officer to let them know what the Captain had advised and why. It took some time to convince the mother although the father agreed once the Gurkha officer had reminded them that the battalion pundit was also on board and that he could give the correct blessings as the body was tipped overboard. The mother eventually, through tears, acquiesced and Jason told the Captain, whose only stipulation was that the burial had to be done outside Burmese territorial waters. On the following morning, a small coffin, draped with the company flag, diagonal white stripes on a blue background, was blessed by the pundit before being tipped overboard, with all 10 GR leave men parading in sympathy.

Jason, feeling a weight off his shoulders, went to amend the nominal roll of families of 10 GR. He hoped that the Port Authorities would not query the amendment. Burmese was not one of his languages so he could not be as convincing as he otherwise might have been. *Leave it to chance!*

Tuesday 18 November1952, Rangoon: Being tied up alongside the quay was unpleasantly hot, even as late as mid-November, and boring once the novelty of seeing stores loaded and unloaded had worn off. The Gurkha officers asked their OC Troops if the men and families could stretch their legs on the quayside. 'I'll find out,' Jason had said and was told, several hours later, that, yes, they could exercise themselves – between two and four o'clock in the morning. The offer was politely declined.

Mr Dhruba Kumar Oli called his assistant, the Vice Consul, to his office. He was Mansing Basnet, whose round, honest face had an expression of permanent surprise as though he could not quite believe where he had found himself. But, in fact, he was a shrewd operator. The Consul had given him the letter to read and now he needed to discuss the most sensible course of action. Two heads were better than one for occasions such as this. 'Mansing-ji, the boat with the mutinying soldiers should be safely tied up by now.'

'Hajur, I have checked and yes it is.'

The two men looked at each other, both knowing what was in the other's mind. 'You have read the King's letter, haven't you?' the Consul asked, knowing the answer but wanting to lead in gradually to what was in his mind and, also, on his conscience.

The Vice Consul nodded as the Consul knew he would. Words were unnecessary.

'You know I cannot go myself but there was nothing in the letter that forbade you to go, was there?' Past tense, with the letter burnt and its ashes blown away. 'His Majesty wants himself and our Calcutta Consul briefed, doesn't he?' A nod. 'It would be, what, provident to find out from any British officer in charge, there must surely be one, who even maybe in danger of his life.'

Yes, that made sense and, in fact, both men were bursting to find out everything about this whole unprecedented and amazing matter.

'Hajur, that is certainly so.' Now they were both implicated the Consul felt happier. 'Suppose you asked me if you could go and see for yourself. That way I wouldn't have tried to make you go, would I?' Oli wheezed in his cunning and excitement.

The Vice Consul shook his head. 'No, Hajur, that is true. There will be families on board and if your wife and mine went with me in the car it would let the mutinous soldiers see we had just' – he emphasised that word – 'come on a courtesy visit.'

The Consul smiled. 'Yes. I like that. See to it.'

The consulate car was a recently bought Ambassador, a clunky, steady machine. 'I'll drive. Those Port Authorities can be difficult people but there should be no trouble in our getting into the dock area with our diplomatic ID cards and the car's diplomatic plates and if you, Consul-ji, ring them up before I leave, it will make that doubly sure.'

The Vice Consul drove to the main gate of the docks where he was unexpectedly given a cheery wave through into the dock area when his diplomatic and the two ladies' ID cards were shown. He knew the name of the boat so was given an entry pass and told what quay to drive up to. Eventually, with car parked and locked, the three Nepalis came to the gangway and, showing diplomatic cards once more and the one signed by the dock authorities, were taken to the Purser's Office.

'I am the Nepalese Vice Consul and these two ladies are the consul's wife as well as my own. I wish to see the British officer in charge of the Gurkhas on board, if there is one.'

'Yes there is a British captain. I will call him.' The purser pulled the Tannoy microphone over and, in English, twice called out, 'Attention please, attention please. Will the OC Troops please report to the Purser's Office now.' He put the machine back and asked the trio to wait.

Jason, wearing plain clothes, came down the stairs opposite the office, smiled at the three waiting people and asked the purser what was wanted. On being told he turned towards the three visitors but before he could introduce himself the man said in English 'I am Mansing Basnet, Vice Consul of the Nepalese consulate, here in Rangoon. These ladies are the Consul's wife and my wife.'

Jason made namasté in return and automatically replied in Nepali, 'I am Captain Rance, the OC Troops. I'd have put on uniform to welcome you if I'd have known you were coming so please excuse my casual dress.' He surprised and delighted all three Nepalis by his charming smile and linguistic fluency. 'So you want to visit the leave party …'

He was interrupted. 'Leave party, did you say?'

'Yes, that's right. That what we call them and I am in charge of them. Before we start off I must warn them. Please wait a moment.'

On the Tannoy he announced 'Troops to go to their boat stations and families go to their cabins, please. We have official Nepali visitors who have come to meet you and this will it make it easy for them to see everyone.' He repeated the message, finishing off 'Thank you.'

They made their way slowly around the boat stations, Jason leading but not saying much and letting the Vice Consul do the talking. Surprisingly there was not nearly as much talk as the OC Troops had expected – *snooty?* –with, Jason noticed, the Vice Consul looking at the men rather more than speaking to them. The women with him said nothing. Not having experienced anything in Kathmandu or of Nepalese functionaries Jason merely thought how different it was, far from the way British officers behaved in Gurkha battalions.

After each group was looked at Jason told the men to stand down and carry on with whatever they were doing. 'Now to the cabins, Hajur,' he told his three visitors.

It was the women's turn to talk but, again not much was said. They called the children over to them, surprised and a little nonplussed when some of them ran to Jason and grabbed him around his, not their, knees. Nothing was said about the sea burial in the dead girl's cabin: it would have been an intolerable intrusion into the parents' privacy to have had the matter referred to.

At the end Jason asked them if they would like to accompany him to the lounge and have either some tea or coffee. 'No, we must go back. I want you to come with me.'

'No, sorry Vice Consul saheb. I can't because we are only allowed off the boat between 2 and 4 in the small hours and that only on the quay beside the boat. Otherwise of course I'd accept your invitation.'

'I can get you through all formalities,' answered the Vice Consul, authority in his voice.

'Then I can't get back,' Jason remonstrated.

'I'll bring you back. They'll let you in all right.'

'If that is really so I'll have to tell my senior Gurkha officer where I'm going to and that I'll be away for an hour or so and then I'll be ready to go with you.'

That done the four of them went down the gangway and walked to where the car was. They got in, both women sitting in the back. They drove along the main roads through the town, Jason seeing how much dirtier and poorer Rangoon was than towns in both India and Malaya were and no different from when he had seen it at the end of the war. They reached an enclosed area dotted with wooden huts surrounded by a wire fence which he recognised from when he had been there after the Japanese had surrendered. There was a sign hanging from a metal archway, '66 Transit Camp' and underneath that sign another, smaller one, with 'Nepalese Consulate' written on it,

They drove on in, came to and stopped at one of the huts. The ladies got out and disappeared. The Vice Consul took Jason inside and told him to sit down and wait.

The furniture was simple, a few chairs. small tables and a cupboard. Before much longer two men entered and the Vice Consul said, 'Captain, this is the Consul, Mr Dhruba Kumar Oli.'

Jason stood up and said, 'Consul saheb, I am Captain Rance, OC Troops on the *Eastern Queen*.'

Namastés were exchanged as were introductory remarks also. Then, unexpectedly harshly, the Consul said, 'Captain saheb, why have you spoken incorrectly?'

Jason took a step back. 'Incorrectly? I am so sorry. I have never spoken to a Consul before. If I have used a wrong word, please forgive me.'

The two Nepalis looked at each other, almost in dismay. 'Sit down,' Jason was told. The Vice Consul went to the cupboard and pulled out a bottle of whisky. He called a servant to bring three glasses and a jug of water. He poured one to the brim, put it on a table by their guest's chair. Jason looked at it in dismay and left it untouched. The other two, with glasses more normally filled and watered, sat down. 'Cheers!' said the Consul.

Jason lifted his glass, raised it to his lips to satisfy hospitality protocol then put it on the table, where it remained, untouched. The two Nepalis glanced at it but said nothing inappropriate.

That was not their way, but they spoke with each other quietly, taking no notice of their guest. 'You say none of the soldiers looked unhappy or threatening,' Oli said to Basnet, loud enough for Jason to hear.

'Not one of them did' Basnet replied. 'They behaved normally. Polite and respectful. Nobody could take them for anything but typical passengers.'

'And the families, the womenfolk? None offensive?'

'No, none. The little ones went for the Captain saheb and clutched his knees, not our women's.'

'Could the message have been wrong?' *A terrible thought: challenging the King!*

'Oli-ji. Ask our guest, listen to his answer and make your own mind up.'

The Consul turned his gaze on Jason and said, 'I asked you why you had spoken incorrectly, not because you addressed me incorrectly, which you didn't, but because you had told my Vice Consul, Basnet-jyu, that you were in charge of a leave party.'

Jason stared, almost rudely, at the Consul. 'But what else should I have called them when that is what they are? We no longer use the word "furlough" as in British Indian days. Sorry, I don't understand you, Hajur. Where am I wrong? Using the English name, not the Nepali one, for them?' His dismay was palpable.

The two Nepalis looked at each other again, baffled it seemed, and the senior openly asked his junior, 'Shall we tell him?'

'Yes, on balance, I think we should.'

The Consul faced Jason. 'Why I queried you was because we

are under the firm impression that the Gurkha soldiers on board are not leave men but a whole battalion that has mutinied so have been dismissed by the British government as unsuitable for any further service and therefore are being returned to Nepal in disgrace for discharge. Are you saying that is incorrect?'

Jason laughed as politely as derision permitted. 'Oli saheb, that is outrageous nonsense. How and where did that come from? Please tell me.'

The Consul gritted his teeth, wheezed rather than sighed and said, 'The battalion was recently in northeast Malaya. The information we had said some place called Kelantan.'

That was too much for Captain Rance. He put his head back and, to the astonishment of both the others, laughed out loud. 'No, no, no, Hajur Consul saheb. There's been a dreadful mistake, a misunderstanding quite how or why I have no idea. Let me explain: until this very last month, there had been no Gurkha troops serving in that part of Malaya. During that time, I, with my A Company, 1/12 Gurkha Rifles, were sent there in place of a Malay Regiment unit, from the 7th to the 23rd of October. In fact it was all rather a rush to get to Singapore docks on time to be OC Troops. So with that you can make up your own minds about that report being genuine or not.'

At such an obviously truthful answer there was no reply. Blank looks were on each face as they shook their heads in bewilderment. Never had either of them been in such a mental whirl.

'Can you tell me from where this nonsense came from, please?' Jason asked. 'See if you can track it down. Deliberate or accidental?'

'It was a personal message from the King of Nepal,' said the Consul, wheezing heavily. 'I can only presume, a guess mind you, he had to take it at face value and, being afraid of having so many Communists in Nepal and wanting to find out, warned us about it because, by then, the boat would have left Singapore.' He looked at his Vice Consul, with a lift of his eyebrows. A nod. 'I was told not to visit the soldiers on the boat but we were so appalled by something like this happening I felt we had to find out. That is why we've invited you here. I took a risk in sending Basnet saheb …' He broke off and wiped his forehead with a handkerchief.

Jason saw he was worried. 'When I get back to Malaya I'll try and arrange for a copy of our monthly newspaper for the soldiers, *Parbate*, to be sent to you. That way you will be able to keep track of events.' He had a disturbing thought. 'How many other people do you think have had similar wrong reports? There was no suspicion of anything like this when we were in Singapore.'

'I can't tell you. I have no idea at all.'

'What would be your reaction if I asked you for permission to tell the British embassy here in Rangoon about it?'

The Consul looked uneasy, pondered, then said, 'Only if you say you have heard it as a rumour from the Burmese and do not, I say again, not mention us or the King.'

'Hajur, you can trust me, one hundred per cent. Please may I use your phone once you have given me the embassy number?'

It was given, grudgingly. After a delay in getting through, Jason asked to speak to the Defence Attaché.

'Lieutenant Colonel James Heron speaking,' came the crisp

answer.

Jason recognised the voice of his first CO in 1/12 GR when they were made into a Gunner Regiment. 'Colonel, you'll never believe it. It is Captain Rance this end.' He tilted the phone so that the two Nepalis could hear what was being said.

'Where are you calling from?'

'From a phone outside the dock area.' On hearing that the Consul looked at Jason with renewed respect.

'And what might you be doing in Rangoon, may I ask?' The question was asked almost in fun.

'I am OC Troops of a Gurkha leave party, sir. There will be some men who'll know you. Could you come to SS *Eastern Queen* for a chat later on today or maybe tomorrow? We sail early morning on Friday.'

'Yes, I'll do that. It's slack now and I'll enjoy meeting up with you and hearing all your news.'

After that there was nothing left except for Jason to be driven back to the boat, leaving his full glass of whisky still untouched, hardly saying a word as they went. Their parting was not unfriendly but a touch frosty: no one likes losing face to a stranger, especially a Nepali in authority.

The Consul was in a quandary; how to let His Majesty know that there had been a mistake without letting on that the troops had been visited. A diplomatic 'white lie' was the solution. As ordered, he would write a strictly secret personal letter to the Consul in Calcutta giving all the details of what Captain Rance had told them after he had been invited to the consulate on what was seen as a friendly visit. They had come to the conclusion that it was most likely that such a monstrous untruth was not just a mistake in correspondence but more likely to be a plot to embarrass His Majesty. 'I therefore suggest,' he wrote to his opposite number, 'that before you write your report to His Majesty, which you are duty bound to do, you make a thorough search among your staff to see if there is anyone likely to have been responsible. If that turns out negative, put your "eyes and ears" to work to find out who could be responsible for such disinformation.' Between them they felt it better not to give the letter to Captain Rance to deliver but to put it in the next diplomatic bag bound for Calcutta, even though it would be much slower to get there. Even though no perpetrator was found in the Calcutta consulate, the King was greatly relieved at the news.

Thinking about all that he had experienced earlier on while trying to get to sleep, Jason's mind turned to his phone call with his one-time CO ... then it scratched at something slightly unusual said to him on another telephone, years, was it, or months, or even weeks ago? ... then it came as he suddenly remembered a curiously ungrammatical remark made by Sergeant Padamsing Rai when he was talking to him the morning A Company left for Gemas. He had mentioned about going to Kelantan and following that referring to the leave party. It was then his answer that came back to him, 'No sir, that is more than all' and the tone of voice it was said in. He turned it over and over in his mind and decided to tell Ah Fat everything that had happened during the day, as well as mentioning that strange remark before, finally, dropping off to sleep.

After his routine duties Next morning Jason took Ah Fat to his cabin and told him what had passed in the consulate. 'I can't understand it. It came "out of the blue" and really shook me as it was me with my A Company that had been up in Kelantan earlier this month. How *could* anything like this have happened so quickly and yet so far away?'

Ah Fat looked at his friend. *Yes, he really is worried!* 'Jason, let me remind you about Operation Tipping Point ...'

Jason, taken by surprise, interrupted with a squawk, 'What's that? Say that again. Operation what was it? You never mentioned anything like that when you gave me your background reasons for going to Calcutta,' he remonstrated.

Ah Fat had the grace to look abashed. 'No, nor I did,' he confessed. 'My going to the very centre of a big Communist spider's web *and* meeting the spider himself will be the "tipping point" in their struggle, hence the operational name?'

'Got it. Carry on please. I'm sorry to have interrupted your flow and glad I did.'

Ah Fat resumed his briefing. Face screwed up in concentration he continued with 'there is a Gurkha at the back of the "from inside" part of the scheme, a Padamsing Rai I think was the name mentioned at the Politburo meeting ...'

At that name Jason shot up from his reclining position. '*P'ing Yee* I interrupt once more. I too am guilty of omitting something that could prove vital in our understanding of this.'

It was Ah Fat's turn to look surprised. 'How come?'

'There is a Padamsing Rai, a prisoner on board this ship of

ours, being repatriated under arrest on another charge. I had to ring the OC of the Gurkha education school in Singapore with a message from my CO. He was out and Padamsing Rai answered. It was to him that I said I was going to Kota Bharu and after that about the leave party. It was only last night that I remembered how his answer struck me as being so unlike his normal correct English grammar.'

'And what was it?' Ah Fat prompted.

'I finished off by saying "That is all I have for you. Have you anything for me?" and his answer, in a suggestive tone of voice, was "No sir, that is more than all." It was so unlike his normal correct English, he is a Darjeeling scholar, that it could have a second, inner, meaning to him but not to others like us.'

'Yes, it is certainly a coincidence, his name being the same and the slip of the tongue. Not to follow it up would be crass. How shall be go about it? Ideas, please.'

Jason bit his lower lip as he thought. 'Can you remember if there was anyone special at that Politburo meeting who was told to make contact with a certain Padamsing Rai?'

'Yes, there was. Now let me see…who was it?' With puckered brow he searched back. 'Ummm. Yes, it was the courier from Kuala Lumpur, who said he would go to Singapore; Xi Zhan Yang whose alias is Ah Ho.,'

'Got it,' said Jason excitedly. 'I'll take you down to the cell and you will talk to Padamsing, saying you are Xi Zhan Yang's brother,'

'I'll say Ah Ho which is the name he uses when talking to outsiders.'

'Better still. I'll tell the duty Corporal Red Cap' – he had to explain what he meant as Ah Fat did not know what 'Red Cap' referred to – 'that you need to speak to him. Only mention his present condition if he brings it up.'

'And have you any particular questions you'd like me to ask?'

'Well, what do you suggest? You have more background than I have.'

Ah Fat's smile was triumphant. '*Shandung P'aau*, yes. I'll give you data for your own Operation Tipping Point. At the Politburo meeting we were told that there were some other Nepalis, now Gurkha soldiers, behaving similarly but no details about them were known. I'll find out from this Gurkha who those other renegades are. He's bound to know them. I'll tell him that as he himself will no longer be in Malaya I'll have to contact the others to help them in their good work, so to give me their names and units. How about that?'

Jason leant forward and shook his friend's hand. 'Spot on. Couldn't be better. And as for the idea of my own Operation Tipping Point, that's a real brainwave,' and he laughed delightedly. 'Let's do it right away. Also try and find out where he got the idea of the discharged battalion from. If we could find that out it would help enormously, solving the problem at its origin. No need to look anywhere else. I'd like to have something definite to tell the DA who's coming round later on today' and Jason told Ah Fat how he had asked for him so he could let Calcutta, Singapore and the War Office know about his meeting in the Nepalese consulate.

'Righty ho! On our way then. Give me a pencil and a piece of paper and off we go,' said Ah Fat and the two of them went down to the brig. Jason beckoned to the CMP Corporal on duty, sitting smoking and looking at an old newspaper, and very quietly said, 'Corporal, as OC Troops I have brought someone who happens to have been affected by the prisoner's approaches, shall I call them, and wants to come to some settlement before we reach India otherwise he will start civil proceedings. I have brought him down to talk to Padamsing. Please let him in, on my authority as OC Troops.'

'No sweat, sir,' and beckoning to Ah Fat, took him to the door of the brig, unlocked it, looked inside and said, 'A somebody come to see yer.'

The renegade Gurkha was both startled at the unexpected interruption to his solitude and happy to be able to talk to someone he hoped would be sympathetic. When a Chinese man came into his cell he just knew that someone had come to help him. The CMP Corporal pushed his own chair inside so both men could sit, and Ah Fat waited till the door was shut before sitting down and saying 'Comrade Padamsing Rai, I have heard all about you and your work from my brother.' He spoke in English.

'Your br...brother?' the Gurkha stammered in surprise and confusion, the word 'comrade' giving him a clue that the visitor was not worried about anything 'down below'. 'And who is your brother?'

'Ah Ho. You met him in Singapore, didn't you?'

'Yes, yes, I did. He rang me and fixed a meeting at the Balmoral in Ulu Pandan.'

On target! 'I heard that you were being sent to India before you could fully carry out your task and so I managed to get a passage and, at the most convenient time, come and see you as we have unfinished business.'

Yes we have, the hapless prisoner thought sadly.

'You have started something by telling him about the mutinying Gurkhas on board and have scored a victory. I myself don't know any details but you have made a significant advance in our struggle. We must build on it. Now, in Malaya, only your fellow comrades can carry on the good work you have so nobly started. I have come to get their details so, without anyone else knowing we have met, except in the Politburo after I return of course, we can continue with your good work.'

Padamsing smiled joyfully. 'So my work won't go amiss and even though I won't be in Malaya any more, the work can continue. Yes, of course I'll give you the names. I don't have pen or paper,' and he spat moodily, 'but you must have.'

Ah Fat took the pencil and bit of paper out of his pocket and gave them to Padamsing. 'You write them down as I will have difficulty with the spelling.'

The Gurkha wrote down six army numbers, names and units, smiling as he did. 'They are my secret squad.' He handed the pencil and piece of paper back with a deep sigh of satisfaction. Ah Fat put them in his pocket. 'Your list will be safe here. And, in any case, were anyone to read the names they won't mean anything to them, will they?'

'No. Thank you sir. I am happy now.'

'And thank you very much, Comrade. I'll take care of everything so you need have no worries.' He turned as if to go, hesitated, and turned back 'Yes, there is one other point I need to have details about: where exactly did you get the information about the mutinying battalion from? I don't think you ever told my brother, did you?'

Padamsing just knew he was with someone he could trust. His morale had recovered from being rock-bottom by now being able to get the other people to carry on with the good work. 'To be perfectly honest I did rather exaggerate,' he said with a lop-sided grin. 'I changed a company going to Kelantan to a battalion and a leave party to a mutinying battalion. Nothing else. Your brother had put so much pressure on me to get concrete results within days when that was, quite frankly, impossible so that was the only way I could manage to give him an answer. He had threatened me if I didn't, said I was bound to the Party. That phone call I had with a Captain Rance, you won't know him but he's on board, would have been a God-send had I believed in a God – which I still don't?' he added, with a rueful chuckle. 'I hoped that by the time there was any reaction to my telling your brother something that was not yet quite true it would be true enough.'

Ah Fat inwardly gulped at such naivety but, being the splendid actor he had become, said, 'Yes, that was a wise thing to do, especially as your other Party workers were not as far forward as you, were they?

The renegade shook his head. 'No, sadly not. You are quite right,' he said with a sigh.

Ah Fat blessed his inspired guess as he got up to leave, thanking the prisoner once more as he did.

'Is there anything you can do for me when we reach India?' he was asked, almost pleadingly.

Ah Fat shook his head. 'All I can say is that I don't know why you are in this cell. It is nothing to do with me. Provided you have only offended the British military and not us, there's nothing to worry about.'

He took the chair outside and thanked the Corporal for it. Jason had been in earshot but unseen. They went up to his cabin where Ah Fat gave him the list.

'You've done well. You probably realise this is a great victory for us...' He was interrupted by the Tannoy announcing, 'Attention please, attention please. Will the OC Troops report to the Purser's Office.' The message was repeated.

Jason mopped his brow. 'Only just in time. As my father used to say: "just in time: born in the vestry"' and left the cabin with the list of names in his pocket.

Lieutenant Colonel Heron, a thickset, affable man with wavy black hair, penetrating blue eyes and hawk-like features, was at the Purser's Office when Jason arrived and saluted him. 'Great to see you sir,'

'Yes, and you too, Rance. I was indeed surprised to get your phone call yesterday. I was elated to have contact with one of my old battalion and intensely intrigued at such an unusual invitation.' He glanced at his watch. 'I have an hour. I'd like to wander around the troops but I expect you'll want to tell me why I'm here first. It may take some time so let's go to the lounge, have a coffee and a talk.'

Before moving off he thanked the purser and Jason led him to the lounge and ordered two coffees. 'Nothing stronger, sir?'

'No, coffee's fine – and, yes, a bun of sorts won't go amiss.' They took their cups and 'buns of sorts' to a corner and sat down. Jason looked around, making sure there were no eavesdroppers. He first told his one-time CO that, although he had phoned from the Nepalese consulate, he had not mentioned it lest the two Nepalis be embarrassed when they met him. He then plunged into his story.

James Heron listened intently, only interrupting when the background to a point was unknown to him. It took more time than he had expected to explain and, at the end, Jason dramatically produced the list of the other six renegades. 'Take this, sir. I've already come to think of any action you take as the start of our version of Operation Tipping Point.'

'My, but you have done a good job of work, Jason. I congratulate you wholeheartedly. You must have some most valuable sources to know what was debated in the Politburo.'

'Sir, you know my background from when you were my CO. Is there any need to ask more?' He shook his head.

'Yes, quite right. I shouldn't have asked. But talking of background, I was always impressed by your ability in the jungle. What do you put that down to?'

'Sir, apart from experience in walking and working in it from an early age, I always plan for three aspects: a firm base, an alternative and a reserve. That way I'm hardly ever lost or at a disadvantage.'

James Heron nodded his appreciation. Jason continued 'and knowing, as the good book puts it, which roots, fruits and shoots are poisonous and which are not when one has run out of rations and is hungry.'

His late CO smiled broadly as Jason added, 'and finally, as the late Grant Taylor said when he was chasing Al Capone, "there are two kinds of gun men, the quick and the dead".'

The Defence Attaché shook his head, grinning broadly at such unexpected wisdom. 'What else have you to add before I go off?' He looked at his watch. 'Just time to walk round the decks and see if there's anyone I recognise.'

'Before we do that, sir, I'll ask you in case I forget: may I presume what I think you will do with that list?'

James Heron chuckled. 'Knowing you, that's what I expected you to do.'

Jason looked slightly embarrassed, grinned and said, 'Get the list to the correct people in Singapore and Malaya – and Hong Kong as the unit of one of those names is there – warn Calcutta that the passengers on this boat are a normal leave party, just in case they might have had an alert. And, this will be up to you, sir, let the War Office know as well, also mentioning the King of Nepal's concern.'

'No worry there either, the FARELF Int boffins will do that in any case. Are you going back to Singapore?'

'Yes, sir. I am OC Troops for the return voyage also.'

'Well, I'll see if I can't meet on your way back and give you any reactions from my report. One thing I do know is that the Int boys will be after your source like a pack of dogs after a bitch on heat to hear what you managed to do in Calcutta.'

'Colonel, you can help me here. Just tell them, from me regarding sources, "no names, no pack drill".'

The Colonel stood up. 'Now that is what I call a really, really valuable visit and I am truly grateful for all your efforts.'

'And I, too, sir, for your coming to take the load off my shoulders. Now, a quick wander round the decks.'

One person the ex-CO knew was his chief clerk, Gurkha Captain Hemlal Rai, fluent in English. He was renowned for having killed three leopards near his home village before enlisting. Lithe and strong, he had an unusual aptitude for walking more easily on sloping ground than on the flat. When annoyed, his eyes had no pity in them. During their few words he said that he had had a letter from home saying that there was a man-eating leopard waiting to be shot. 'So instead of two-footed shikar, four-footed for a change,' said with a characteristically charming smile on his face.

'Mind you don't come a cropper!"

'No worry, sir. My brother, Jaslal Rai, a sergeant in 1/10 GR, is also going on leave and we'll be together.'

'Well, best of luck. I am pleased we were able to meet up again.' He looked round for Jason. 'It really is time to go.'

Jason escorted the DA as far as the gangway, saluted him and watched him until he was out of sight.

Before they docked at Calcutta Jason and Ah Fat put their heads together once more in the hope of making a joint plan. 'What neither of us must not forget,' said Jason 'is that, to me anyway, it seems as if the idea of the Gurkhas having to be disbanded is nothing but a very large red herring. Yet, however tenuous or strong such a link might be, the spider – if indeed he does exist and does operate in Calcutta – will be in the dark about Padamsing's unintended confession so, whatever else, the mysterious spider in his equally mysterious web will have no idea whatsoever of your Politburo's idea.'

Ah Fat nodded his head emphatically. 'True enough, so true that if I play my cards correctly I can either ignore going to the Mystery Man altogether or...'

'Telling him a load of nonsense so getting him to waste time in following false trails and I don't know what else,' Jason interrupted excitedly.

'That gives us almost endless scope, doesn't it? What can we think of, I wonder?'

'Oh, I am sure we'll come up with something.' Jason sounded more optimistic than he felt. 'If you do not contact the Hakkas with the purser it will get back to the Politburo and you'll be in grave trouble. Once you have found the spider in the web, even if you do nothing, the mere fact of being able to report it officially should be a tremendous personal bonus for you.'

They tossed a few more ideas around and made out a provisional programme. Ah Fat was ready to go with the purser, possibly as soon as after work on the second of the six days they would be in the port. Jason calculated that, if they docked in good time, the men would disembark that day and if they sailed late on Day 6 the new leave party would embark that same day. That meant that Days 3, 4 and 5 were free for any plans to be acted on.

'Since it is so indefinite, we will have to put on our snail's eyes and react to anything negative instantly so as not to waste any precious time.'

Gurkhas are not good sailors and everyone was glad when the ship docked. Jason was met by Major Dougie May – always known as Muggy Day – OC of the Gurkha Transit Camp out at Barrackpore, some miles from Calcutta itself. He was a tall, lanky man, with a mediocre brain and no hope for any more promotion. He was loyal, hard-working and completely dependable. With him were two members of the Calcutta police who took charge of Padamsing Rai to escort him up to the eastern Gurkha depot in Darjeeling – what a homecoming! The two Red Caps, hand-over receipt safely pocketed, decided to spend nights on board but to visit the city by day.

It was early afternoon when the OC of the Transit Camp met the OC Troops. 'Give me the paperwork and I and my chaps will look after everything,' said Dougie, who knew Jason from Malaya. Jason, ready with them, gave them to him.

'No trouble on the way over? None of us quite understood the message the DA sent from Rangoon.'

Now was not the time to go into details of what happened there. Jason took a side step from the truth. 'Muggy, we had a burial at sea. A little girl died before we reached Rangoon. I told the Defence Attaché about it and I suppose he over-reacted. I've noted it in the documents I've given you. Put it down to a Self-Adjusting Balls Up, a SABU.'

That satisfied Muggy.

'Well, I must get everybody away from here to reach the Transit Camp by 1600 hours. Nowadays large groups of coolies from the jute mills come to demonstrate against us outside our camp. We have had to close down two smaller gates and have asked for a civil police guard outside the main gate as we are only allowed to guard ourselves inside the camp. I have had to order extra buses to take the leave party in one fell swoop rather than wait for empty buses to return. That will save an hour coming back here, some time reloading and an hour back to the camp.'

'What's all that in aid of?'

'They are demonstrating against our men being in the British Army. They will tell this lot not to rejoin after leave and they try to intimidate returning leave men and their families. I think it also happens up in Darjeeling but I'm not sure.'

'Well, we have had an echo of that in Malaya and that is why we had a Gurkha prisoner. He is one of those who enlisted to try and make things difficult for us. We expect to have the others arrested before long. But it's dreadful that it's happening in both places.'

'It is, God rot their souls. Bad cess to them all. No time for gossip now. See you in the Mess this evening. You go ahead in that car I've arranged for you.'

'That's kind of you, Muggy. One night only though' as Dougie May hurried off to get the passengers on shore and into their busses. Before Jason went and collected what he needed for the night he sought out Ah Fat and told him about the coolies at Barrackpore. 'So the sickness is real here. You need to know that for whatever happens to you in your quest.'

'Jason. You are a born disseminator. It could be that I can get you a meeting with whoever it is I will be meeting. Are you game?'

Jason grinned wickedly. 'Grist to my mill, Flat Ears. Game,

set and, hopefully, match.'

Tuesday 25 November 1952, Gurkha Transit Camp, Barrackpore, Calcutta, India: As Jason was being driven up to Barrackpore, he queried the driver, a Nepali civilian, about the crowds that the OC had mentioned to him on the docks. 'Oh those blighters,' sniggered the driver. 'They have no idea what it's all about. All they are interested in is the 8 annas they get paid for the half hour of shouting. None of us knows who is behind such nonsense. I think they are probably jealous because the leave men are paid better than they are.'

'That could indeed be why,' countered Jason. 'What else have you to tell me? I have not been to Calcutta since 1948.'

The driver didn't answer for a while as he concentrated on the swirling traffic. Only when it thinned out did he resume his conversation, which was local and not all that edifying.

At the camp Jason was shown his room. After bathing and changing he went for a walk. Around the time he thought the crowds would come baying to the main gate he went to see for himself – and found nobody. He went to the Corporal Guard Commander and asked him when the crowd would come. The Corporal grinned and said, 'Saheb, they won't come.'

'But the OC Saheb said they would.'

'Oh yes, they did but a day or so ago their leader came and asked me, I was on duty then, if we would fire our rifles at them when they started shouting. I told him we wouldn't if we couldn't hear them. So they went to an open space about two miles away and shouted their heads off without fear and of course we heard nothing.' The Corporal grinned derisively. 'They don't know we don't have any weapons. They won't come back.'[15]

Before their evening meal Jason had been invited to the Gurkha Officers' Mess for titbits and a chat. It was a joyous occasion and the time passed on wings. He looked at his watch and got to his feet. 'Sahebs, I must be off now. I have much enjoyed meeting you all. Thank you.'

Jason and Dougie had not met for more than two years and had a lot to catch up. After supper they settled down to serious talk, there being so much to catch up on. Dougie had been the Assistant Military Attaché in Moscow before being posted to Barrackpore so had missed all the excitement of Operation Janus and was agog to hear about it. At the end he shook his head in admiration. 'You and your men should get a gong for what you did,' he observed.

Jason slid over his answer and, although Dougie felt something was not quite right, he made no comment. 'Let me hear about Moscow. It must be a complete one hundred and eighty degrees different life from the regimental one.'

So, Dougie told him. One of the stories he recounted was how the Attaché, a Major General, always managed to produce reports that were of such use to the War Office and Foreign Office. He said that those Russians with whom he spoke never knew how much classified material they had, unwittingly, given him. "It is knowing how to behave when having a meeting with the Russians and their inevitable and non-ending toasts. No one has

---

15 This was what your author was told by the Guard Commander when he was at the Transit Camp at that time.

ever seen me worse for wear afterwards as I always come back sober, however many toasts I have had to drink, proposed both by him and by me in return. I'll let you into my secret. Half an hour before going to their compound I would go home, open two tins of sardines, drinking the oil as well as drinking a pint of milk. That so thickly lined my stomach I could always out-drink any Sov under the table, never getting drunk myself. I'd always go in my official car with an escort, British of course, from the embassy. After about twenty minutes the Russian's brain would snap open, out would come the secrets for a few minutes, five or ten at the most, then he'd collapse. I would get up, go to the door, be met by the inevitable watcher, escorted to my car and be driven back. Once home I'd put my fingers down my throat and get rid of the muck I'd had to drink. Unpleasant but most effective."'

Jason listened avidly, knowing it was possible he'd meet the 'spider', an MGB man surely, before sailing back to Singapore *and I know I can't drink that amount but* ... 'Muggy, that certainly is one way to hold on to the initiative in enemy territory' and he nodded reflexively while Dougie went on and on ... till just before midnight.

As they left they saw the orderly yawning. '*Keta*, it's late. You'll have two hours extra duty pay at the end of the month,' said Dougie.

'Good night, Muggy,' said Jason. 'I'll be off after breakfast tomorrow. I'll pop into your Paymaster and get some rupees. I don't have an Indian bank account so I hope he can give me an advance of December's pay. You'll be busy and I need to get back to the boat so let's say our farewells now.'

'Farewell and good night, Jason. It's been great to catch up.'

Wednesday 26 November 1952, Calcutta: Ah Fat had told Law Chu Hoi he'd be in his cabin awaiting a call for when the purser was free. At 1030 the steward knocked on his door and told him to go to the Purser's Office. Law Chu Hoi had his own pass and made out another one for Ah Fat, written and stamped as an Assistant Purser on the *Eastern Queen* which he showed to the Dock Police. Outside the gates they hailed a taxi, driven by a Sikh, and the purser told him to go, as fast as was safe, to the near end of South Tangra Road.

The Sikh grinned and in Hindi said something that sounded derogatory but neither passenger understood it. They drove on in silence and once the taxi had reached the first temple they came to at Tangra the purser ordered it to stop. He and Ah Fat got out and Law put his head through the driver's window and asked, in English, 'how much?'

The taxi had no meter and the price was obviously exorbitant. 'I'll pay you half now and you can take me back to the docks in about half an hour when you'll get the other half.'

'And pay waiting time?' asked the rapacious driver.

The purser nodded and led Ah Fat into the temple and out the other side and strode off to a tannery not all that distant. Once there he went inside and made for the manager's office where he found the man he was looking for, Wong Kek Fui. He had a blunt demeanour, with a long nose, flared nostrils, a prominent chin, a big moustache and a wispy beard. They greeted each other warmly. The purser spoke Hak Wa and as Ah Fat could get by in it there was no problem of communication when Ah Fat was introduced.

'Time is short, Wong *Sin Saang*. I've brought my friend who has come all the way from Malaya to meet you and your contact. As he has to go back on the same boat we need action now. Can you manage to look after him? I have to go back now as I am busy.'

'Too busy for a glass of brandy?'

'Never too busy for that' and just within the half hour he returned to the waiting taxi and sped away.

'I was warned that a visitor might come but had no idea when or who. I expect the contact will see you but he is a proud and irascible red-haired running dog for all his political acumen so don't be surprised at being not all that welcome. He seems to look down on anyone who is not the same as he is, a Russian. I don't have a telephone number for him as he rings me, never the other way round, he's such a cautious fellow. We will have to go to his place without any warning. Are you ready?'

'Of course, after such a long and complicated journey I must be, mustn't I?'

The tannery had a truck and the Hakka told Ah Fat to get in. He drove out of the area on a different road and although Ah Fat had never been to India what little of Chinatown he saw was incongruous when compared to what he and the purser had driven through already. 'If, after you have handed me over and I need to return, may I ask where we're going?'

'Yes, of course you must know. It is the Soviet consulate

in Alipore Park Road. There is a man there who is known as the Rezident, a Russian word I believe, a man who calls himself Leonid Pavlovich Sobolev. It took me a long time to learn how to say that!' He swerved dexterously to miss a wandering buffalo, just managed to miss an on-coming car, served back and again just missed another vehicle which was driving on the wrong side of the road. Ah Fat wiped his sweaty hands on his trousers and hoped the journey wasn't too long.

The Hakka parked his vehicle down a side street, locked it and said, 'Come on. Follow me. Try not to show any surprise at what happens.' They walked into the main road, reached a building that was guarded by thick rails, went up to the front door and rang the bell. Nobody answered until the fifth ring and the door was opened by a European, presumably a Russian, who recognised Wong Kek Fui but of course not Ah Fat.

'What do you want?'

'I have a messenger from Malaya I need to meet the Rezident.'

'Name?'

'You know mine. His is of no interest to you.' Such a bald answer satisfied the functionary. 'Wait here. I'll tell the Rezident' and a few minutes later he came back. 'Come on in but make it quick as he seems to be in a bad temper.' He led them to a visitors' room. 'Sit down and wait.'

A burly, uncouth-looking man came into the room, looked at Wong Kek Fui and said, 'And no warning again?'

'Mr Sobolev. If I could I would. This man has just come from Malaya and has been told to report to you.'

Leonid Pavlovich Sobolev, uncertain whether his security had been breached, was neither gracious nor forthcoming. Ah Fat had yet to learn that the only people a Russian can be on really friendly speaking terms with is another Russian, and then not always.

The Rezident eyeing Ah Fat, creased his lips disdainfully and muttered 'another slit-eye.' Ah Fat, uncharacteristically, felt his gorge rise. He turned away from the Rezident and said to Wong Kek Fui, 'Stand up and make for the door. I'll follow you.'

'Where are you going?' called out a startled Rezident.

Ah Fat spun round and spat out 'I have made an uncomfortable and long and lonely journey to report to you as I was told to by the Politburo of the Malayan Communist Party about your helping us and I do not expect to be insulted and spoken to as a piece of shit. I'll go back and tell them you are nothing but a fraud' and, reaching the door, turned the handle.

'No, no. Don't go.' *Bloody little man.* 'Come back and we talk as friends.'

Pretending reluctance Ah Fat and his companion went back and sat down. 'You say you come from where?'

'Malaya.'

'And that you were told by your Politburo to come and see me, the MGB Rezident in Calcutta? That is not likely. My security is much better than a pile of unknown Chinese knowing who I am.'

'My Politburo knows nothing about you personally or your rank. Only that somewhere they don't know is a big controlling spider in a web that links us comrades up together.'

At that the Rezident merely grunted and asked 'What is it your Politburo wants from me and how does it know about me?

Of course I am willing to help but first I need to know how it is you know about me.'

'Nothing as such. It knows that Comrade Cheng Geng knows Comrade Law Chu Hoi and I was sent on his ship to come to here. He does not know you but he knows that Wong Kek Fui knows where to bring me. He took me to Tangra where he introduced me and he has now brought me to you to introduce me to you. Now are you satisfied?' *I have never spoken like this before but it seems to be working* Ah Fat thought as he saw the Rezident look relieved.

'That I accept. And what help do you want from me?'

'We understand that you are helping to manipulate Gurkha soldiers serving in Malaya to be converted to Communism to get them dismissed by the British government as not wanted and, at the same time, if any of them do stay in Malaya to have them sent to Sarawak, if you know where that is, to quell any trouble there. Once there the MCP can recuperate what losses they have suffered so go on to victory.'

The Rezident nodded. 'Yes, that was one of my many tasks. I gather one battalion has already joined us and been sent back to Nepal. Did you come with them?'

Ah Fat nodded. 'My Politburo is satisfied with what you have done so far over in Malaya. The people who you influence, even if not directly, are doing a good job and so there is no need to increase whatever you are doing.'

The Rezident looked satisfied. Ah Fat thought furiously, *how can I further disillusion him? How can I use Jason?* 'As you cannot get about like any normal agent may I make a suggestion for what to do here in India?'

'What do you know about what is happening here?'

'Don't tell me we don't know about the jute mill coolies at Barrackpore?'

Such a detail shook the Rezident over whose face flashed a look of surprise.

Yes! Got it! 'I have a trump card I would like to take from up my sleeve and offer to you' and without going into details he suddenly stopped talking. *Let the oaf resume the conversation!*

The Rezident was not used to being spoken to like this. Being spoken to 'in his own coin' was a rarity. He waited for his visitor to resume. He waited in vain. Like any bully he relished the initiative.

'And what is that?'

'Unknown to the British Army there is a captain, an Englishman, who has taken over the Darjeeling Gurkhas' task of getting the Gurkhas in Malaya on to our side. He came over on the same boat with me and is returning in a few days' time. He told me he wanted to increase the effort over here. He seems to think that there may be an Indian representative you can let him contact to give him some of his ideas and tell him the result of his efforts, which he feels must be considerable.'

As he let that sink in he saw a gleam in the Russian's eyes. 'And his name?'

'He is masquerading as a Captain Jason Rance. I don't know the name he was given at birth before he was made an in-depth agent of your party. He will only work with you on the understanding you keep it a secret as, so far, he is under no suspicion whatsoever.'

'When can he come here and meet my representative?'

'Let's say the day after tomorrow or the next day. If not then there will be no other opportunity.'

'Let's make it the day after tomorrow. Sobolev reached for a note book and looked up a number. He found it and dialled. The phone was answered but Ah Fat was unable to hear what the answer to the Rezident's question was, 'Where are you and can you come and see me? Yes. An emergency ... of sorts. The day after tomorrow? Good. About when? Not before four o'clock in the afternoon but definitely not later than 5. Good. I'll tell my visitor to be here then.' And quite obliviously he said, 'Good night, Mr Bugga,' as he put the phone down.

'Do you think you can come here by five o'clock on the day I've arranged with your "friend"?'

'If I don't it will mean something most unexpected has happened. But yes, of course.'

Ah Fat got a taxi back to the dock area and arrived at the time Jason stepped out of a Transit Camp vehicle.

Jason had worn mufti when he travelled to the Transit Camp as it was forbidden to wear the uniform of a foreign army unless one was a diplomatic soldier. He was allowed into the dock area with his official ID card. He also had a certificate saying he was the OC Troops. He greeted Ah Fat who took him to the safety of his cabin and told him exactly what had happened earlier on that day. 'I have no idea who he phoned but he spoke in English and said that there was "an emergency ... of sorts" with a gap in the middle of the sentence and not to come before 4 but not after 5. Oh yes, he said good night to a Mr Bugga.'

'That's an Indian name, surely. The Rezident sounds just how I have always imagined such a person to be,' Jason commented. 'But how unusual for such a secret set-up to masquerade as a normal diplomatic office.'

'I disagree. Who would imagine such a place would have such a secret task. As you English might say, "no cloak and no dagger" so nothing secret.'

Jason grinned. 'Point taken. What else have you for me?'

'Fasten your seat-belt. I have managed to get you an invitation to meet him the day after tomorrow. Our man said at five o'clock so let's aim for about half past 4. I have billed you as a deep, deep cover Soviet agent. Is it possible for you to act the part?'

'Flat Ears, as I once heard it said, "the only way of discovering the limits of the possible is to venture past them into the impossible." Providing the Rezident took you sincerely, and those kinds of people would never think such was a ruse, I won't be suspected.'

'I like it and provided we get there before this Bugga person – what an unfortunate name! – it could foil any plot they might hatch out to our disadvantage and give us some initiative, something we may be glad of.'

'Yes, this is new for both of us, isn't it? For once I can tell you something new. Listen to this …' and out came the story he had heard from Dougie May about the toasts and how to guard against ill effects. 'He didn't offer you anything, did he?'

'Of course not,' Ah Fat spat out. 'I'm not a European white

but a coloured Asian so it takes an effort for such a man even to be talking to one such as me.'

Jason nodded ruefully. 'I'm afraid that is true,' omitting that the reverse could also happen and had happened to him more than once. 'That means I'll be expected to drink toast after toast with him, and, as a non-drinker,' he sighed heavily. 'I'll have to look around for sardines and milk, although I expect butter will do just as well.'

'Cheer up, Jason. I've got another idea that has just come to me. I believe these people only drink vodka. Were you to say that vodka disagrees with your stomach so you've brought your own bottle of brandy ...' Jason held up his hand but Ah Fat carried on. ' ... don't interrupt. Just listen. My idea is to fill it with cold tea, brewed to the colour of the brandy. That's why I didn't suggest gin or whisky.'

'You mean we drink toast to toast but pour our own?'

'Well, why not?' and both roared with laughter.

'Does that mean I'll have to buy him a bottle of vodka, do you think?'

'N ... no, I think not. He may have his own sort and much cheaper that anything you could buy in Calcutta which, for all I know, is dry, like the rest of India is, so I have been told.'

'You are full of ideas,' said Jason admiringly. 'I too have another idea. That is go to the main book shop and try to find an English-Russian dictionary or phrase book, learn a few words and come out with them at the correct time.'

Ah Fat nodded and pursed his lips. 'Yes, that might pay dividends. You never know, it could come in useful. As you said earlier, this is new for both of us. And yes, on the face of it, I advise you not to let anyone hear you speak Chinese. Only use it if absolutely necessary.'

It was Jason's turn to nod agreement. 'None of the ship's crew knows I speak it. As you know the purser better than I do and as the staff seem to know that you do, do you think you could get hold of a used brandy bottle that still has its label on and fill it with tea? Make up some story to suit the occasion. If I leave you to do that I can go and look for an English-Russian phrase book or dictionary.'

'One other thing, Jason. I don't know how much Indian currency you have spare but if you can't walk to the Soviet consulate in Alipore Park Road to have a look I hope you have enough for a taxi to take you there. As it probably won't be marked as such outside, they are such secretive devils, you can ask the taxi driver, who's bound to know or ask. What I have learnt about such places is that they have a large array of aerials sprouting from the roof so that could be one way of recognising it.'

'Yes, I have enough money. I paid the Transit Camp Paymaster a visit before I left. I'd better give you some as getting the bottle and tea ready will be easier to get with an extra rupee to flash about.'

Later on, Jason came back empty-handed, there not being any such phrase book and also, without knowing the pronunciation, it would have been of little use even had he found one.

Friday 28 November 1952, Calcutta: They decided to go to

Tangra during the early afternoon as there was nothing else to prepare, except for Jason to find a phrase book and Ah Fat to get the bottle of 'brandy' ready. They found which bus went there and, although it was unusual for any European to travel by local bus, both of them thought that if they were seen arriving in a bus it might create a better impression of 'comradely solidarity' than if they went there by taxi. They got out of the bus at the porticoed entrance, dodged round a white bull chewing the heavy garland of zinnia, cannas and jasmine drooping around its neck, and saw a local guide – or was he a guard? Ah Fat went up to him and asked where the office was.

Cantonese and Hak Wa, being almost interchangeable, Ah Fat was understood. 'Do you want to see Cheng Fan Tek? If so, you will find him ...' and he gave them instructions how and where to go to his office.

Ah Fat thanked him. Jason kept quiet, listening carefully to what the Hakka guide was saying. *Not all that different, is it* he told himself.

They found the office building and Ah Fat asked for Cheng Fan Tek and was immediately shown into an inner sanctum. They found a tall man, probably in his fifties, with shrewd eyes and a wispy beard sitting at a table. As they were escorted in he got up, surprise in his eyes. 'Please come in and sit down.' He turned to the clerk who had ushered them in and told him to bring tea.

Ah Fat introduced himself and Cheng Fan Tek said who he was. 'And him?' cocking an eye at Jason.

'Oh, a *gwai lo* who wanted to come along and see what sort of place Tangra is.'

After a bit more desultory conversation 'may I ask where you have come from?'

'The *Eastern Queen.*'

'How clever of you to find me without Comrade Law Chu Hoi coming with you.'

'Oh, I met up with him two days ago but there was no time to look around. I want to see part of my motherland so far away and in India.'

'And will you be going to see Comrade Sobolev?'

'Yes, later on today.'

'I expect Comrade Wong Kek Fui will go with you. I have not been warned.'

'That is not in my hands but in Comrade Law's.'

'And what nationality is this ugly man with you?'

'English. He is a hidden comrade.'

The Hakka made a moue of disapproval. 'All red-haired devils are smelly and unkempt. I don't like them at all.'

Ah Fat grinned back at that remark. 'Some are worse than others.'

'It doesn't matter to me but I know that even if this running dog with you is one of us, Comrade Sobolev hates all non-Russians and will try to trick him into confidences with drink. Looking at this ugly lout I would be happy to see him drown himself in drink, better still in rat's piss.'

Jason grinned inside himself. Turning towards the Hakka he said, 'Why not pig's piss. Better if you were drowned in it but not with me. You uncouth *Fei Toh*.'

The effect was one of open-mouthed disbelief. Clearly he did not like being called a bandit. 'But why did you not start with our language, although you only talk another dialect?'

'*Paan chue sek lo foo,*' feigning to be a pig, I conquer tigers, said Jason. 'and if I have any more rudeness from you I'll tell Comrade Sobolev to have you castrated, that is if you have anything at all down there.'

There was an awkward silence then Jason said to his friend, in English, 'Let's walk away proudly, saying nothing at all.' And that is what they did.

As they made their way back towards the main road they looked up when they heard the clatter of wings as a skein of wild duck circled overhead as it flew towards the lower reaches of the Hooghly.

The Hakka, Cheng Fan Tek, incensed at being spoken to in such a fashion and not having been briefed of anyone other than a Chinese from Malaya needing to be taken to the Soviet consulate, was also deeply suspicious. He felt he ought to check so he picked up the phone in his office and asked the exchange to put him through to the Purser's Office in the SS *Eastern Queen*. The operator, presumably a new man, did not know that the boat could be rung up but, having been given the number, made the connection. After several rings the purser answered, in English, giving his job and the name of the boat.

'Law Chu Hoi, it's Cheng Fan Tek speaking.'

'Is this wise?'

'I must speak to you. You can tell me if it is wise or not.'

'What's the trouble? Make it short. We never know who's listening, even here.'

'You know the comrade from Malaya who has to be taken to a certain place?'

'Yes, of course I do. I took him there yesterday.'

'Well, he came back today with a *gwai lo*. A *gwai lo* who speaks our language.'

'I can't think who you mean. There is a *gwai lo* on board but he speaks only English and *Loi Pai Yi Wa*, the same as the *Goo K'a bing* speak. I have never seen him speak with the comrade from Malaya. No, it must be someone different.'

'Thank you, Comrade. It is always wise to check up.'

'Yes. I'll ring off now. It's safer.'

Cheng Fan Tek put his phone back on its stand. *Who can he be?*

237

5

Friday 28 November 1952, Calcutta, India: Ah Fat had done a good job with the bottle and tea. Despite the tea/brandy ploy, both of them felt that in case liquor was forced on Jason to an extent he could not decently refuse, it was prudent to get enough butter for three large spoonfuls and a small jug of milk as 'absorbers' to be consumed before they left the boat. At three o'clock Jason ate the butter and nearly choking on it, washed it down with the milk. The tea-filled brandy bottle looked like a new one with its neck neatly stuck up with something that looked enough like the real one at a cursory glance. Putting it in a Nepalese bag that he hung from his shoulder, the two of them moved out of the dock area, telling the superintendent at the gate who they were and they might not return until after dark.

They found a taxi and were driven to Alipore Park Road, arriving at the Soviet consulate just on four o'clock. They rang the doorbell and the door was opened by a non-smiling, pressed-lipped man who took them to the visitors' room, complete with the compulsory large picture of Lenin. They were soon joined by two Russians. One introduced himself as Leonid Pavlovich Sobolev, the First Secretary, Political, not as the Rezident, and the other, a burly, uncouth-looking man who introduced himself as Dmitry Tsarkov 'another member of this consulate'. Being a wartime casualty, his gait was ungainly, having had his left leg amputated below the knee. No one outside his unit ever knew that his CO had said he looked like a lavatory brush draped with a discoloured flannel. Ah Fat, who had not met Tsarkov when he had first visited the consulate, was not introduced. *A mere Chinaman ... why bother?*

Gritting his teeth, it was now Ah Fat's turn. 'Comrade Sobolev, let me introduce Comrade Jason Rance. I won't tell you his real name because, like you, he guards it well.' Sobolev took Jason by complete surprise by stepping over to him and giving him three kisses, right, left, right. He had enough sense to try and emulate the Russian, hoping his disdain for such a greeting wasn't too obvious. He merely made a formal bow to Dmitry Tsarkov and kept silent. Tsarkov mumbled something in passable, albeit guttural, English.

'I am expecting another guest,' said Sobolev, glancing at his watch. He had never owned one before being able to buy one in Calcutta and was inordinately proud of it. 'But we can have a drink and a toast before he comes.'

Jason and Ah Fat were told to sit down. Vodka and glasses were brought in and put on small tables only in front of the two Europeans. Jason took the brandy bottle out of his bag and said, 'Comrade. I don't have many weaknesses but one I do have is that vodka upsets my stomach so, against normal Russian habits, I have taken the risk of bringing my own drink. I nearly brought you a bottle of vodka but I did not know what your favourite kind was but even if I had known I would not have found a bottle as this place is dry.'

The two Russians glanced at each other. 'You think you will be poisoned, then?' asked Sobolev, in a nasty bullying tone of voice. It was clear that he had already had quite a lot to drink.

'Not by you, Comrade, ever, 'Jason said, and Ah Fat added, 'True, Comrade, it really does have a bad effect on him.'

Before the First Secretary proposed a toast to their meeting Jason said, 'as comrades, all four of us must have a toast at the same time. My friend here is under doctor's orders not to touch liquor as he has a duodenal ulcer. Please bring him a soft drink.'

The Rezident didn't argue but the look of disdain on his face was indicative of his dislike of drinking with a non-white person.

All four of them stood, toasted British and Russian solidarity with the Russians tossing off their drinks in one and Jason merely 'going through the motions'. An attendant poured another lot into the Russians' glasses and Jason poured a little more into his own from his own bottle. Ah Fat, with glass still half full, did nothing. Nobody noticed that the attendant, feigning uninterest in the proceedings, unobtrusively stayed within earshot, with a deceptively bland look on his face.

Then Dmitry Tsarkov proposed a toast to Soviet and British amity, followed by Jason's toast to the victors of the Great Patriotic War and so it went on, without stop, turn by turn. Jason, who only pretended to finish off what was still in his glass, had a hard time thinking of something new to toast.

The door opened. Everyone turned to see who it was. They saw a Bengali, dressed in a shantung suit and wearing a 'Bombay bowler' pith helmet, even indoors. He looked about thirty years of age, was heavily hirsute, had a slight 'outward' squint, a puffy face and pock-marked cheeks. He had pendant ears, with a heart-shaped birthmark under the right one. He wore a long moustache to cover a slight hair lip which made his labial consonants awkward to understand. He looked round and smiled. 'I am thinking you are drinking, are you as drunk as a skunk? A "drunken Russen"? As one spy to another I say, introduce me, you MGB drunkard.' It was not the type of opening greeting any of them expected.

Sobolev, by now near his limit, took violent exception to such an opening gambit, even in supposed fun. His face contorted with rage and the two men glared at each other. Then the Russian calmed down enough to say, 'This is Mr Bugga, Vikas Bugga, one of us in India, a black man. He is the one in charge of the mutinying Gurkhas. Let him have a glass of vodka. Oh yes, these two here are a Captain Rance, or so he says, and Comrade Ah Fat, or so he also says.'

Mr Bugga with his glass of vodka moved over to where Jason was standing. The urge to toast Sobolov overtook him again and he proposed another one to the mutinying Gurkhas.

Jason, his world, for the fraction of a second, dropping a dimension and becoming paper thin. had concentrated on Vikas Bugga's accent. Pretending a certain unsteadiness, he leant over the Indian and, in Hindi, said, 'I am a friend of Padamsing's. He is doing a great job. You chose him well and there's no need to bother about him and the others. He says that without doubling their pay the coolies will stop shouting, so please do so. As it is, with so little incentive, they are now shouting so they can't be heard in the Gurkha camp.'

Vikas Bugga knew that there were no extra funds but he could not say so. He merely thanked Jason for his information.

Sobolev didn't understand what was being said. *Intolerable!* His temper snapped and in Russian he shouted '*ja ne ponimáju, chto govorít ètot chórnomazyi ubljúdok.*'

Vikas, who had some Russian, understood that to mean 'I don't understand what that nigger bastard is saying' which naturally infuriated him but, sensing a golden opportunity, before he could answer, Jason leant over towards him and, using his ventriloquism, made him say, 'You Russian bastard. You are black inside. I am like Queen Victoria, all pink inside.'

In his fury the Rezident answered in Russian. '*Ty nazyvájesh' menjá chórnym vnutrí?*' Vikas understood that to mean 'You call me black inside?' Then another outburst, '*Ty nichtózhnaja málen'kaja chórnaja svin'já.*' You insignificant little black pig. The Rezident's notion of consular diplomacy was injudiciously elastic.

The two angry men flickered their eyes at each other like lizards' tongues.

Vikas Bugga opened his mouth but Jason was quicker to answer. 'Oh, go to hell, you worthless piece of dog shit.' Jason's accent would not have passed muster were the tension in the room not so strained. The effect was electric: the Rezident stuttered, glared, took a pace towards the equally surprised Indian who, although without any alcohol inside him, had been unbalanced at what he thought he had heard himself say. 'Call me black, you black bastard? You insignificant little pig. How dare you talk to one such as me like that?'

The enraged Russian looked at the Indian with fanatical,

bent-on-one-thing-only eyes and threw his glass hard at him, hitting him on the nose, actually bending it, and on one cheek, making him bleed copiously. Sobolev turned back automatically to the vodka bottle on a table beside him, picked it up and drank from it in one long gulp. The bottle fell from his hand as his rage and drunken state got the better of him, causing him to lose his balance. He had reached his tipping point and, gasping, collapsed onto the floor with a thump and passed out.

For Ah Fat time stopped like a broken clock as he witnessed such gross and unimaginable drunken behaviour.

Tsarkov had also been drinking toast for toast but had stayed silent and relatively sober. Now he suddenly realised what had happened and sobered up: a trusted Indian ally – and there were no other Indians like him – who had been so insulted he'd most likely have a grudge against the Soviets for the rest of his life. With the Rezident so disgraced in front of the Indian with a bleeding face and the new English comrade by his insensitive and unnecessary conduct, there could scarcely be any trust in any further collaboration. Before he could call for someone to look after Vikas Bugga's face the attendant had dashed away and brought back a first-aid box and had started to repair what damage he could. The face was in a mess and needed stitching and the nose needed straightening.

'Come and lie down. I'll send for the consulate doctor,'

Eyes downcast, Mr Bugga was led away.

Jason looked round and saw the silent assistant. Feeling he knew how to maintain his role he said, 'Either give me a consulate vehicle to take me back to my boat or order a taxi. Now.'

The assistant, with a strange look on his face, left the room. It was a curiously long while before he came back and said that the consulate car was waiting for them. 'It took me a little time to alert the driver, hence the delay. I hope you comrades will forgive such behaviour. It is not how we like to comport ourselves with guests such as you. As loyal party members I ask for your total discretion about this evening.'

Jason solemnly assured him of his reticence as did Ah Fat. An envelope was slid into Ah Fat's hand. 'Please give this to the purser when you get back.'

Neither passenger said a word as they were driven back to the docks fearing that the vehicle, being the consulate car, was 'doctored' or, at least, the driver briefed to report back anything reportable he'd heard. As they got out they thanked the driver, showed themselves to the duty superintendent and walked to the *Eastern Queen*. They were in time for the evening meal. Jason's stomach, still feeling the result of butter, milk and cold tea, was not receptive to too much food. In the lounge they had a couple of cups of coffee before going to Jason's cabin to talk over the visit.

'*Shandung P'aau*, what on earth made you become a circus clown? We could have learnt a lot if you had not called toast for toast and then made that wretched Indian not know whether he was punched, bored or countersunk.' Ah Fat was very proud of that phrase but seldom had the chance to use it. 'As it happened, we learnt nothing. Rather a waste after all that build up!' He was disappointed but tried not to show it.

'In a way, *P'ing Yee*, I agree. What I was aiming for was those few minutes between reticence and collapse when there might have been a windfall. Alas Vikas Bugga came in just at that moment and the Rezident, being the oaf that he is and very near his "sell-by date", was in no mood for any unknown non-white person to learn any secrets. My aim then was to make verbal chaos and the Russians to lose face, regardless of how it affected the Indian. In fact I told him that the coolies were not doing their job properly and here I improvised by saying they needed twice the money, my hope being that party funds can't meet the extra expense. I also told him that Padamsing was doing a great job and so were the others so there was no worry there.'

'So, what now?'

'I feel that by what you on board with the purser and I today have managed to accomplish will result in the Communists not realising they have reached their tipping point for failure so they'll go on expending energy needlessly.'

'Could be,' said Ah Fat, 'but what shall I say to the Politburo?'

'That's a good question. You must not lose any points there but gain a few. I am sure you'll find words enough to satisfy them. Fool them with that mutinying battalion! You were given assurances that everything in India was being taken care of and that there was no more worry.'

'And in Sarawak?'

'That's nothing to do with you so, again, no worry.'

'That cheers me up. *What* a day!'

Before they went to bed Jason asked about the envelope that was given to him as they parted.

Ah Fat took it out of its pocket. He saw the ink on the envelope was smudged and that it had been only half sealed. *Written in a hurry! Why?* 'Jason, I am suspicious. I have a feeling that there is bad news inside.'

'We have our coffee kettle here in the cabin so let me steam the envelope open and read the letter before putting it back and resealing it before giving it to the purser.' Jason filled the kettle and put it on to boil then deftly held the envelope over the steam and gently prised it open and gave it to his friend to read.

Jason heard his friend gulp. 'Read this,' Ah Fat said vehemently, thrusting the letter into his friend's hands. Jason took it and read it, aghast as his eyes travelled over the hastily written English. The purser was ordered to get both men thrown overboard with no one else knowing about it. 'Essential for the Party. Don't ask questions. You will be rewarded.'

'Unbelievable,' breathed Jason. 'What will you do with it?'

Ah Fat shook his head, almost in a trauma. *If the ink had not been smudged and the envelope only half stuck down!* 'I can't think. What do you suggest, Jason?'

'Nothing now. When we disembark go to the Captain, give him the letter and tell him to do what he thinks fit.'

'On the face of it that might be the best thing to do. Let's sleep on it.' They bid each other good night and Ah Fat went to his own cabin.

What neither man would ever know was that the attendant, the silent witness of the proceedings, was the only one in the consulate who was a Department S's undercover representative, so more powerful than anyone else there. His report reached the office in number 1 Derzhenskii Square, resulting in the soon-to-be-ex-

Rezident's sojourn in the prison in the Lubyanka building, where Leonid Pavlovich Sobolev found himself not long afterwards. Dmitry Tsarkov was more fortunate: he was posted to the MGB HQ where he could be kept under observation, pending another report on his conduct.

So, unbeknownst to those in the consulate and in Department S, or anywhere else in the MGB set-up, Operation Tipping Point was scuppered by the organisers of the whole scheme: not a SABU, a Self Adjusting Balls Up, but a NABU, 'N' for non-adjusting.

Friday 28 November 1952, somewhere on the East Coast Railway, Malaya: The Director of Operations had been impressed with what A Company, 1/12 GR, had done during and after the railway ambush and decreed that it should be taken off its framework operations and go back and examine that area once more. What had excited him was the possibility of there being more weapons caches in that area. The cache had been cleverly found by a member of the clearing patrol who had hidden behind some thick undergrowth for a call of nature. As he squatted he noticed an unusual change of colour in the vegetation. He had investigated why and found where the cache was. A British battalion had been sent to the same area after A Company had been withdrawn from Kelantan but now was due to return to England. No more hidden weapons had been found. The area was taken over by 1/10 GR and extended so much that it needed more troops to cover it. That resulted in Jason Rance's company being called back there.

The CO of 1/12 GR called Major McGurk to his office and told him that A Company was being sent north to work under command of 1/10 GR. 'I'd rather have you with me, I must say, but apparently the Director of Operations doesn't like to waste knowledge of what has already been gained. He somehow thinks that the high standard shown by A Company in finding where weapons had been cached can be repeated.'

McGurk nodded. 'I understand, sir. Have there been any troops in that area since A Company were there?'

'Yes, from reading the Intelligence reports it seems that a British battalion was while 1/10 GR was on its re-training. It had a fatality when a corporal was killed patrolling the railway after another train ambush. It has now done its three years and is getting ready to return to England. 1/10 GR has taken its area back again and its area of operations has been increased. They don't have enough troops to cover it and that it why I have been told to send A Company back to cover where they were before, on the eastern end of 1/10 GR's area.'

This time A Company moved by road convoy as far as Kuala Lipis, escorted by armoured cars. It was a long and hot journey that took more than a day. They stopped over at Tactical HQ of 1/10 GR.

The CO of 1/10 GR called Major McGurk, gave him the background and briefed him on his task. 'We have been operating in this area for a couple of years so it will help if I give you a guide,' he said, having been warned that the Major was on reserve duty so out of touch as well as it being useful for local knowledge and liaison with battalion HQ if needed. 'As ordered to, I am sending you to the area that your company, then under Captain Rance, was ambushed when moving by rail. I also want you to patrol the railway line. I feel sure that the company will react well to you if you listen to anything that is advised by senior ranks.' The new OC looked a bit askance, feeling he was being adjudged as not up to the job.

'Don't look like that, please,' said the CO, sharply. 'You are not yet in practice and it is only common sense to listen to those up-to-date with Malayan jungle tactics. This is Counter Revolutionary Warfare against guerrillas, not a full-scale war as it was in Burma.'

Major McGurk expressed his thanks and after a few more details were tied up, met the guide, a Rifleman Pahalman Rai, and took him to his Company HQ. Although he had been passed over for promotion, he was a strong, steady man in his early thirties and was especially chosen because he had worked as an officer's batman so 'knew' the *gora* sahebs, understood their foibles and was used to hearing 'mangled' Nepali so was more likely to understand what Major McGurk was trying to say than a soldier who had not worked closely with a British officer.

On his return to his battalion Rifleman Pahalman Rai gave this report: 'we were walking along the railway track. I was not far behind the Major saheb and at a mile stone at the side of the track, I saw him turn round and talk to somebody in English. I saw nobody there. The Major saheb spoke severely, turned round to look at me then turned back again. He seemed visibly upset. I did not know why but learnt that he had seen a British corporal, without a weapon, leaning on the mile stone by the side of the track. He had wanted to know who the soldier was and why he was there. After he had turned to look behind him, he looked back again but the man had vanished. That is why the look on his face was strange.'

It so happened that the British company patrolling that had been attacked in that area and had a corporal shot and killed by the guerrillas but the OC had no means of knowing that.[16]

The company thrashed around as ordered by the CO of 1/10 GR and eventually returned to base in Seremban without any guerrilla contacts – or finding any more cached weapons. Only the OC and his guide knew about that strange incident.

Sunday 30 November 1952, Calcutta: With the arrival of the returning leave party on the docks and Major May handing over the required documents, Captain Rance's life returned to what passed as normal, something he was glad of. On the face of it everything appeared as it should: their recent visit to Tangra now seemed infinitely remote and the abnormal happenings in the Soviet consulate were more like a bad dream than reality having actually stared him in the face. Now the job he had been sent on seemed almost an anti-climax: but how welcome, with, he hoped, nothing unexpected to upset the customary routine on the return journey+.

Muggy Day broke into his thoughts. 'So, Jason, it's back to the battalion once more. I'll be glad to get back although this

---

16 Rifleman Pahalman Rai's story is on page 219 of *Gurkhas at War: In their own Words: The Gurkha Experience 1939 to the Present [1999]*, edited by J P Cross and Buddhiman Gurung. Major McGurk told your author that he had said, '"I invoke you in the name of God to tell me what you are doing and who you are." I had no prior knowledge of the casualty.'

job has its good points. I can get up to Darjeeling now and then and enjoy the cooler weather and having a blanket on my bed at night. I am sorry you couldn't have stayed longer with us but I expect you wanted to wallow in the bright lights here, relaxing and enjoying yourself. I wonder if you got up to any mischief you shouldn't have?' and he gave a smile … of, what? Jason thought, forgiveness?

'Mischief? If I did it was not the kind you might have been thinking of?'

'Jason, stop talking in riddles, one of your more arcane habits.' He looked at his watch. 'No time to be gossiping,' and he went into last-minute details about the draft.

'Time to be off, Jason. Happy journey' and he turned to go, then turned back. 'Oh yes, the mob of coolies shouting outside the lines. You'll be interested to hear that last night, for the first time in I don't know how long, the police reported that no coolies had gathered anywhere. The only excitement was a banging in the cookhouse that went on all night and some of our more fanciful men thought it was a particularly noisy ghost!' He laughed. 'Guess what?'

'No idea.'

'A jackal had got into the cookhouse, sniffed out a smelly tin that attracted it, put its head inside and got stuck. Trying to escape all it did was to bump into table legs and I don't know what else. When the early morning cooks went in they saw the wretched animal, got hold of it and pulled the tin off. The poor thing was so bemused by then it didn't run away but just sat down and looked lost.'

Jason laughed. 'And what did the cooks do? Kill it?'

'No. They thought it had suffered enough so they let it slink out.'

They shook hands and Jason saluted his senior officer, a grin on his face at such an unlikely story.

But there were no grins either on any Soviet faces, embarrassed as they were, or on the battered face of Mr Vikas Bugga. The doctor had put his face under local anaesthetic, cleaned it before stitching him up and straightened his nose, his patient having stated he didn't want to keep it bent as a badge of humiliation. 'Take it really easy for a couple of days,' the doctor advised him. 'Certainly stay here the night,' and he told Dmitry Tsarkov to fix a bed up. Before the doctor left he told Vikas Bugga where his clinic was. 'Come round in a couple of days for a new dressing and, when the time comes, I'll take your stitches out.'

Bugga, whose now-straightened nose and bruised, stitched cheek, were hurting him, merely nodded. It was less painful than trying to speak. He wasn't hungry or thirsty for some hours and then eating was almost impossible, despite the pain killers he had been given. The Soviets gave him thin soup to suck through a straw: being ashamed of their Rezident's behaviour they tried to make up for it as best they could, certainly by paying all the medical bills.

As the Indian lay in bed that night he went over and over in his mind's eye how strange it was that he had heard himself speak when he knew he had not even opened his mouth. The Communist in disguise, now what was his name? had told him about Padamsing, how well he was doing. How had he known? That was a mystery. And the coolies being paid twice the amount. Party funds didn't allow so much. If Padam was such a success maybe they didn't deserve a rise: maybe they could be dispensed with altogether. Yes, that was the answer. Early next morning he would tell Dmitry Tsarkov, or write it down on a piece of paper if talking was still difficult, to contact his paymaster and tell him to stop payment that very day. That decided, the only unsolved matter was his speaking when he knew he hadn't. What sort of party trick was that? Whatever else, he was happy that his choice of upsetting the British Gurkhas, Padamsing Rai, was doing sterling work over in Malaya. That at least was one, even if the only one, positive outcome of being told there was some sort of emergency. His face started aching and he managed to swallow some more pain killers, helped down with the water in a glass by his bed. He drifted off into a befogged sleep.

Ah Fat had been shocked by the behaviour of the Russians. Having had no experience of them he had not realised how differently they behaved from the British he had seen and grown up with in Malaya. Sure, he had seen some of the tuans drunk but never being so incapable that they lost all sense of dignity and of face: 'face', that display of public potency which makes for personal prestige. And the more he thought about that extraordinary letter that had been so furtively pressed into his hand ... *What witheringly bad tradecraft. Could it have been that the inborn superiority of the white man believing that a coloured native would automatically obey him?* Such a thought made Ah Fat shudder. *I know everyone can't be as good with Asians as Jason but even so …*

He thought of Jason's idea of his giving the letter to the Captain and hoping that any executive action would result in the communist purser being sacked. Of course, without knowing what was in the letter he could deny all knowledge – that was completely natural – but even the thought of being capable of such an action was, surely, damning in itself? What he'd do was to make a copy of it, give that to Jason to do with it what he thought best as well as giving the original to the Captain. He spoke to Jason about it once matters had calmed down enough for the OC Troops to relax.

Jason frowned as he thought it over. 'I don't like the idea of you personally giving the letter to the Captain, altogether too risky if there were any follow-up. I think you must make a copy of the letter to give to any of your contacts you think ought to see it. Why not make two and give your Party one? Show them just how hard it is to talk to the Russians. You can blame Vikas Bugga for interrupting but, please, no mention of me. Yes, put the letter in its envelope into an outer envelope, no covering letter, with the Captain's name on the outside. We'll have to get a third and non-involved person to deliver it or, better still, say, leave it on the bar in the lounge when the barman is not looking. If you think that is difficult, I'll give it to one of my Gurkha officers to put it on the bar of the second-class lounge. No one could ever suspect any of them being involved.'

Ah Fat thought it over and nodded agreement. 'Doing it on the last morning just before disembarkation will be the best time,' Jason added.

Tuesday 2 December 1952, somewhere in the Cameron Highlands, north Malaya: Members of the Politburo were discussing matters at a routine Plenum. News, generally, of Security Forces activity was casting a pall of gloom. 'It is some time since Comrade Ah Fat left us,' said one of them. 'I do hope his journey will be successful.'

'Of course, we all do,' added the Secretary General. 'He is one of our most trusted operators. I have known him all these years. His wartime work was in every way a success. He is the most trustworthy' and, confused by what he had not quite meant to say, 'he is no more trustworthy than any of you are. He is only a cadet member of the Politburo, quite why not a full member I don't know, but there it is.'

An uneasy silence ensued. Everyone knew, in the heart of his heart, that life in the Politburo was always on a tight rope, however hard one tried for it not to be.

Chien Tiang, chief confidant of Chin Peng and propaganda expert, looked up from reading a piece of paper in his hands. 'I think what we originally decided was that his work took him to various places, and, in this instance, distant and unexpected ones, for such long periods he was apt to miss Plenum sessions so be unable to cast his vote. As a non-voting member his advice could well be sought but we could never count on his being present when we were voting'

Heads nodded and it was agreed that if anyone could find the spider in the web and get it to work for the Party, Comrade Ah Fat was the man. Their attention was switched with the arrival of a courier and his escort with various documents. The meeting broke off till these were read and put into their various files in the office. After that normal boredom set in as there being nothing positive to do, unless one calls 'waiting for something' positive.

Sunday 7 December 1952, Rangoon: The voyage was a soothing antidote to the events before the returning leave party's embarkation. Both Jason and Ah Fat gave the purser a wide berth, feeling that if they were seen too much together it might get back to the MCP Politburo to Ah Fat's disadvantage. They only visited each other's cabin when none of the staff were about. *Tradecraft!* Also, who knew if the Hakka Chen Fan Tek in Tangra might, just, have met up with the purser and told him that Captain Rance spoke Chinese? So, although on the surface all was quiet, the two men were on their guard. Thus they came to Rangoon in slightly cooler weather but with same movement restrictions.

Sunday 7 December 1952, somewhere in east Nepal: The Chief Clerk, Gurkha Captain Hemlal Rai who had told Colonel Heron about the man-eating leopard, and Sergeant Jaslal Rai, a smaller edition of his elder brother but with thicker hair, were by now back home enjoying their leave. Both were keen shikaris and, as the villagers had seen recent leopard pug marks, they arranged for a goat to be tied up to a tree beside a little-used track where the villagers had said and had built a machan up a large tree, from where they could get a good shot at the marauding animal.

Both brothers, with loaded guns, climbed up to their hiding place well before dusk and sat, silent. There was a full moon. Around half past ten they heard footsteps coming from both ends of the track they were sitting above.

'Keep quiet,' muttered the elder. 'Most unusual. Smugglers? Robbers?'

'Can't be normal village people, I'll be bound,' whispered the younger. 'They keep well away when there's leopard shooting.'

A short distance off both lots of footsteps came to a stop and a noise like a bull frog was made from one end. This was echoed from the other. The footsteps cautiously resumed and two pairs of men met under the machan. One in each group stood back and the other two moved forward, gazed at each other and embraced.

As Jaslal peered down through the bamboo slats of the machan he saw that one was much shorter than the other. Hemlal laid a restraining hand on his brother's arm and gently squeezed it, a sign to remain utterly silent.

The shorter man spoke and Sergeant Jaslal, who had been an instructor in the Gurkha school, nearly gave their position away by his violent jolt when he heard the voice of one he knew too well and thoroughly despised for his habits.

'Padamsing?' The taller man asked softly in English. 'Is this really you after so many years?'

The renegade Gurkha had gone into east Nepal to try and whip up support among leave men for his campaign that had been so unhappily disrupted and had had a message to meet, name not given, at a certain place. At that question he turned and recognised the monk, Lee Kheng Kwoh, who had seduced him when a lad in Darjeeling.

The familiar voice of ex-Sergeant Padamsing Rai answered, 'Mijhar! Mijhar Lee Kheng Kwoh, my boyhood hero! Yes, it is I. I have come to meet you as your unnamed instructions told me to. I did not let any local villager know I was coming here: I made a recce by myself, with my own escort.'

They embraced again. 'Same as I did,' said Lee Kheng Kwoh. 'We can talk here. We won't be disturbed. The villagers stay indoors at night, especially with the man-eating leopard I've been told is wandering about.

He then called out softly: 'you two others go back down the track you came up and, if anyone comes, turn them back.'

In the moonlight the two shikaris saw them turn round and disappear.

Padamsing said, 'Now we really are on our own, aren't we?' He leant over and kissed his companion with a whispered titter that sent shudders down the two brothers' spines.

'Comrade Padam, you are just the same as you were all those years ago.'

'Yes, the same me, older and a bit sadder.'

'Tell me where you've been since we last met in Darjeeling all those years ago, when you were still young. I heard that you were going to subvert British Army Gurkhas. Did you manage to?'

Before he could answer they heard the bleating of the tied goat, disturbed by the guard who had frightened it. 'A goat? Here? Why?' muttered the one-time Sergeant in alarm.

The monk gave an un-monk-like curse. 'Those stupid villagers! A goat and no shikaris! What fools they are. Excuse me a moment.' He went up the track towards the renewed bleating, saw the tethered animal and told his guard to keep an eye on it and to take it back with them when they left.

Back under the tree the renegade Gurkha said, 'Mijhar, to answer your question. I was so nearly successful. I really was. I had it all going so smoothly that I felt sure they would be useless for British imperialism.'

'"So nearly successful"? What exactly do you mean?'

I mean "personally" successful. I had to leave the operation in the hands of others. I was wrongly…' and here he felt he could not mention the real reason even though the monk had been responsible for his all-male proclivity.

'That was highly unfortunate. So then, what happened?'

'I transferred my work to Patna, in India, and was making great headway with the MGB comrade there, but he changed his mind. I felt so let down I just knew it was time to stop working for the Soviet Communists and transfer my loyalties to you. I will try to organise an army in the hills to persuade people that the Nepalese government must be overthrown, and our men being recruited in foreign armies prohibited. Now it's time to eat.'

He opened the haversack he had been carrying. 'I have some chapattis and tea, Mijhar. The tea is as you like it, weak, unsweetened and without milk. I remember learning that in Darjeeling.'

'Yes, you are known for your good memory.'

On the machan the younger man put his mouth to his brother's ear. 'We are armed. We could kill both so easily. Let's shoot them.'

Hemlal again laid a restricting hand on his brother's arm. 'No, too risky and one is a monk. Can't do it. Our hill men are too sensible to react to scum like that. Thank goodness there are so few of them. Let them go away without learning about us.'

'So, Comrade Padam,' the monk said some few minutes later, it being impolite in Chinese society to talk while eating, 'these are my orders. I will help you to get arms from the Chinese or, if you think it easier, you can do it yourself on the Indian black market – I'll fund you – and gather villagers and where possible leave men and open a campaign against the Nepalese government for recruiting Gurkhas for the British Army and, where possible, try and influence Indian-domiciled Nepalis to do the same.'

'Yes, it means I can continue our Party's policy.'

'Exactly that. My sincere wish to help you will in no way diminish as I carry out my new task, which is taking Assamese comrades to China for training.'

'That I fully understand. Time to move off. Put those eating bits and pieces away.'

The two men stood up and moved off together, followed by their escorts, the monk's leading the goat.

When they were out of earshot Hemlal said, 'No goat so no leopard. Let's get down. We'll try again tomorrow or the next day.'

'Shall we report this to the police?' Jaslal asked his elder brother once they were back home.

'Yes, I think we ought to. Leave it to me.'

History doesn't relate whether they were successful with the leopard but does relate that the ex-Sergeant was unsuccessful in his attempt to start a rebellion. The Royal Nepal Army was deployed against him and, after nearly being captured, he managed to escape.[17]

Monday 8 December 1952, Rangoon, on board SS *Eastern Queen*: '*P'ing Yee*, I'll be visited by the Defence Attaché some time while we're tied up and, possibly, someone from the Nepalese consulate. I think it'll be wiser not to introduce you to them, but if you'd like to meet either I'll merely introduce you as someone I met on board. What think you?'

They were sitting in Ah Fat's cabin. '*Shandung P'aau*, one never knows how things spread. An innocuous meeting can raise serious doubts among the suspicious people I have to live with, questions, questions, questions; why? why? why? That lot won't believe anyone who says it's raining unless they go outside and get wet themselves. No, I'll stay out of sight. What did you teach me? "Out of sight, out of mind!" so, even if I were to pass by, we don't know each other.'

'Fine with me. We've got ourselves to ourselves until we reach Singapore. But tell me, how much has our purser friend seen us together, do you think? Bound to have done with our cabins being next to each other. Is he suspicious? He has never, to my recollection, heard us speaking Chinese to each other or even talking in English together except possibly for perfunctory small talk.'

---

17 He did manage to start an armed insurrection against the Nepal government. All of 15 years later your author was shown bullet marks in trees where there had been the decisive fire fight that drove him off to hide in India. He died a pauper with a huge drink problem in 1974, a hero for Bengali university campus students.

'He thinks I am a dedicated comrade. What he thinks of you, Jason, other than being one of the hated British running dogs, bad-meat-smelling, red-haired, long-nosed imperialist colonials so never to be spoken to unless he has to I can't say.'

Jason laughed uproariously at that. 'Let him continue to think that way. Only if he approaches me, or hints otherwise will I let him revise his options ...'

'Attention please, attention please, will the OC Troops report to the Purser's Office,' came over the Tannoy.

'Talk of the devil, me to him or him to me' said Jason as he went to his own cabin to put on his uniform. Properly dressed he went downstairs, if that, he wondered, was the correct nautical terminology. He saw it was Lieutenant Colonel James Heron who had come to meet him. Jason threw him up a salute although his one-time CO was in mufti, was introduced to his wife, a small, prim-looking woman who had a nun's eyes, steadfast, innocent, devout, and shook hands with her. 'Welcome aboard. I hope you don't have to rush off as we have a lot of cud to chew, at least that is why I expect you have come to see me.'

'You'll remember my wife from Seremban,' Colonel Heron said. 'She said she'd like to meet you again so I have brought her along.'

Jason did remember her. She gave him a modest smile.

He smiled back and mischievously asked her, 'We didn't by any chance meet last week did we?'

'No, Captain Rance. I think you have me muddled up with someone else. Indeed no and why would you think so?' she answered demurely as though almost expecting such a ridiculous question.

'Because you don't look a week older than the last time we met,' said gallantly and inaccurately.

Mrs Heron, face bland, smiled enigmatically and answered innocently, "I expect those wrinkles round your eyes were there long before the sea breeze on this voyage made them deeper.'

Jason realised he'd been outclassed.

Seeing his embarrassment, 'but I'm delighted to meet you again.' was her tactful rejoinder.

Her husband joined in, 'Jason, on, on, on. There is a lot to fill each other in with so let's go somewhere quiet where we can talk.'

'How about my cabin? I'll ask the steward to send up some coffee. Snacks?'

'No, coffee is enough for both of us, thanks.'

Jason, as politely as he could, asked the purser for that to be done, 'as a one-off, special favour and I'll reward the steward.' The answer was a grudging nod.

Up in the cabin with cups of hot coffee, Mrs Heron sat on one of the two chairs and the Colonel on the other. Jason sat on his bunk and the Colonel started off by saying he had done all that he had promised, alerted HQ FARELF, copy to the War Office, in a top secret, coded telegram, told Barrackpore – 'you call him Muggy Day I hear' – that the leave party was normal …

'Yes, he queried it. Asked me why such a message was sent. "Any trouble on the way over?" None of them quite understood the message you sent. I thought it wrong to go into details of what had happened in Rangoon so merely told him it was that he might have heard of some difficulties about burying the little girl at sea and the message was sent in case echoes of it somehow reached him.'

James Heron nodded approval. 'That was quick thinking. Now, can you let me know what happened in Calcutta?' and for the next twenty minutes the elder man sat riveted, forgetting even to drink his coffee, as Jason told him, in detail, what had happened. At the end both man and wife gasped in amazement. 'What I won't pass on is your link with your boyhood friend. That must mean continuously closed lips. He helped you, or rather you him during Janus, didn't you? Saved him from death when he was tied to a tree and tortured.'

Jason nodded. 'Even we don't talk about that between ourselves. I know he is eternally grateful.'

'So the Rezident was as angry as all that! Must be a hard case. According to the briefing I had before coming to this job I expect he'll be for the chop, and as my chief clerk once said, "a good riddance of a bad rubbish". And do you think that your talk in Hindi – I wish I was as fluent as you! – really managed to put paid to the coolies' shouting?'

'Yes, sir, it does seem so. As we wished each other farewell Muggy Day said the police had reported that the coolies had given up going shouting outside the camp.'

'And that dreadful renegade? How can they enlist such people?' He answered his own question, 'of course it's not something that's looked into when recruiting, is it?' The question, being rhetorical, was left unanswered. 'Let me get the chain, not of command but of passing information correct: the Malayan Communist Party Politburo link tells a man in Singapore who meets the purser, either of the SS *Eastern Queen* or of the SS *Princess of the Orient* who goes to Tangra where an already detailed man goes to the Soviet consulate and tells the Rezident?'

'Yes, tenuous, sir, but you've got it correct.'

'Is it always as tenuous, do you think?'

'Can't say, sir, but it seems that in the consulate there are no Chinese speakers, nor Hindi either, but the wretchedly named Mr Bugga speaks good English and seems to understand some Russian. Maybe an English-to-English coded overseas phone call is made but knowing the Soviet insistence on security, if one is, it will be kept to a coded and innocent minimum.'

'I agree that'd be the way they'd play it.'

They stared at each other, and the Attaché said, 'that ventriloquist ability has the status, almost, of a secret weapon, doesn't it?'

'I hadn't thought of it in such terms but, yes, I agree.'

'Now I must write a report on it, or do you want to write one when you get back to Malaya?'

'No, sir, no, no. My report will merely mention the dead child and the prisoner in the brig whose hand-over certificate to the Calcutta police was given to the Red Caps. I don't want to write about anything else, sir. I am but a humble OC Troops. Such a report will come so much better from you.'

'Right. In that case give me some paper and I'll sit at your table and rough out a report here and now. I have plenty of time. I'll be able to check with you that the details are correct.'

In first-class cabins some company note paper is in one of the drawers of the table and the Attaché set to work. Jason leant forward and said to Mrs Heron, 'so much shop and so boring for you. Now tell me how you like Rangoon'. She started off but was interrupted when the Tannoy blared asking the OC Troops to go to the Purser's Office 'now please'. He excused himself, saying he'd be back as soon as he could and went to the Purser's Office. There was the Nepalese Vice-Consul, Mansing Basnet, this time with no wives.

They greeted each other with the namasté and smiles. 'Can you come and see us at the consulate once more, Rance saheb?'

'So sorry, Vice Consul saheb, but the British Defence Attaché is in my cabin and I've told him I'll go back and finish our talk when I can.'

'Now, that's a pity but never mind. Can we talk in the saloon?'

'Saheb, a good idea, with a little refreshment to repay the hospitality I received from you on my way to India.'

Once seated the Vice Consul asked if there was anything else about the rumour of mutinying soldiers.

'Yes, I can tell you how if all started and what happened after we sailed away from Rangoon.'

The Vice Consul leant forward, as if almost literally hanging on Jason's words. They spoke in Nepali: 'The cause of the trouble was in the ship's brig as not being wanted any more in the British Army. It was a matter that gentlemen don't discuss. However, I managed to have him interviewed by someone he had no suspicions about and it transpired that he had started the rumour because the Communist party had ordered him to do so.'

Mr Basnet, utterly surprised by Jason's reply, stared at Jason in shock. 'One of our men did that?'

Jason nodded. 'But he isn't a hill man. He's from Darjeeling.'

The Vice Consul made a sour face of disgust. 'And now? Where is he?'

'He was handed over to the Calcutta police who escorted him to the British Depot in Darjeeling. There they will have discharged him by now, having paid him all that he was due. Where he is now I have no idea.'

The Vice Consul mulled that over. 'Thank you, Rance saheb. You did well to find out all that. It is a disgrace, that's for sure. I will tell the Consul all about it and he will write a report to His Majesty and I am sure will include how you personally handled everything and I know he will be well pleased.'

Rance thanked him. 'Please remember me to the Consul saheb and the ladies' he said as he saw Basnet get ready to go.

'Of course. I'll be off now.' Jason escorted him to the gangway, saluted him[18] and went back to his cabin. Colonel Heron, a quick worker, had his draft ready by the time Jason got back there. 'I'll tell you what I've written. Sit down and listen.' He read it out.

There were only one or two slight corrections to be made. Satisfied, the Colonel again thanked Rance for a sterling performance and said he'd now go back to the embassy and 'deal with this properly'. As they passed the Purser's Office the Attaché said, 'Jason, I can't remember hearing you speak Chinese when I was in the battalion. Speak to the purser in it.'

Jason knew the purser was a Hakka but could probably understand Cantonese. Without thinking of any repercussions,

---

18 Your author met the Vice Consul 42 long years later in Kathmandu and they discussed the whole incident once more.

he addressed him freely, talking about the difficulties of various dialects.

The purser, normally disconcertingly reticent and graceless, was almost stunned and only stuttered his answers. Jason turned to the Colonel and said, 'I was speaking in Cantonese. He's a Hakka, hence the difficulty.

'It's all too difficult for me,' was the rejoinder. 'So, off we go. I don't know when we'll meet up again. One never does in this man's army.'

'Colonel, before you go I must tell you that I was called away to meet the Nepali Vice Consul. I told him how the whole mutiny business started and that there was nothing in it as far as Gurkha troops were concerned. He said he'd tell the Consul who would forward the news to His Majesty.'

'And nothing about Calcutta?'

Jason shook his head. 'Not a word, except to say the renegade man was handed over to the police there.'

'So that's that', the Colonel said as Jason escorted his visitors to the gangway, shook hands, saluted and waited there until they were out of sight. He went and walked around where the men were lounging or talking then back to his cabin where he told Ah Fat all that had passed – 'nor did I mention your name once!'

Law Chu Hoi, the purser, was a suspicious man. There was something about that tall Englishman he simply didn't trust. He had no idea he spoke any language of the Middle Kingdom. *That must have been the man Cheng Fan Tek asked me about. I'll have to ask Comrade Ah Fat if he knows about this*, he cursed under his breath.

Friday 12 December 1952, Soviet Embassy, New Delhi, India: Vikas Bugga, still with a sore face and a blatant scar on his cheek but now able to talk, wanted to complain to the Soviet Ambassador, Kirill Novikok, about his ill treatment in the Soviet consulate in Calcutta. At the gates the duty guard, an ex-Indian Army soldier, asked him his business. 'Personal, with the Ambassador,' Vikas answered, his voice more than difficult to understand.

'Go inside to the front desk and ask there,' answered the guard and, opening the gates, let him pass through.

In the room next to the front door the duty security person, at this instant a woman, watched Vikas Bugga walk in. She had brown hair, porcine eyes narrowly set together, rimless glasses and a pink slash where her lips should have been. She wore cheap black shoes, thick stockings and a prim brown dress. The entrant went up to her and, not wanting to speak Russian, asked her in English if he could have an interview with the Ambassador. That shocked her almost beyond belief. In her stuttering English she said 'no' and shook her head violently.

At that Vikas Bugga took out his party card and showed it to her. 'I want to see the Ambassador because,' he pointed to his face, 'your Rezident, Sobolev, Leonid Pavlovich, in your Calcutta consulate, drunk, threw a glass at me. I want to complain and have recompense.'

The use of the word 'Rezident' without the word 'comrade' before it was enough to make her realise that the woe-begotten man standing in front of her was, possibly, someone to listen to. But she had to check. She asked her visitor the Rezident's name again and Bugga gave it and his junior's.

She wrote something down, beckoned to a man who had suddenly appeared, and Vikas understood her to tell him to take her note to the Ambassador's office. The Indian was asked to go and sit in the visitors' room. In a surprisingly short time the messenger who took the note appeared in the doorway and beckoned him forward. They went upstairs and once more the Indian was asked to wait, this time in a room next door to the Ambassador's office. After a short wait he was joined by two men, one of whom said he was the Ambassador. Both were middle-aged and intelligent looking, with pleasant faces. No Soviet ambassador was ever allowed to interview a stranger without an MGB representative accompanying him: that was what the second man was. Kirill Novikok's English was as good as Bugga's. He asked what the trouble was and why, he, the Ambassador rather than a secretary, should be bothered.

Vikas Bugga, angered at the implied rebuke, 'jumped in at the deep end' with a full and unstoppable complaint of what had happened. Both Russians listened without interrupting. 'Your Excellency, I have been a card-carrying party member for many years.' Mr Bugga concluded his relentless monologue. 'I have even been told that Comrade Colonel General Zdhanov has mentioned my name to the Politburo. I have always trusted the Russians to behave properly even though vodka toasts are a permanent feature of your hospitality. But never this,' pointing to his injured face. 'My trust in you and your party has been damaged for ever. Likewise when he said to me "*ja ne ponimáju, chto govorít ètot chórnomazyi ubljúdok*" and "*Ty nichtózhnaja málen'kaja chórnaja svin'já*" I was deeply and permanently insulted.' He stood up, picked up his party card from the table where he had put it down and said, 'Here you are. Send it back to your Politburo where I know my name is known. I am no longer a member. Now no glamour of hammer and your sickle is fickle. Good bye.'

What the Ambassador tried to say merely gurgled in his throat as both men watched their furious visitor leave the room.

Outside, near the gate, the duty security woman saw him spit: she did not know it was in disgust. Whatever repercussions took place after that was not his concern, then or ever.

Friday 12 December 1952, Singapore: The SS *Eastern Queen* tied up. Jason went into his friend's cabin. 'We must say good bye here. Tradecraft! It has been wonderful to have had so long together. Where will you go after you disembark?'

'I think you know Reggie Hutton from 1948?'

'Yes, I met him then.'

'I must brief him on everything that has happened and give him the copy of that letter, the one you'll give to a Gurkha that will be picked up. After that I'll go to KL, have a couple of days with my family, pick up my Bear, talk to C C Too and, with a straight face, report back to the Politburo.'

'What will you tell them?'

'I am a master at feeding them false news with a straight face. I don't know quite how I'll tackle it but have no doubts, I'll manage.'

'Where is that letter?'

'In my pocket. Do you want it?

'I think I'll take it to the Captain myself when I go and thank him for his help with the dead child on the way out. I'll tell him I found it on my bed.'

'So long as the purser doesn't see you give it to him!'

They smiled at each other as they shook hands before parting.

As soon as the gangways were in place, the Movements Warrant Officer came on board to meet the OC Troops. 'Good voyage, sir? No problems?'

'Apart from the ill girl dying and being buried at sea, none except the ship pitching, tossing or rolling, whichever it is that the experts call it' Jason answered with a grin. 'Here are the regimental nominal rolls' and he handed them over.

The two Red Caps came up, saluted Jason, who thanked them for their work, and gave the prisoner's hand-over receipt to the Movements Warrant Officer. They drove off in a Provost vehicle that turned up to fetch them.

'Right you are, sir. They are mine now. You are free to move off.' He looked at his clip board. 'Yes, here is a warrant for your train journey to Seremban, but an open ticket for a sleeper. We couldn't book a sleeper because we didn't know timings so no berth has been booked.'

'No worry. My thanks for thinking of me.'

'Let's go to the Purser's Office and you can tell the men the order of disembarkation.'

Off they went. Jason asked the sulky purser for the Tannoy. 'This is your OC Troops speaking,' he announced. 'I am handing over to the Movements Warrant Officer. I want to say good bye to you. It has been pleasant being with you. Now this is the order of getting off this boat ....'

At last all were off. The cabin steward brought Jason's luggage down to where he was in the lounge. Jason had some Malayan currency on him and gave him a decent tip. From the way the man smiled it must have been a deal more than normal.

'Keep an eye on my luggage for a few minutes, will you?' he said to him. 'I have a job to do.' Smartly dressed in uniform, he made his way to the bridge, telling those who tried to stop him that he was duty bound to say farewell to the Captain. The Captain was in his cabin with some Port Authorities and Jason had to wait a while till he was free. He was then invited in.

'Captain Lam Wai Lim. I have come to thank you for all your help when we had that burial at sea on the way out. I don't think I thanked you properly then.'

'Oh, Captain Rance, I am so glad you took my advice.'

'The dead girl's parents were also glad to have made, how shall I call it, a clean break. Gurkhas keep so much inside, it would have been almost unnatural for them to have thanked you.'

The Captain bowed his head in appreciation.

'Sir, just one strange point for you. I found this on my bed in my cabin when we left Calcutta. I thought I wouldn't bother you as we were moving but now we are tied up and you are free to see me, I can give it to you with a clear conscience.' He handed the letter over.

The Captain opened both envelopes and read the letter. A puzzled frown creased his face. 'But, how strange. How ... '

'Sir, I rudely interrupt. I have absolutely no idea so it is useless your asking me. I bid you farewell.' He saluted, made his way back to collect his luggage and left the boat as quickly as he could.

Neither Jason nor Ah Fat would ever know that Captain Lam Wai Lim was shocked to the core when he read the inner letter, though they both guessed he probably would be. The purser could not explain the letter that was signed by Dmitry Tsarkov and had the Soviet consulate address on it. He could truly swear on oath that he personally had never been to the consulate, which was, of course, perfectly true, but that could not hide the fact that the letter was addressed to him, Comrade Law Chu Hoi, Purser, SS *Eastern Queen*. Despite passionate protestations of innocence, even wishing he had known about it earlier, it was the 'Comrade' that stuck in the Captain's gullet even more so when the purser eventually admitted his allegiance to the Party. He lost his job although the purser of SS *Princess of the Orient* kept his.

The last of the returning leave details was getting into the coach provided to take them to the Transit Camp as Jason, seeing no other transport, quickened to board it. 'Sir,' the Movements Warrant Officer called out to him. 'Please wait. I have something for you.'

And miss my transport! The Warrant Officer joined him. 'I have just had a phone call in my office. A staff car is coming to fetch you. You are wanted to go to Tanglin, GHQ, and meet someone.'

'Do you know who and why?'

'No, sir. No details. The car will be here shortly. It will have a pass to come to my office. Come and have a seat till it arrives.'

The car drew up there and then. The driver, a locally enlisted Malay, got out, went over to Jason and saluted. 'I am to take you to GHQ, Tuan,' and gave him an envelope.

Jason pleased him immensely by answering in fluent Malay, thanked the Warrant Officer and got into the car. He opened the envelope, eyebrows lifting as he read the letter. It was from the Military Assistant to the Commander-in-Chief. 'You are to report to GHQ. Please come in plain clothes. Walk behind the main block where there is a wire enclosure. The gate is locked. There is a bell. Ring it. You will be met and taken inside. Tell nobody your actual destination. If asked, say it is a debrief from your last operation. Have your ID card ready. When you have finished come and see me.' It was signed illegibly by a Major someone-or-other, MA to the C-in-C.

Exciting. Unusual. Another challenge? Even so, I'd rather go back straightaway to my company, my battalion home, time to sink once more into the seeming infinity of jungle work, sweaty body, aching limbs, taut nerves and a camaraderie seldom found elsewhere.

Jason reached for his suitcase and asked Mr Hutchinson if he could use his office to change into mufti. Dressed as a civilian he bade the Movements Warrant Officer farewell, got into the car and was driven to GHQ. At the car park he got out, thanked and dismissed the driver. He went round the back of the main building and there was the gate in the wire. He walked up to it, saw the bell, pushed the button. A civilian escort soon came and asked to see his ID card. He examined it minutely, saying nothing. He opened the gate and beckoning Jason to follow. They went along a short concrete path, flanked by two wire barricades, to another gate where he rang another bell. There he was wordlessly handed over to a second escort. Again, no word was spoken, merely the new man's finger beckoning him to follow along behind. *Spooky!* The two of them went to a red-brick, one-storey building, the outside door of which had no handle. The silent escort rang yet another bell. A Judas hole opened and an eye peered at them. The escort left and the door opened. A middle-aged man, again without speaking, beckoned Jason to follow him down a passage to another door and knocked.

'Come in,' came a voice and, slightly dazed by now, in Jason went to be greeted by a grizzled, middle-aged civilian with a ferocious expression on his face, sitting at a desk. Another man, tired-looking and lanky, also in plain clothes, was sitting in an arm chair and introduced as 'coming from the War Office', with no other details.

The expression of bewilderment on Rance's face showed his interlocutor it was time to tell him why he had been called in. Jason, innately wise, did not ask any questions about whom and where he was, nor was he told.

'I have called you in because I have had a lengthy letter from Lieutenant Colonel James Heron whom you so adequately briefed in Rangoon. So important do we consider your report that my guest' and he nodded to the officer from the War Office, 'that London also wants to hear you say it all again *and* answering what questions we put to you.'

Jason could not answer some of the questions, one being the size and number of the array of aerials on the roof of the consulate and another were there any obvious microphones in the room. Others came easily: descriptions of the Russians, the Indian, the contacts in Tangra and the purser.

Jason answered all of them convincingly, until they came to Ah Fat. He looked at both officers. 'It would be an insult to question your probity, the more so as you are trusting me. I have never told anyone more than that he and I were boyhood friends in Kuala Lumpur pre-war, that we played together and that is how I learnt Chinese and Malay, that he fought with our stay-behind people against the Japanese during the war. Isn't that enough?'

It plainly was not enough. Both men shook their head. 'No. How was it he was on the boat in the first place, went to Tangra and had an interview with the Rezident?'

'I have never told anybody why. There is someone in Police HQ in Kuala Lumpur who knows the story and only he. I never tell anybody because, if it got out, it would mean a long and painful death for him, which nearly happened before but I managed to rescue him at the last moment. I am not ready for that to happen ever again`.'

'You mean he is a double agent?' It was the man in the chair who asked.

'And a non-voting member of the Malayan Communist Party Politburo.' *Spell it out for him. London won't know what MCP means.*

'Understood and accepted.' Both men spoke together as though they had practised beforehand.

Satisfied at last, they thanked him for all the data and details he had provided. 'Unique,' said the man from the War Office.

'Just one more question before we go to lunch,' the man sitting at the desk asked. 'How did Vikas Bugga manage to be so unexpectedly rude and uncomplimentary to the Rezident?'

Jason grinned. 'Another top-secret matter lost.' They looked at him quizzically. 'I am a ventriloquist and I chose the words for him.'

The other two roared with laughter. 'That deserves lunch. Come.'

They took him by car to Ulu Pandan, to an eating place named Balmoral. The only thing that did surprise Jason was when the man who had sat behind the desk said, 'Our lot had this place built.'

Jason met the MA, a cavalry officer who wore his handkerchief up his sleeve and his watch on the inside of his wrist. 'Home and dry?' he asked with a wink.

'Not home yet but, surprisingly, dry – or at least I think so.'

'Strange that you should use that phrase, "not home yet". There is going to be a large seminar on jungle fighting in a week's time and you're needed to get the subjects straight before we start. We have your CO's permission for this. You will live in Tanglin Mess. You will get back to your battalion in time to enjoy Christmas. Here are the details …'

Friday 12 – Monday 22 December 1952, Singapore and Malaya: Ah Fat's journey back to MCP's HQ was not straightforward. He was now nearly back in his own stamping ground and, although admittedly Singapore was not where he normally worked, he felt he had a duty to Reggie Hutton to visit him once more, as promised. On leaving the dock area he walked to the nearest café. Inside he saw that there were booths, curtained off so that there was privacy if needed. He ordered a snack and a coffee, took his plate and cup to a table next to the window and, looking outside, slowly nibbled and sipped. He 'felt it in his bones' that, somehow or other, he would be checked up. Tradecraft was essential. Movement caught his eye: he saw a Chinese man nonchalantly moving up the pavement on the other side of the road, as though he was looking for something – or somebody. *Could be anyone, couldn't it?* he asked himself.

He was just about to ask if he could use the phone in the café, when he saw the man return, talking to ... yes! none other than Chen Geng. They crossed the road, making for the café. Quick as a flash he picked up plate and cup and went to the end cubicle, drawing the curtain but leaving a gap for him to look out of.

The two men came in, ordered something at the counter and came to sit in the next cubicle. Their snacks were brought in. 'Don't disturb us,' Chen Geng said. As soon as the waiter had gone out of earshot the two started talking. Ah Fat listened carefully.

'Did you see the comrade come off the boat?' Chen Geng asked.

'No, not off the boat. I went to the place where visas are shown and the man there said, "Yes, an Ah Fat has already left us. I have no idea where he went. That is not my job as his passport was in order."'

'I have had an order to contact him. There's nothing serious but the Politburo in Malaya want to make sure he was on the boat, that he came back.'

'You mean that they fear he might have decided to defect?'

'That's putting it bluntly but yes, I presume that is what they meant.'

'But he has returned. There can't be any chance of him defecting, can there?'

'No, even though he was operating openly, not revealing his true identity.'

'So, do you want me to continue looking for him? From your description I could recognise him.'

'I can't think it necessary. Those people hiding in the jungle get inflated ideas. And fears, too. What I'll do, no need to tell you the details, is to get a message through to them saying that all is well.'

'Is that enough? Do you need to tell them when he'll get back?'

'Not at all. He operates in his own fashion. There are certain places it's safe for him to go and certain other places where he has to take great care. A man like him can find his own way back. If the Politburo can trust him to go to Calcutta and back, it has to trust him to go from Singapore up country back to base.'

'Yes, that makes sense. And, if he has to join the Politburo in the jungle, he'll need to wait for an escort. It could be sometime next year before he gets back.'

Ah Fat could hear cups being put back on their saucers. 'Another cup?' Chen Geng asked.

'No thanks. I'd better go. I have other matters to look into.'

'Yes, so have I. Let's say good bye and leave. I'll pay.'

Ah Fat heard them get up and leave their cubicle. Peering through the gap in the curtain he saw them move out into the road. *I'll wait a while. Let them get right away.*

Finding a phone would not be easy so he risked asking at the bar if he could use theirs. 'Only for local calls. I'll time you and you can pay me at the end.' He still had some local currency, so he agreed. He knew Reggie Hutton's number and rang it.

It rang for quite a while and Ah Fat was on the verge of putting the phone back on its cradle when, to his relief, Reggie Hutton answered it. '9928 speaking.'

Ah Fat turned his face away from the bar man and, speaking softly, said, 'Mr Hutton, have you your hat on. Is it inconvenient if I come and see you?'

'No, certainly not. Do you want to be picked up?'

'It would be expedient. I am now in a café near the dock area. I'd like to be picked up where you picked us up before. Give me half an hour.'

'Is that necessary?'

'I think so. Tell you why when I see you' and rang off. 'How much is that?'

The barman told him, and Ah Fat paid. 'Does a bus from anywhere near here go to the railway station?'

'No,' and the barman told him where to go to find one that did.

Ah Fat thanked him and left. He flagged down the first empty taxi he saw and told the driver to go to the railway station and once there, waited for Reggie Hutton's car to pick him up.

At Reggie's place it was talk, talk, a meal, talk and, finally, bed time. Reggie was overwhelmed with what he was told. This is much larger, broader, bigger and more frightening that I had ever thought,' he said. 'What do you think will happen to Sobolev and Tsarkov?'

'Oh Reggie. That's beyond me. I have no idea.'

'Well, from what I know of their system I expect that certainly the Rezident will disappear and the other punished. And that unfortunately named Indian, Vikas Bugga?'

All Ah Fat could say was 'your guess is as good, or as bad, as mine.'

'And your friend Jason Rance. His future? Will he be chased by Soviet representatives over here, do you think?'

'He was billed as Jason Rance being a working name, he being a closet comrade. I can't imagine anything unpleasant happening to him. There's one cool man who can look after himself.'

'So now you will go back to your jungle base. Oh, what happened to your Bear? You haven't mentioned him.'

'There was only one ticket for me, nothing for him, so I sent him back to his family. I'll catch tomorrow's day train to KL, pick him up and back to base it is.'

'And C C Too. Will you meet him?'

'Originally I had intended to but that means a delay and really I should show my face as soon as I can now. Is there any way of your briefing him, even though all I've told you is outside his territory.'

'I'd rather you did if you could. There are some questions I might not be able to answer.'

So, Ah Fat agreed and, it being bed time, both of them turned in, Ah Fat glad that the bed was still and not moving.

At KL Ah Fat met up with his Bear. He was tempted to spend a few days with his own family. He went and saw C C Too and gave him a detailed briefing and it wasn't till the following Wednesday that the two of them moved north. On Monday 22 December, fortunately having met up with a courier and escort, the two men reported back to the MCP HQ. They were delighted to see them and agog to learn what he had found out and what would the future now hold.

It only now occurred to Ah Fat whether to tell them the truth or let them live in false hopes. 'I'll brief a Plenum, Comrade Secretary General, as soon as you can arrange one. But now, so delighted am I to be back, please let me relax for a day or so.'

They fixed a Plenum for two days later. That gave Ah Fat plenty of time to consider what to say. He realised that they would not have heard the false news of mutinying Gurkhas nor about the Barrackpore coolies. He'd merely talk about the meeting in the consulate. In fact, whatever he did tell them, as far as he and Jason were concerned, both Operations Tipping Point had been a success. *Yes, and for them let it be a failure.*

Having made up his mind, he knew how best he would manage the Plenum. There was a smile on his face when he went to sleep that first night – and on the second. And a broader one, a grin, after the Plenum, there being an inverse ratio to their gloom and his inner joy.

Monday 22 December 1952, Seremban, Malaya: Captain Rance travelled by day train to Seremban so it was evening by the time he reached the battalion. The meeting in Singapore, which everyone had judged a success and had congratulated him on his wonderful display of knowledge, had been hard work but worth it. But back in Seremban, in the battalion lines once more, Jason really did feel like coming back home. He put his kit in his room and went to visit A Company, had a talk with Major McGurk, who garrulously kept the conversation to his weird experience and how stimulating the men were before going round the barrack rooms and letting the men know he was back, little realising that they knew that already.

That night in the Mess he was asked by all and sundry how matters had panned out. 'Lucky devil,' one said, 'Bugger all to do except sun bathe on the First Class deck. You were really on leave, both ways, with the Queen paying your fare, board and lodging.'

'Quite right, but jealousy will get you nowhere,' was Jason's laughing reply. 'Tell me what's been happening around here.' *Anything to keep away from my doings!* It was a happy evening, banter and counter banter. The Adjutant told him that the CO would like a word on the morrow, after orders, around 1215.

The CO welcomed him back. His main interest was the two wartime Gurkhas Jason had rescued. 'Yes, the Singapore High Commission had approached the Indian High Commission because the two men were in the Indian Army when they were captured. They, in turn, contacted GHQ Indian Army for their repatriation. I gather GHQ will contact their Record Office to find out details of back pay. It will take a while to work out how many years they will get it for. Until Indian Independence or when? The two men were especially allowed to go back by air. They could well have overflown you as they went.'

'I am delighted to hear that sir.'

'And the journey to India and back? No trouble?'

Jason thought out his answer. 'I spent a pleasant night with Muggy Day. I met the Attaché in Rangoon: as our first CO in 1948 that was a pleasant bonus. I am sorry I couldn't get back earlier but the symposium kept me down in Singapore.'

'Yes, of course I agreed to what they asked. What was your main point?'

Jason thought back over the past month while the CO waited for his answer.

'We discussed many tactical issues and I was asked a number of questions about how I had managed with my men. I think I gave adequate answers. And then I had a brainwave. Not that I would or could write a book about any of what I've managed to do.' The CO gave his company commander a quizzical smile – OC A Company's written reports weren't up to staff work standard. 'I'd dedicate it "To the Security Forces, especially remembering those whose home ground Malaya is; Malay troops, Malay Police and especially our Gurkhas, whose skill and tenacity reached the tipping point in the Emergency in our favour."'

'Isn't that premature?' asked the CO, dubiously.

'Only that from the way matters are going in Indonesia and French Indo-China, Malaya will be the only country where the

Communists will have lost on ground of their own choosing.'[19]

The CO asked Jason what examples he had given and he said, 'I mentioned various points about Janus. You may think I finished up a bit pompously.'

The CO smiled. 'Well, let's hear it so I can judge.'

'I said, if ever I'd write a book about it, which of course I never will, I'd dedicate it thus:

And should you ask, where do they live
These men with skill superlative
Who showed superb initiative
Enhanced their name, achieved success
And gave the 'baddies' no redress?
– The Jungle is their home address.

The CO grinned: 'Just as well you'll never write anything, Jason.'

---

19 Communism was also beaten in a territory of their choosing in the Dhofar province of Oman, 1970-1975. One of the key factors was that the campaign was developed 'in the service of the Sultan' and working with the grain of local Islamic belief.